A WOMAN'S WORTH

"A masterpiece."

—KOLA BOOF, author of *Flesh and the Devil*

"*A Woman's Worth* is a masterfully written story where Price-Thompson not only demonstrates her writing talent with prose that makes you read a sentence twice because of its beauty, but she also provides a compelling not-happily-ever-after story that will keep you flipping the pages. . . . You will be treated to a novel that will have your heart pounding, your eyes tearing, and a story lingering in your mind long after you've read the last page."

—*Quarterly Black Review*

"P̶   se veers from eloquent to pu̶   ugh, making this a charged pa̶

—*Publishers Weekly*

"Price-Thompson has a keen ear for spoken cadence for evoking a scene—its hues, humidity, pulse and scents—all the while keeping the tension taut."

—*Ms.* magazine

CHOCOLATE SANGRIA

"A wonderfully written novel that demands attention from page one."

—ZANE, author of *The Heat Seekers*

"[A] heart-wrenching tale of love and family . . . a fable on the consequences of keeping secrets and betrayal."

—*USA Today*

"Vivid, striking prose, heartfelt and authentic. *Chocolate Sangria* is a thought-provoking book that examines sensitive issues among people of color."

—MARCUS MAJOR, author of *4 Guys and Trouble*

BLACK COFFEE

"A racy tale of romance and ambition in the military."

—*The Washington Post*

"Price-Thompson has set this novel among a seldom-written-about group, African Americans in the military. . . . [She does] an excellent job of showcasing a lifestyle not often glamorized by contemporary novelists."

—*Booklist*

"[*Black Coffee*] puts a literal spin on the war between the sexes. . . . This is not a lighthearted, sweet-talking love story, but an energizing slice of ultra-contemporary romance."

—*Publishers Weekly*

Knockin' Boots

Knockin' Boots

A Novel

Tracy Price-Thompson

One World

Ballantine Books | New York

A One World Books Trade Paperback Original

Copyright © 2005 by Tracy Price-Thompson
Reading group guide copyright © 2005 by Random House, Inc.

Published in the United States by One World Books,
an imprint of The Random House Publishing Group,
a division of Random House, Inc., New York.

ONE WORLD is a registered trademark and the One World
colophon is a trademark of Random House, Inc.

ISBN 0-345-47723-5

Printed in the United States of America

www.oneworldbooks.net

2 4 6 8 9 7 5 3

To Daddy . . . Greg, you are so much more
than my husband. You are my best friend.
Thank you for all that you do for me
and our children and for the life
we have built together.
I love you.

TT

You ain't gettin' paid, you ain't knockin' boots
You ain't treatin' me like no prostitute

—*Salt-n-Pepa*

Sexual addiction can be characterized by the repeated, compulsive seeking or performance of sexual acts despite adverse social, psychological, and/or physical consequences.

The Players

THE SEX TOY

This shit ain't normal, I told myself as my husband moved against me, moaning and thrusting to a steady rhythm. I felt his breath heavy on my neck, his tongue licking my earlobe, his hands cupping my hips as he held me firmly and rode me from behind.

"My turn." The voice of the strange man in front of me was deep and thick with arousal, reminding me of his presence and of my role. At my husband's command, the two of them had made a sandwich out of me. They were the bread, and I was the meat.

THE SELLOUT

I wouldn't touch a black woman with a ten-foot pole. Don't swell up! Quincy Jones, Taye Diggs, Wesley Snipes, Kobe Bryant—they were down with me too. They knew the deal when it came down to sisters. Corn bread, collard greens, hogmaws, and chit'lins! Mouths too foul, fingernails too long, weaves too big, and way too much drama in their blood.

THE DIVA

If these hips could talk they'd be speaking in tongues! It was Friday night and my shit was on. I'd ducked out of work early and swung by my apartment to jump out of that hot-ass military uniform, then I hit High Street and got my hair did and my nails did, and my feet did too!

THE DOG

I am an addict. I'll lie, steal, and fight to feed my addiction. I am an addict, and there ain't a 12-step program in the world that can ease my pain. I'll stay out all night long, fuck over my best friend, deceive my boss, whatever it takes to keep my jones fed and my sins secret, I'll do it.

Knockin' Boots

CHAPTER 1

EMILE

Corn Bread, Collard Greens, Hogmaws, and Chit'lins

I knew Fancy was a freak when I married her," Kevin said as we sat chewing hot wings and sucking down brew at a corner table at Fort Dix's All-Ranks Club. All eyes were on the dance floor, where Kevin's wife—dressed in a candy-apple thong under a sheer black minidress—was rolling her body all over some twenty-year-old corporal, grinding him into the ground. The beat was slow and funky, and at Fancy's urging the corporal grabbed two handfuls of her sweetly rounded hips, pulled her close, and dry-humped her like a horny teenager at a red-light basement party.

Fancy was fine, if that was the kind of woman you went for. She had a classic ghetto-fabulous body—junk *all up in* the trunk, juicy breastesses that looked like two ripe coconuts, tiny waistline with a bright tattoo and a perfectly pierced navel. She was even pretty in the face if you could get past the chewing gum and that bottom lip that stayed poked out all the time, but women like her didn't raise my pressure. I wouldn't touch a black woman with a ten-foot pole.

Don't swell up!

Quincy Jones, Taye Diggs, Wesley Snipes, Kobe Bryant—they were down with me too. They knew the deal when it came to sisters. Corn bread, collard greens, hogmaws, and chit'lins! Mouths too foul, fingernails too long, weave too big, and way too much drama in their blood. Not to mention the ratio of video hos to hoochies. But Kevin was my brother, the only family I had, so I nodded and went along with his program. Still, it had to hurt coming home from a monthlong deployment in Iraq and busting your wife getting her swerve on up in a club.

"I mean"—Kevin licked hot wing sauce from his thumb and shrugged his rationalization—"this is a crazy lifestyle us soldiers live. Marching off to all corners of the world at the drop of a dime. A woman like Fancy needs hands on her. Lots of hands. On her ass, in her hair, between her legs . . . you just can't put chains on a woman like her and expect her to hush up and hold still."

I just looked at him. Kevin had always been a little slow, even as a kid. Dig. While his wife was out dancing in the club, I'd driven the fifty miles round-trip to pick him up from the Philadelphia International Airport where he'd been waiting for hours. Thirty days of doing dirt just hadn't been enough for Ms. Fancy Pants Lawson. Instead of greeting her man with some sweet-smelling hair and a set of clean sheets, she was out there rubbing that stuff on the next soldier.

"So what are you saying, Chief? You're not going to roll out there and snatch her up? Let her know you're back from the desert and you've peeped her?"

Kevin just grinned and licked more sauce off his fingers. "What for, Emile? I know where my woman sleeps at night. 2651-B Cedar Street. Let her have her fun now. She'll make sure I have mine later."

Fools and flies, I thought and put on my hat and scooped up my car keys. *I do despise.*

These days, the more I trifled with fools, the better I liked flies.

————

KEVIN was real laid back for a man who had just witnessed his wife putting the moves on another man. Why he would even marry a woman like Fancy was beyond me. As if we hadn't learned enough from Lil Mama and them growing up. How much more of that could he take? Everybody knew Fancy was scandalous. A real skeezer, always running the streets. Hitting on men at unit functions, getting her swerve on in Kevin's bed while he was away on temporary duty. Rumor had it that she swung both ways, and judging by the company she kept, especially that firecracker Staff Sergeant Sparkle Henderson, I could imagine it being true.

Kevin needed to learn how to put his foot down, but then again he was accustomed to stomaching a lot. We'd both been raised by our foster mother Dirty Sue, a skeezer extraordinaire who was as black and greasy as they came.

I don't know how the state of Missouri allowed Dirty Sue to get her hands on one orphan, let alone two. She did a job on us in every way imaginable, and since Kevin was a pretty boy and Dirty Sue's daughters, Lil Mama and Teesha, dug his muscular body, those nymphs just about used it up.

I was a fat wheezing kid, so I wasn't prone to getting much

more than a foot in the ass, but Kevin was their stud. He'd caught the drips twice in the sixth grade and chlamydia in the seventh, and to this day he swears that's the reason he never fathered any children.

Dirty Sue and her brood had tortured me too, but in different ways.

Every evening at five thirty I'd listen through the screen door as she marched up Brunson Hill Road, dressed in her housekeeping clothes and messing up my name. Our house was at the end of Catfish Row, and neighbors on both sides of the street would sit outside on their porches, fanning themselves and enjoying the Dirty Sue Revue.

She'd be mad to the max. Cussing the whole neighborhood out because the state required foster parents to have their own source of income, and thus some type of gainful employment. "Emil-Leeeee!" she would holler. "Emily! Em-ill-*Lee*! You hear me calling you, you corn-fed, crispy-critter, dark-vader, liver-lipped sonna-bitch! Answer me with your wide-ass self. You better have my goddamn dinner ready by the time I climb this hill, boy!"

Humiliated, I'd leave the pork chops simmering in gravy and stand out on the porch wheezing and biting the insides of my cheeks until my mouth filled with blood.

Almost twenty years later I could still feel those cheap rings on her fingers as they swung past and dotted my eye. I still pictured that nasty combination of bacon, chicken, and pork-chop grease congealing in a coffee can on top of the stove. My nose stung at the scent of black smoke as she dipped a hot comb in a can of Royal Crown pressing oil, and then wiped it on an old cloth and country-fried her nappy hair. My heart crawled into my throat when I heard her voice, juiced up and deep in her cups, making Emily out of Emile and screaming for every underfed bully in the neighborhood to have a go at the fat foster kid. Yes, Dirty Sue had done a job on us, and some things never changed.

As I drove into the military housing area I glanced at my foster brother and best friend from the corner of my eye. Our country was at war with Iraq, and as one of the army's top demolition instructors, Kevin's expertise was in high demand. He'd recently been handpicked to deploy to Tikrit as part of a special explosives ordnance team, and had spent the last month traveling all over Iraq training coalition soldiers on the detection and removal of land mines, booby traps, and other unexploded ordnance.

My status as a soldier was a little different. I'd taken advantage of being an orphan and earned a free ride to the state university, where I majored in chemistry. During college I met a pretty redheaded girl from Wisconsin who introduced me to the joys of healthy eating and physical fitness, so I took up running and weight training, lost the extra seventy pounds that had had my ass dragging the ground, and then joined Kevin on active duty as a college-optioned infantry officer who went through basic combat training and then straight into Army Officer Candidate School.

I'd kissed all the right asses and landed a great position at the Twelfth Army NCO Academy, where I commanded a company of Noncommissioned Officer Educational System instructors. Commanding at the academy came with its fair share of issues. You know the deal. If soldiers ain't complaining then they ain't training.

Especially that troll who ran my supply shop. Staff Sergeant Sparkle Henderson. Stupider than a damn soup sandwich. Ate the hell up! Had training profiles coming out of her cargo pockets and skipped out of work early every other day, but the way Kevin treated her you would have sworn she was that Beyoncé girl or somebody. Come to think of it, the two of them did favor each other. Between the blond weave and their asses hanging out everywhere, Sparkle Henderson and Beyoncé could have passed for sisters.

"Thanks for picking me up, man," Kevin said as I pulled up outside his base quarters. He got his duffel bag from the trunk of my car and I waited until he slammed it closed.

"You straight?" I asked, hoping he didn't go inside and pull out a couple of bouncing bettys, then set up an ambush for his nasty wife.

Kevin nodded and slung his duffel bag over his shoulder. "I'm good, my man. I'm just gonna go inside and get a shower and wait on my honey to get in. Say hi to Becky Ann for me."

I smiled at the mention of her name, and suddenly I couldn't care less how much crap Kevin took off of his wife. I drove away with a weak feeling in the pit of my stomach just thinking about my princess and how right she was for me. Becky Ann Grantley. Freckled nose, clean, strawberry-scented blond hair that hung down to her waist, even teeth, slim hips. Just perfect. Kevin might not have learned anything from living with the likes of Dirty Sue, but I sure as sugar did. There were too many trifling and confused black women running loose, and I, for one, could do just fine without them.

CHAPTER 2

SPARKLE

I'll Take Your Man

*I*f these hips could talk they'd be speaking in tongues!

It was Friday night and my shit was on. I'd ducked out of work early and swung by my apartment to jump out of that hot-ass military uniform, then I hit High Street and got my hair did and my nails did, and my feet did too!

Raising the drop-top on my Nissan 350Z Roadster, I pulled into a parking space outside the five-story apartment complex and turned off the ignition. After giving my face a once-over in the rearview mirror I rechecked the address and grinned. Yep, this was it: 4040 Westlake Drive. It looked just like he'd described it, red bricks and wide balconies. Adjacent to the building, I saw a slew of brothers taking it to the hoop under the bright lights of a curbside court. I shivered at the sight of all that delicious man-sweat dripping from their chests and decided to have me a little fun.

I stepped out of the car flashing my dimples and pearly whites and looking as fine as I wanted to be: eighty-dollar lavender shorts that showed off my *ass*ets, matching cross-strapped halter top that looked more like two Band-Aids covering my nipples, and four-inch heels that complemented my toned thighs and shapely calves.

I slammed the driver's door loud enough to be noticed, then switched around to the front seat of the passenger side and retrieved the tray of cookies I'd baked. After glancing over my shoulder to make sure I had an audience, I "accidentally" dropped my keys and then, balancing the cookies, I s-l-o-w-l-y bent over to pick them up.

Them brothers nearly broke that basketball court up! You should have heard the whistles and the roars! I laughed out loud and waved, because that was the exact reaction I'd been expecting. A curvy sister like me always got big-time attention. Men just loved me! Women hated me on sight. I wonder why?

"*Beyoncé!*" one of them yelled, then dropped to his knees. "*Please have my baby, Beyoncé!*"

I let that noise go right over my head because Beyoncé's young ass didn't have a thing on me. With their damn-you-fine calls still ringing in my ears, I strutted my stuff toward the front entrance of the building. The name beside intercom number four said REID, and I gave it two quick jabs and waited. Wiggling my booty to adjust my satin thong, I slung my purse over my shoulder and caught a whiff of Danger as it wafted up from my cleavage. Gary Reid didn't know it yet, but he was in big trouble. I'd met him at the All-Ranks Club a couple of weeks earlier, and after giving his cream-colored, hazel-eyed, six-foot-four body a look-over and actually enjoying the smooth brand of yang he was talking, I had decided he'd passed the Sparkle test and taken his phone number.

Gary and I discovered that we were both at the club that night to celebrate a mutual friend's birthday. He also told me he worked swing shifts as a hospital electrician, which was great because I didn't date military men anymore. Servicemen were some of the biggest hos out there, and me and my best friend, Fancy Lawson, could testify to that. Sailors had them some poontang in every port, airmen a hoochie in every hangar, and a soldier sure 'nuff had him a freak-mate in every foxhole.

Gary seemed legit, though. He was on call for the hospital most of the time so he said it didn't make sense to try to reach him at home. He'd jotted down his cell phone number and we'd spent crazy hours on the telephone, me talking dirty and being my naturally scandalous self, and him describing all the ways he could put the zoom-zoom-zoom in my boom, boom!

I sailed past the buzzing door with a bounce in my step. Boyfriend better be packing enough ammo to back up all that pillow talk because I was ready to get laid out lovely tonight.

Gary told me he shared an apartment with his grown niece, and since I'd let it be known from the jump that I wasn't looking for nobody's damn husband, he had no reason to lie. Don't get it twisted—I *will* take your man. It's just that I'm not on a happy husband hunt. I've never gone out actively looking to attract a married man but hey, if his wife ain't swinging her hips the right way and he's offering me something I can use . . . Well, like I told Gary, I believe in sticking my titties in a niggah's face. In being direct and up-front. Let me know the name of your game and then Miss Sparkle will decide whether or not you get to play it.

Their apartment was on the second floor but I bypassed the stairs and took the elevator instead. Why sweat if I didn't have to? Gary said his niece was a nurse who worked long shifts at the same hospital as him, and since neither of them was ever home for very long they decided it would be cost-effective to simply share an apartment.

Whatever. I didn't need all the details. Work your business, baby. Work it.

Gary was standing in the doorway when the elevator opened.

"Gee, baby." His words were like a moan. "You look delicious. Here." He stared at my cleavage and handed me a single rose, then kissed my cheek and stepped back to let me inside. "This is for you."

I took the rose and giggled 'cause I had turned him on without even trying. "And these," I said, handing him the small tray of cookies I'd baked the night before, "are for you." I checked out his package. He was dressed in some FUBU gear that at thirty-five, I thought he might be a little bit too old to be sporting but at least he had a fresh haircut and smelled good.

Inside the apartment was spacious and airy with sliding glass doors that led to a balcony. Gary led me through the foyer and into the living room and believe me, Miss Sparkle's eagle eyes were busy picking up every little detail along the way.

There was definitely a woman living up in here, up in here. And sistah-girl was holding it down with style too. Their place looked almost as good as mine. Almost—but not quite. Not many honeys had my kind of flair.

I stood in the living room where the lights had been dimmed and D'Angelo was singing in the background. Vanilla-almond incense hung in the air and tickled my nose.

"Have a seat," Gary said, then snapped his finger and smiled. "—Oops! Almost forgot. I got something for you." He dashed out the room and I heard a refrigerator door open and slam. A moment later, he was back.

"If I remember correctly," he said, untwisting the cap on an icy bottle with a brightly colored wrapper, "this is your favorite, right?"

I accepted the cold wine cooler and took a sip. He placed a plastic coaster on the cherry end table and handed me a napkin, skinning and grinning and eyeballing me like I was a slab of barbecue ribs. I could have gone for a bite or two of him as well, because he was even finer than I'd remembered from the club. He sat down across from me and scooted up close in his chair.

"So, where's your niece?" I asked, still looking around. Miss Niecy had skills. The curtains on the glass door had been hand sewn, and the fabric matched the doilies covering the end tables.

"She's working tonight," he said, and glanced over his shoulder.

I nodded toward an eight-by-ten photo that was behind the glass of their wall unit. "Is that her?" The young woman had thin lips and a big smile. Cute, but not as fine as me.

"Yeah," he said. "That's my niece."

Smiling again, he spread his legs and reclined in his seat with his hands behind his head. Y'all know I couldn't help it. I looked down at the Lugz on his feet and my heart leaped. Hello! Them jokers had to be at least a size thirteen. And his hands. Oooh *weeee*! Palming basketballs would be no sweaty-dah. But when my eyes crawled into his lap (yeah, you know I had to go there) I almost jumped up and did the splits!

Sparkle hit the Lotto! Sparkle hit the Lotto! I was dancing inside. Old boy was packing a *pow*! I could see the print through his jeans. It was fat and long and laying against his thigh. It was so big it looked like his pants were choking it to death.

"You like what you see?" he asked, doing that LL thing and running his tongue back and forth over his bottom lip. His skin looked like vanilla cream and I wondered how the curls of his mustache would feel on my tongue.

"The question is," I countered and quickly came correct. (*He* was supposed to be drooling all over *me*.) "Do you like what *you* see?" (Never let 'em forget who the queen is.)

"Know what?" He stood and faced me and his crotch was bulging right in front of my eyes. "I like what I see and what I feel." He took the wine cooler from my hand and put it on a coaster before pulling me to my feet. I was a tall sister but he made me feel tiny. I let him take me into his arms, and naturally we began swaying to the music.

Gary lowered his head and pressed his mouth to mine, and then lightly stroked his tongue back and forth across my lips. I nearly died it felt so good. I felt him nibbling and probing, teasing and tasting, and before I could stop myself I pulled his juicy tongue between my lips and sucked it like a piece of strawberry candy.

We stood there kissing and grinding like two kids. I've been known to go for what I want, so while his hands were all over my booty I took a few liberties of my own. I let my fingers climb up his biceps and shivered at the strength I felt in his arms. Down, down, skimming his tapered waist, teasing his flat stomach, and sliding my fingers just inside the waistband of his pants.

I heard him moan but his tongue never stopped. Our kiss was sexy and passionate, and I let my hand drop lower as I searched his inner thigh for that torpedo I'd seen bulging below his groin.

"Wow," he said, pulling away and leaving me empty-handed. He brushed his thumb against my pouting lips. "So sweet . . . so fine. I bet you taste good all over."

"You got that right," I said, smiling.

Stepping away from me, he stretched and nodded toward the balcony. "It's a beautiful night, baby. The stars are sparkling in the sky, just like your eyes."

Now, if that wasn't some of the corniest mess I'd ever heard. Yeah, I knew my name was jazzy and brothers on the prowl were all the time trying to get prolific with it, but damn if Mr. Gary didn't just go and make me feel special!

"C'mon." He took my hand and picked up my wine cooler. I started walking toward the sliding doors, but he led me toward the right. Toward the bedroom.

Nice, I thought, looking around at the mustard-and-brown décor. The room was totally neat. Too damn neat. African art on the walls, fake bearskin rugs on the floor. A small desk was in the corner, but except for a computer monitor and a cup filled with pens, there was nothing there that gave the room an ounce of personality. No shoes or clothing laying around, nothing on the dresser except a lace runner and a lamp. Not a thing was out of place, and you know Miss Sparkle looked. At the foot of the king-sized poster bed was another sliding glass door that led to a smaller balcony.

I waited as he opened the door and then followed him out-side. We were on the second floor, right over the basketball court. So close it looked like I could reach out and grab a rebound. I put my purse down on the inexpensive patio table and looked down over the railing. There was something about black men chasing a ball that just did it for me. Sent me swinging. I had been prepared to play hard to get with Gary for at least a good hour, but he'd crept up behind me and my treacherous coochie started twitching.

"It's hot out here," he whispered in my ear. "And you're hot too."

The brothers were running up and down the court. Talking shit and throwing 'bows. Gary leaned against me until the railing pressed into my midsection. I could have sworn I felt his erection poking a hole in me and I loved it. I was enjoying myself immensely when I felt something vibrate against my hip. I looked around.

"Damn," he said. He pulled his cell phone from its clip holder on his waist and peered at the number. "It's my sister. My niece's mother," he explained and flipped the cover shut. He set the phone down on the table. "I'll call her back later."

I nodded, then turned and leaned against the railing once more. He pressed himself against me and I swayed back. Biting my neck gently, his hands traveled up, cupping my breasts and teasing the pebbles of my nipples. Now, unlike some sisters who step up in a brother's den and then jump all righteous when he tries to get him some, I knew why I was there. Miss Sparkle had baked the cookies and now she was ready to see how fast they could crumble.

I reached back and took his right hand off my breast and pulled it down between my legs. He caught on real quick, and in less than two seconds he'd slipped his fingers under the crotch of my shorts. I put my head back and worked my hips in small circles and I didn't care who saw us. The voices below, the pounding of the feet, the bouncing of the ball, all they had to do was glance up and we would be cold busted. That shit turned me on!

Minutes later we were back in his bedroom and I was doing a striptease. Off with the halter! Off with the shorts! Off with the thong! I stood in front of him wearing nothing but my sandals and a smile.

"Damn," he breathed thickly. "I ain't never seen a woman built as fine as you."

Holla!

He pulled the mustard-colored comforter off the bed and swept it into a corner. Then he sat down on some bright purple sheets and unbuckled his belt, and before I knew it he'd kicked my thong and eighty-dollar short set under the bed, then jumped out of his pants and slipped between the sheets before I could even see what he was working with. I went around to the other side and propped myself up on some pillows on top of the sheets. Lying next to me, Gary caressed my breasts and tickled my navel with his tongue as I moaned out loud and my toes curled in my sandals. I slid my hand down his chest and trailed my fingers through his pubic hair. Anticipating the best, I opened my hand and reached for his bone.

Patting around, I searched for that log I'd seen poking through his pants and if I wasn't so horny I would have cried. I'd been tricked! There must have been a banana in his pants because there was nothing in his drawers! At least nothing worth mentioning, let alone worth touching!

Gary reached into a night table drawer and pulled out a condom. I almost laughed out loud when he slid it on. Not only was it busting a sag, it was about three inches too long and drooping over at the tip. Ladies, can we say dickless? I was so disappointed. So disappointed.

"You're gonna love this," Gary panted and rolled me on top of him, then just as quickly flipped me over and pinned me in a half nelson. For the next ten minutes I felt like we were playing Twister. I got sheet burns on my elbows and a crook in my neck. He grinded against me, tearing out my pubic strands and giving me hair bumps. He twisted me up and put some moves on me I'd never even heard of. I was sweating like a dog and ready to cry uncle by the time I found myself facedown and tail-up at the foot of the bed. We'd turned 180 degrees and Miss Sparkle was dizzy and disoriented.

"Bottoms up, baby!" He pulled me backward by the hips until I was on my elbows and knees, doggie style. I felt his tiny pee-pee poking around my coochie preparing to take the dive, and then a door slammed in the apartment and we both froze.

Boyfriend moved quickly, like he'd done this before. He cursed out loud and leaped over my body. His feet had barely touched the floor before he grabbed my arm, flung open the glass door, and tossed me outside. Then he put his finger to his lips, *sshh,* and slammed the door in my face.

"Wait . . . a . . . min . . ."

A second later, the door slid open a crack and a bright purple sheet sailed out.

The door slammed again and I heard the lock turn, and that's when it hit me. That fucker had played me. Played me hard! I was locked outside on his balcony wearing nothing but my shoes!

I lost it. Straight lost it. I screamed and cursed and called him every low-down name in the book. It took a couple of seconds before I realized I wasn't the only one hollering. I turned and looked down at the basketball court and saw the brothers, fists raised, arms pumping in the air. "*Dayum*, what a brickhouse! C'mon, baby!" they were yelling. "Jump, baby! Jump! We'll catch you!"

Humiliation wasn't the word! Those kneegrows had jokes! I grabbed that purple sheet and held it up to my neck.

Should I wrap it around my waist and jump? Or should I tie it to the balcony post and slide down it like a fireman? I spotted Gary's cell phone on the table. Ignoring the comments ringing out below me, I grabbed the phone and dialed the digits of the only person in the entire state I knew I could trust. "Fancy!" I screeched when she finally answered the phone. "Girl, come and get me!"

CHAPTER 3

FANCY

Freak Nasty

This shit ain't normal, I told myself as my husband moved against me, moaning and thrusting to a steady rhythm. I felt his breath heavy on my neck, his tongue licking my earlobe, his hands cupping my hips as he held me firmly and rode me from behind. Despite myself, I sighed and pushed back against him, enjoying the pool of wetness he had created between my thighs. I hated that I loved him so much. Hated that I could allow him to treat me this way.

"My turn." The voice of the man in front of me was deep and thick with arousal, reminding me of his presence and of my role. At my husband's command, the two of them had made a sandwich out of me. They were the bread, and I was the meat. Like the others before him, this man was tall and good-looking. He sat facing me, naked and beautiful, perched on the edge of my glass dining table, and for the life of me I could not remember his name. My hands left prints on either side of his muscled thighs, and I watched as he stroked himself, then took my submissive fingers and guided them around his shaft.

This just can't be normal. My husband's hands were no longer on my hips. Caressing my shoulders, he urged me into a slight bend, then pushed downward on the back of my head. I knew what he wanted and as usual, I obeyed. With my lips wet and wide, I took the strange man into my mouth and raised and lowered my head to the same beat that was being pounded out behind me. The sex was raw and primal. Two penises. Two tongues. Four hands. *Nasty Fancy.* The sounds and smells were incredible. *Freak Nasty Fancy.* I felt my clitoris clenching, my orgasm rising even as the shame of it hammered away at my heart.

I was damn good at what I did, and the man in front of me finished first. Groaning out his climax, he pushed me away and held his still-hard penis in both hands. My husband was more patient. Clutching me against his chest, he controlled his strokes, waiting for me, and moments later we exploded together: me crying out loud with tears in my eyes, him whispering his perpetual promise into my ear. "This the last time, baby. I swear. This the last time."

———

HIS e-mails usually came once a month and told me exactly what to do. Ran down the scenario in so much detail that I didn't have to think at all: just shake my ass, pick up the men, and execute the commands. At first I thought it was fun. Sexy. Exciting. Monthly sex games, love play. Nasty Fancy had finally met her match. I must admit, I got a lot of pleasure out of it for a while. Kevin's eyes alone could bring me to multiple orgasms so you know his sex was good. According to all the relationship articles I'd read there was nothing wrong with adding a little spice to your marriage to keep it fresh. To keep your man happy. Right? Besides, I was proud that my man trusted me enough to share his most intimate sexual fantasies with me. Lord knows I had more than a few of my own. But then Kevin became more demanding. His cravings more bizarre.

It wasn't long before my quest to satisfy my husband had led me into some sort of vicious sexual cycle, and now I was getting nervous because the e-mails were coming more frequently and each time I opened a new one the scenario was more twisted, the instructions more perverse.

The shag rug from our living room had been spread out on the dining room floor, just as Kevin had instructed. He'd watched from the shadows as me and the man, whose name I now remember as Mario, had come in and began fooling around. Minutes later, my husband had joined us.

And now, with the young man gone, Kevin lit two candles and lay me back down on the plush rug. The group games were out of the way and he was ready for the main event. Even above the scent of the candle and the odor of two men, I could smell my own sex. I watched the shadows flicker across my nipples and illuminate the sun-ray tattoo that encircled my navel as I tried hard not to cry.

He kissed me, his mouth hard and demanding. His penis pressed into my side as he pinched my nipples painfully, and then shoved three fingers inside of me without warning.

This just ain't normal.

I arched my back and bore it. I was sore, but I knew better than to resist. Turning him down was out of the question.

He'd be furious for days. Give me the silent treatment and make me pay for it in a million little ways.

"Look at me," he demanded. His fingers were like fire moving in and out of me and I shuddered at the harshness in his voice. I opened my eyes and met his steady gaze as he urged me into a familiar game. "I don't know who the fuck that niggah was who just left out of here, but you better tell me exactly what happened, Fancy. Go 'head, baby. Tell Daddy everything you let him do. Tell me everywhere he touched you. Where you put your mouth and what he tasted like. And I promise you, baby. I promise. I ain't gonna get mad."

CHAPTER 4

KEVIN

Love Jones

I am an addict.

I'll lie, steal, and fight to feed my addiction.

I am an addict, and there ain't a 12-step program in the world that can ease my pain. I'll stay out all night long, fuck over my best friend, deceive my boss, whatever it takes to keep my jones fed and my sins secret, I'll do it.

My addiction has affected my cash flow, my mental health, and my standing in the church. My addiction has kept me on my toes, scheming and conniving as I figured out unique ways of getting my needs met. Tonight my addiction had once again led me to use my wife to satisfy my urges, and I was mad as hell when the telephone rang and interrupted my flow.

"Keep going," I told Fancy as I moved on top of her. "What else he do?" I asked, my nuts straining for another burst. "You let him put his tool in you, too, didn't you!"

Ringgggggg.

To my surprise Fancy pushed against my chest and scooted from under me. Cold air hit my hammer and I cursed.

"I gotta get that, Kevin. It could be Mama. You know Lavish is sick."

I couldn't care less about her sick sister. I grabbed at Fancy's arm but she pulled away and reached for the telephone sitting on its brass stand. "Hurry up, baby," I whimpered. My hammer was so hard the tip throbbed. I stuffed the blanket between my thighs to keep it warm. "You know how much I need you."

I thought I heard Fancy suck her teeth, but before I could react there was a click and sounds from the speakerphone filled the room.

"Fancy! Girl, come and get me!"

Sparkle Henderson. Now, that was one fine chick. She was my supply sergeant and Fancy's best friend, but I'd been admiring her ever since the days when we were stationed together in Puerto Rico. I figured she'd be chilling with some lucky man on a Friday night, but there was so much background buzz it sounded like she was calling from a club or something.

"What's wrong?" Fancy shouted. "Where are you?"

My hopes were beginning to dwindle but my erection stayed true.

"Girl, I'm locked outside. On a balcony! Butt naked! Fancy, please come and get me. I'm on Westlake and Dumont. On the balcony right next to the basketball court!"

Fancy flicked on the overhead lights and screwed up her face. "What's all that noise? Who are all those people?"

"Girl! Who you think?" Sparkle shrieked. "Niggahs! Niggahs down there on the court lookin' at my naked ass! 4040 Westlake, Fancy. Hurry up, girl. And please bring me some clothes!"

———

WHEN Sparkle called there wasn't much that could keep Fancy from answering. And I couldn't blame her. I swear that girl had some type of mojo on both me and my wife. She was just that fine.

I let Fancy leave without much of a fuss. The night was ruined anyway, and besides, I was getting bored with the setup and needed to think of something different. Lil Mama and Teesha had turned me out at an early age, and despite the love I had for Fancy we both knew that I could never settle for having sex only one way. I needed constant stimulation, variety, diversified activities.

I was one of those guys who'd always had it pretty easy in the ladies department. God had blessed me in a lot of ways and I'd never had a problem getting the trim. I must have slept with more than three hundred women in high school alone, and coming from a town the size of mine sometimes that meant I had to double-dip: I hit the daughter and the mama too.

Back then brothers used to sweat me. Stayed on my tip hoping to get a shot at my sloppy seconds. And I didn't mind. Why should I care who fucked behind me? I seldom went back more than twice, and I never got jealous if my boy wanted to take a splash in the pool I'd just climbed out of. It wasn't like I was capable of having a relationship or anything. I just had a hungry monkey and needed a nut from as many different women as possible.

By the time I was sixteen I'd learned that I had something really special in my pants. Women passed out just from sniffing my vapors, and the way I sexed them kept them coming back for as long as I wanted. Problem was, I never wanted them for very long. It never failed. I'd hit them two, maybe three times, and then nothing. They could suck my toolie all night long but I couldn't come if they paid me.

Now, that might sound like fun to some guys, but you know what your momma said: Too much of a good thing ain't no good for you. I'd leave them sore and walking bow-legged: pussy so scuffed they never wanted to see me again. That scene got so frustrating that I made it a rule to hit it once or twice, then quit it.

That's when I knew something was wrong with me. I was actually ashamed of myself. Felt like a pervert or something and actually had to downplay my numbers for my friends. None of my boys was getting even a fraction of the trim I was getting. Yeah, they all bragged about banging mucho ass, but none of them seemed to actually *fiend* for it the way I did. I mean, I had to get me a hit in some shape or fashion almost every single day! And in between the women I was masturbating seven days a week. Let Dirty Sue tell it, my palms should have been as hairy as her ass. Yeah, Lil Mama and Teesha had awakened something ugly in me and at one point it almost destroyed me. The sad truth of it is they'd turned me into a street junkie with sex being my drug of choice.

Once or twice I tried to kick it. To tell that monkey scrambling all over my back to leave me alone and take a hike. That's when I learned what a heroin addict must feel like trying to go cold turkey. I did all kinds of things to keep myself distracted, to keep my mind off sex. I barred myself from places where it would be easy to pick up women. I pumped heavy iron in the gym and ran five miles a day. I even made myself join a new church family and serve as a deacon. Didn't work. A ninety-two-year-old church mother passed out after catching me and Sister Carmichael going at it in a balcony pew, and who could blame them when they poured holy water down my pants and revoked my deaconship card.

When I enlisted in the army things went from bad to worse. There were more willing women than I knew existed. Ages eighteen to eighty. Privates to general officers. After screwing around heavily for a few years I got caught in a run-down. Three sistahs. Fort Hood, Texas. Man, I tell you black women will kill you for loaning out their tool. I had my brand-new car spray-painted with the letters O-P-P on all four sides. One of them stole my credit card and took the other two on a shopping spree. The craziest of the three had all of my keys copied and commenced to driving my ass crazy. She'd sneak into my apartment while I was at work and unplug my refrigerator and leave the door open so my food would spoil. Or I'd pull my car nose-in to a parking space at work, and she'd come past and back that baby in. Or worse, move it to a new spot altogether and have me outside walking up and down the lanes and scratching my head until I found it.

Just fucking with my head.

And then I got orders for a permanent change of station to Fort Riley, Kansas, hooked up with Fancy, and decided to get married. She was the only woman I'd ever met who could keep up with me in the sack. Who didn't think my fantasies were perverted and who could actually handle my needs. Fancy was my kind of freak. She could come by just the sound of my voice, and believe it or not, there were times when she wore me out and left my hammer so limp I didn't want any for two whole days. Fancy was the first woman I ever really loved, and the fact that she understood my drives and helped indulge my fantasies proved that she loved me too.

But here lately I was having some old familiar urges. Urges that turned my wife straight off. The last time I tried to make her do it she cursed me out and went to stay with Sparkle for a whole week. Soon I'd convince her, though. She couldn't resist me for long because deep down inside Fancy needed to have orgasms the same way that I did.

Kicking the blanket aside, I walked naked into the kitchen and got a beer from the fridge. I carried it into the living room and turned on the wide-screen television. Examining the collection on my wooden shelves, I selected a tape and started the VCR. With the volume turned down, I watched two sisters getting it on with one man. The sisters had beautiful bodies, but it was what they were doing to each other that held my interest.

Chugging back my brew, I stroked up my hammer and enjoyed the show. I pretended I was the brother up there on the screen, watching my girls get down in living color. One looked like Fancy and the other looked just like Sparkle. Sinking back into the soft leather I closed my eyes and relaxed. Moments later I was ten years old again and living with Dirty Sue. Locked in a back bedroom, I lay back and let Lil Mama and Teesha show me the ropes as I fed my monkey until I exploded in my own hand.

CHAPTER 5

FANCY

Be a Ho if You Wanna

I raced down the side streets looking for Westlake. I couldn't believe it. Sparkle had sounded like she was crying mad on the phone. Crying mad! Sparkle and I had only been friends for a little more than three years, but have you ever met a sister-girl who you just *felt*? Our temperaments and the way we went about doing things may have been very different, but almost from the moment we met I'd felt us *click*.

Maybe it was just our chemistry, or perhaps it was because our life experiences came from opposite ends of the spectrum. Sparkle was big city and I was definitely small town. When she wasn't squeezed into her military uniform, Sparkle was decked to the hilt in flash and bling, and for the most part I preferred jeans and a roomy T-shirt.

Sparkle came from a loving family of outspoken women who were comfortable with their sensual selves. I was born in Tempest, Kansas, a preacher's daughter with a whore's body. I'll be honest. I didn't have a single sob story or a stack of excuses for my behavior. Nobody molested me when I was a child. Nobody deprived me of attention or affection. I was just born loving sex, and maybe it was a genetic thing because my sister, Lavish, was the same way. While my father sang the Lord's praises from the pulpit and my mother served as president of the women's advisory board, Lavish and I snuck into the back room and played horsey, doctor, and barstool hussy with a crew of older choirboys at least three times a week.

Nasty Fancy is what the townspeople called me, and for a long time that's exactly who I was. Trembling at the sound of singing voices and stomping feet, I let those church boys hem me up against the wall and touch me wherever they wanted.

It wasn't long before every horny adolescent in my neighborhood was sniffing around my door, and since I was bold enough to sneak into the boys' bathroom during school and give them what they wanted, they had good reason to come back looking for more. I was soaking in the bathtub one evening when my mother walked in without knocking. *Nasty Fancy.* She took one look at the hickeys and bite marks all over my neck and thirteen-year-old woman-sized breasts, and fainted dead away.

But when she awakened she was much stronger. She rallied her church sisters beside her, and along with my father they sat around in a prayer circle calling on the Lord to rebuke the demon that had infiltrated my wanting flesh.

It's not that I don't believe in the power of prayer, because I do. But when it came down to sex, not even the good Reverend Murphy and congregation could pray away the yearning that ached between my legs. When I graduated high school and went to college, education was certainly not the main thing on my curriculum. I majored in sex with multiple partners, and graduated with an advanced degree. Even after leaving college and landing a dream job as a law clerk, I still wasn't satisfied. I took a side gig dancing at a spot called Jugz, which is actually where I met Kevin.

Jugz was a topless bar located on the main strip leading up to Fort Riley. At one time it was placed off-limits to soldiers by order of the community commander, but it went through a change of ownership and all the drugs and thugs were chucked out the back door.

Kevin used to come in alone all the time, and he was known to drop the dollars. I couldn't have cared less about how much he spent. I was there for the thrill of it: one of those women who got turned on by turning men on.

One night Kevin signaled the manager and said he wanted a private lap dance with the girl they called *Freak Nasty*. Needless to say, I took him upstairs to one of the lounges and we broke all the rules. Of course the customers were warned not to touch us. We were paid to tease, not to please. But Kevin was the sexiest man I'd ever seen, and just the sound of his voice and the deep pools of his eyes had turned me on beyond belief. And as I hovered above his lap, my naked breasts grazing his chest, Kevin put his hands on my hips and moved me to a rhythm that was so soul stirring and sensual that it was me who exploded in my pants instead of him.

"I'm leaving here in sixty days," Kevin told me as he walked me to my car after work one night. We'd been seeing each other constantly for three months, and I was already so whipped that I barely knew my own name. He was the sweetest man I'd ever met. He bombarded me with affection, took me out dancing, and sexed me in the most exciting places, giving it to me deep and dirty just the way I liked it. Everything about Kevin just accentuated the freak in me, and for the first time in my life I felt comfortable revealing the scope of my sexual appetites. "Marry me, Fancy," Kevin asked. "And I promise you'll never want to dance for another man again."

Boy, was he right. I married him at a justice of the peace, called my mother and Lavish and told them I was leaving the continent, and the next thing I knew we were climbing on a plane to Puerto Rico, where we'd be stationed for the next three years.

Kevin and I were about a year short on our tour in Puerto Rico when Sparkle arrived on the island. Even though I was a pretty decent photographer and had earned a degree in criminology, jobs off post were scarce if you didn't speak the language, so I'd taken a position as a medical assistant in the sick-call clinic at the base hospital.

While I was inprocessing Sparkle's medical information into the hospital database we struck up a conversation. She called me country and said I sounded like I was from the backwoods of Georgia. She did her best to speak very properly by enunciating her words to the extreme, but I could tell she was faking her dialect, and I could also tell that she was from the North. In her case, the North turned out to be Brooklyn, New York, and I almost laughed because with her flashy blond hair and big ass, she personified almost everything I'd heard about sisters from New York City.

Our friendship progressed slowly, but it felt really good. It wasn't long before we were meeting for lunch and shopping together on the weekends. I don't know exactly when we became best friends, but I can remember the day I knew she trusted me.

Sparkle had her eye on some young guy named Carl she'd

met in the NCO club. Carl had a chiseled body but was known as the U-MOP to most folks: the Ugliest Mother-fucker on Post. As bad as Carl's face looked, his body was mesmerizing and rumor had it that he was swinging a fat bat. That was all Sparkle needed to hear. "If it's that good I'll put a paper bag over his damn head," she told me. "I wanna fuck him, not hang a picture of him in my den."

Sparkle ended up sleeping with Carl a few times, but as soon as the next cutie with a fabulous body caught her eye she jumped ship and sent the U-MOP on his way. That would have been the end of that, except the U-MOP showed up in my sick-call clinic one Friday afternoon complaining that his pee-pee hurt and his testicles were swollen.

I was dialing Sparkle's number while the poor boy was still standing at my desk.

"Oh shit!" she'd screamed into the phone. "And his don-key dick broke the rubber while I was riding that hideous monster! Girl, what am I gonna do?"

"I don't know," I told her, "but he's up here getting tested for chlamydia."

Sparkle was skeeved out. She refused to sit around for al-most a week feeling diseased while we waited for his test re-sults to come back, so we came up with a quick plan. She would come into the clinic on sick call the following Monday complaining of a vaginal discharge. I'd be her chaperone, and when the doctor ordered a swab, I'd be sure to have the proper slide and tray waiting. She'd get tested without going through the rigamarolla of naming names, and thus get her cure.

Well, it wasn't long before I learned that nothing involving Sparkle ever goes exactly according to plan. She came into the clinic like she was supposed to and I set her up in an examining room and gave her a gown.

"I really do have a discharge now," she whispered behind her hand. "Itches too."

I waited until the doctor came in and told her to scoot her butt down to the end of the table then, averting my eyes from her vagina, I positioned myself behind him and hurriedly opened the culture dish.

"You have yeast," the pudgy Pakistani doctor said, peering between Sparkle's legs and then holding the swab in the air. I'd looked up the symptoms of chlamydia and made sure Sparkle complained of having every single one of them.

"Uh-uh." Sparkle sat partway up on the examining table, resting on her elbows and shaking her head. "It's not yeast. Doesn't feel like yeast. Feels like—" She began reciting the symptoms in earnest. "I have abdominal pain, it hurts when I have sex, I've been spotting between periods . . ."

"No!" the doctor insisted. "It is yeast. Look!" he held the swab in the air and waved it under Sparkle's nose. "Yeast, yeast, yeast!"

Two years later we could still laugh about that so hard we both peed. As it turned out, Carl didn't have chlamydia and neither did Sparkle. All of that worrying she'd done over the weekend must have stressed her out and given her a yeast infection.

And now, after some stroke of divine luck had ordained that we both be stationed at Fort Dix in New Jersey, I was the one who was worried. Traffic was pretty heavy, even for a Friday night, but I drove with my foot pressed to the gas pedal and managed to arrive at the address on Westlake less than twenty minutes after she'd called.

I was surprised to find Sparkle waiting in the foyer of the building looking crazy with rage. She was leaning against a tall white man who had nice legs and wore glasses. He was only a pair of contact lenses away from being extremely fine, and I gestured through the glass for him to unlock the door.

"Sweetie!" I rushed to hug her as the guy let me into the building. "Are you okay?"

Sparkle truly scared me. She looked a pure-dee mess. I'd never seen her so angry. She had on a pair of men's plaid shorts and an oversized T-shirt plastered with a popular WB cartoon logo that read: IF YOU SEE DA POLICE, WARN A BROTHER. A pair of lavender high-heeled espadrilles were on her feet and one of the straps was busted.

My friend stepped toward me and dropped her purse. Ignoring her stuff as it scattered along the floor, Sparkle balled up her fists and worked her lips as she tried to get her words out. I reached out and hugged her to me, whispering soothing murmurs as if they would dissipate her wrath. When she stopped shaking, I let her go and saw that her makeup was shot and there was a purple sheet slung across her shoulders. "What happened?" I asked, searching her eyes while the white guy gathered her stuff up from the floor and pushed it back into her purse.

She gave me a look that was so agonizing and evil I was almost sorry I'd asked.

"That asshole—" she began, then covered her face and took a series of deep breaths trying to calm herself. I took her in my arms again. I wanted to rub her hair but it was already everywhere. I patted her back instead.

"Uhm—excuse me."

The white guy standing with Sparkle was offering a shake. I looked at his outstretched hand, then back into his face. "What's going on here?" I demanded. "Did you do something to her?"

"Who, me? No, I was just trying to help. I'm Phil. I live in the apartment next door to Gary's. From what I can figure, his wife must have come home just ahead of me and, um . . ."

"Gary?"

"Uhm, yes. Gary. You know, the guy she came over here to . . . see."

"She came here to see Gary? That fool who drives the white Lexus?"

He nodded, the words tumbling from his mouth. "Yes, that's right. I was just coming in from the gym and saw the crowd swarming under my window. I couldn't chase all the fellas away, but one of them was decent enough to toss some clothing up onto the balcony." He frowned and ran his hand through his wavy black hair. "Things were pretty chaotic for a few minutes, but I managed to climb over my balcony and help her get across to my apartment. She told me a friend was coming to get her, so I thought I'd just come downstairs and keep her company while she waited."

I nodded my thanks, but I was too through. I'd tried to tell Sparkle that things weren't on the up-and-up with Gary. She shouldn't have been in his apartment or out on his balcony in the first place, but with all the crazy crap I'd done who was I to be judgmental? I thanked Phil again, and let him hold the door open for us as we left.

"You can bring me back for my car tomorrow," Sparkle said as I moved some spent rolls of film from the passenger seat and started my ignition. "I'ma pay Gary's ass back, you can believe that, but right now I just wanna go home and wash that asshole's spit off of me."

Wash? What the heck was wash? I'd run out of the house like a bat out of hell with a lot more than spit on me. The memory of Kevin laying on the floor stroking himself flashed through my mind. He'd probably try to jump my bones again the moment I walked through the door.

"Okay," I said. "But you should have listened to me about Gary, though."

"He told me he was single! Said he lived with his grown niece!"

I turned to her. "Sparkle. Come on now. You're too smart to have fallen for that line. How legit could he be when the plates on his car say I CREEP? And please don't tell me that means he drives real slow."

She gave me an evil look and turned away.

I was done. "Okay, girl. I'll take you home. Buckle up and let's fly."

Sparkle put on her seat belt, then hissed, "You know what, Fancy? Gary must have thought Miss Sparkle was somebody's back-alley ho! Do I look like somebody's goddamn ho?"

I reached out and touched her hand. My girl drew all kinds of drama when men were involved. "You are *not* a ho, Sparkle," I said firmly. "You're a woman, just like the rest of us women out here. We're all trying to make it the best way we can."

She flicked her hand in the air. "No, Fancy. Cut the crap. I know how people talk about me. I hear the things they say. 'Staff Sergeant Henderson is nothing but a slut. She's a get-over artist and doesn't give a damn about anybody else. She kisses officer ass and never runs PT. The only reason she made E-6 is because she screwed her way up the enlisted ladder.' "

I swallowed hard. She had a point. That's exactly what they said. But then again, they talked pretty badly about me too. "Okay," I told her, switching tactics, "so what if you're a ho? You can be a ho if you want to." I thought about my crazy relationship with Kevin and shrugged. "Most of us are hoeing for one thing or another anyway. Just because you know how to be an independent woman and stand up for yourself doesn't make you a slut, Sparkle. It makes you strong. Besides, people talk about me all the time. Men write my name on bathroom walls. That doesn't make them right about who I am."

"But why does it seem like every man that I can halfway respect is either hung up on some white girl or is already married? Yeah, I know I'm fine and I can pull a man in a hot minute, but all the brothers who seem like they might be able to handle me are carrying around a truckload of issues! Is something wrong with me, Fancy, huh? I mean, I'm fly and smart and my coochie is good. So what the hell is wrong with me?"

"There's nothing wrong with you, Sparkle, but maybe you should be more selective about who you bake cookies for. I mean, you're bright and sexy, and you have a lot of style. Men are naturally attracted to you. The fact that you talk shit and treat them like dirt doesn't hurt either. They love it."

"Yeah, right." Sparkle sat back and crossed her arms. She still looked angry, but at least she wasn't enraged anymore. "I guess that's why I'm going home to a rubber love stick and four D-cell batteries. Gary knew what my rules were, with his

Vienna sausage, no-dicked self! He could have told me about
his wife. He still might've gotten him some. And my goodness! You wanna talk about a *nasty* somebody? Bringing another woman into his wife's house?" She shook her head,
disgusted. "After what I went through with Lonnie, I'd kill a
man if he did me like that."

"Don't judge all men by Lonnie. Anal-retentive dick-
slingers don't really count."

Sparkle sucked her teeth. "Yeah, he had some compulsive
behaviors, but his asshole wasn't that tight. Besides, his butt
looked scrumptious in that flight suit and he also had a sweet
strong back." She grinned. "Maybe I should piss his wife off.
How about I chuck the D cells tonight, then roll over to
McGuire Air Force Base and throw some rocks at his window? Skinny blond wife or no, you know he'll come running."

"I'm serious, Sparkle," I said. "I think you should chill on
the married man thing, but that doesn't mean you should settle down and start ironing some idiot's socks."

"That's easy for you to say. Even though you keep your
booty up in that godforsaken club like you work there, at
least you have a husband at home who respects you and loves
your last week's dirty drawers."

Oh, if only she knew. Knew the kind of things that Kevin's
love had led me to do. But Kevin was Sparkle's first sergeant,
and in her eyes and in the eyes of most of the other troops,
Kevin was the poster child for the hard-core soldier and dedi-
cated husband. This would have been a perfect time to tell
Sparkle the truth about my sordid life. To tell her exactly why
I was in the club nearly every weekend dancing like a hooker

and picking up men, but every time I opened my mouth to let it out something inside me froze. I was just too ashamed. After all, how bad could it be if I had multiple orgasms each and every time?

"I wish I had a man like Kevin," Sparkle continued, sweeping her hair back from her eyes. "Not just like him—he plays you much too close—but similar. Watch out for that brother of his, though. Emily Pinchback! Any man with a name like a bitch is shady in my book. That Oreo is so into white girls it's a shame. He shouldn't hang around Kevin or any other black man who has a sister for a wife. Bad influence."

I shrugged. "Emile has his issues, but so do we all. Besides, he's my brother-in-law so I try to look past his white-woman fetish."

"You're too damn nice, Fancy, but I love you." She gave a short bitter laugh, then looked at me with wistful eyes. "Do you know why we're such good friends?"

I caught a whiff of myself and the two men I'd had. Discreetly, I closed my legs and rolled down the window to let the breeze blow my funk away. "Because we're just alike?"

"What! Girl, your shit could never be this tight."

"You know what I mean. We're friends because we're alike in a lot of ways. We like the same type of music, the same foods . . . we have a lot in common, Sparkle."

I stopped for a red light at the corner of her house and Sparkle laughed loudly. "No, Fancy. I eat the same kind of stuff a lot of sisters eat. Don't mean they can stand the sight of me. None of that mess is why we're friends. We're friends because"—she put her foot up on my dashboard and spoke earnestly—"because we have the exact same degree of cute-ness. Neither one of us is finer than the other. Yeah, you have softer hair, but my complexion is better. Both of us have big asses even though I think mine is shaped nicer."

Pulling into her parking spot, I killed the engine and sighed. Turning toward my friend I said, "Don't make our relationship sound shallow, Sparkle. Remember, I've seen you naked, tiger booty, and we both know that my ass is rounder and my skin is only messed up right before my period. But I really do love you. Love the hell out of you."

We got out of the car laughing and walked toward her apartment. At the door Sparkle paused. The anger was gone from her eyes and her gaze had turned tender. "Thanks for coming to get me, Fancy. Aside from my girl Sanderella, you're the only real friend I have."

"No problem," I said, reaching out to hug her tightly. "I hope we can always be there for each other."

Sparkle pulled away sharply, then sniffed twice and glared at me with suspicion.

"Damn heffah! You stink like *hell*! Fancy girl! Have you been fucking?"

CHAPTER 6

EMILE

My Sistah!

*B*ack in the day it wasn't cool to be a dark-skinned brother the way it is now. Cats like Michael Jordan, Morris Chestnut, and that skinny brother Taye from *Waiting to Exhale* did me a big solid when they put *brown skin* in the dictionary right beside *sexy,* but even with my honest eyes and nice white teeth, it still bothered me that if the light was wrong you couldn't really tell where my skin ended and my hair began.

By the time I was thirteen I'd tried all kinds of lightening creams. Cocoa Butter, Ambi, Nadinola, Black & White Bleaching Cream . . . you name it, I spent every dime I earned bagging groceries buying it. I'd stand in the drugstore for hours reading the labels and comparing the ingredients. Then, after pushing my purchase down inside the front of my pants, I'd run home and sneak into the bathroom, lock the door, and pray to the gods of beautiful fair skin as I rubbed the creams and ointments into my cheeks, across my forehead, and down the back of my neck.

One morning in the seventh grade I woke up and almost flipped out. I was light all right. But in patches. I looked like a sick dalmatian. Black with white spots. Dirty Sue took one look at me across the breakfast table and smirked. "Oughtta put some Clorox in your bathwater, boy," was her recommendation. "And quit washing your face with the goddamn dishrag."

I was in high school when I figured out that black people had far more issues with my dark skin than white people did. Not one white person had ever called me Bosco or Mudd Pie, or Cocoa Puff even though a lot of blacks had said those things and a whole lot more.

I didn't date at all during my high school years, but I tried hard to make up for it when I got to college. Nancy, Susan, Lisa, Teresa, Cathy, Diana, Helen, I could go on and on. I liked them either blond or redheaded, and the fairer their skin, the better.

"Man, what you trying to do? Lighten up your gene pool?" Kevin accused me when he came to visit me during spring break of my sophomore year.

"You're damn skippy," I told him without shame or hesitation. I wanted my kids to have the best of the best, and since all I could give them was all I possessed, I would have to choose a mother for them who could do the rest. Yeah, they'd still be mixed with black, but at least they'd be light. They wouldn't catch the same kind of hell I'd caught.

I shrugged away my thoughts as I drove down High Street. It was Saturday morning and my watch read 8:20 A.M. as I pulled into the employee parking lot outside of Victory Mall.

The doors were locked but I knew security was already inside. I went around to the back of my truck and unloaded a pulley and two large boxes, and then I beat feet across the parking lot, pushing my merchandise in front of me.

I was the first vendor to arrive, and a guard with ashy cornrows looked pissed that he had to put down his doughnut and get up off his ass to let me in. Did I care? I'd never operated on colored people's time and I sure wasn't about to show up late when it came time to turn a dollar. I had certain habits and rituals to complete, so I liked to get in early and give myself plenty of time to get set up, and by that I meant my pushcart as well as my sales façade.

Saturdays were always busy at "the black mall," as Victory was known. The joint suffered from ghetto gangrene, but I'd be a fool to complain. Six months ago I'd gotten permission from my battalion commander to moonlight on a second job, then applied for a business license and set up a pushcart kiosk. I'd smooth-talked the forty-two-year-old overweight sister who handled vending assignments and landed a spot smack dab between the food court and the mall's only ATM.

Location, location, location!

I had no idea where black people got all that disposable income they were dropping, but man, business was lovely and you'd better believe that seven days a week my cart was open so we could help them spend it.

Most of the clientele I catered to were nothing more than label whores: sisters who spent their last dime to put somebody else's name on their ass. I understood their mentality because I was raised among it, but personally, it was a mentality that I loathed. Why spend on flash and trash when you could have money in the bank?

Playing to their weaknesses I'd hired Ali, a smooth-talking young brother with light skin and wavy hair who manned the kiosk during the week, but on some weekends I worked it myself. And I mean I *worked it.* I turned on the charm and sold designer hats and handbags hand over fist. Everything from Coach to Gucci to Louis Vuitton, and you wouldn't believe how much bank I took in.

Living with Dirty Sue had taught me to adapt to my environment, and standing at that kiosk soliciting sales from black women I became such an actor! It had only taken me a second to learn that it wasn't just dried and dyed leather I had to sell, but the illusion of a community business owner, a together brother who really cared about his customers. That, plus a little flirt-flirt thrown in for good measure, had ensured me a stable base of about thirty sisters who paid my car note and helped make it possible for me to treat my Becky Ann to all the things my military paycheck would never have covered.

Black women reigned supreme in Victory Mall, so I made it a point to wear my BDUs every now and then when I came in. Materialism aside, most women loved the sight of a man in uniform. My motto was *Use what you got,* and if the uniform gave me an edge, made me seem more appealing to these scheming sisters, then so be it.

But the atmosphere sickened me. At least a million times a day I saw Lil Mama and Teesha, parading around wearing fake everything: contact lenses, hair, nails, and even gold teeth. Yeah, these days their names were more like Destiny, Diamond, or Diamante, but they were cut from the same cloth. Talking on cell phones, chasing their wild kids, pushing expensive baby strollers, and putting stuff on layaway that they couldn't even afford to get off. Where did it end?

I even saw Dirty Sue. Or at least a couple of close facsimiles of her. Walking around the mall with her whole purse stuck up in her bra. Showing her age and her ass, still ranting and raving and talking that same old tired black woman shit: "Look at these fat-ass porch monkeys—walkin' 'round wearing they booties in the front of them cheap-ass ho dresses! I just got off work scrubbing the shit out of somebody else's toilet and I'm tore-back-frogdog-drag-ass-ugamoe tired, while these lazy Welfare heffahs 'round here lookin' all *fresh*! Got they hair slammed, they nails bammed, but no Vaseline on them crusty-ass ankles—feets looking like they need to be soaked in a pot of warm Crisco!"

Then the Dirty Sues of the world would suck their teeth and say loud enough for their man to hear, "Damn hoochies got tons of baby powder caked up 'round they necks, and ain't nare one of them even brushed they teef! And they got the nerve to be lookin' at my man 'cause he got a job—and his dumb ass prob'ly lookin' back at them too!"

I shuddered. No, as long as I could help it, I would never subject myself to another black woman for as long as I lived. Kevin got mad and said I was a hypocrite for selling my products in a black mall, but remember, I told you he was slow. The opinion of a man who passed on a free ride through college and married a worm like Fancy didn't hold a lot of weight in my book. Instead of playa-hating, Kevin should have parked himself in my corner and taken some notes. He laughed when he saw the way I manipulated my female customers: talking sexy shit and keeping a verbal barrage going that made them feel good, but stopped short of actually exchanging any digits or committing to a date. I tried to flatter their silly asses to death.

"It's not just that you exclusively date white girls, but you don't even like being black, Emile," Kevin had complained one Saturday afternoon when he came with me to work. "You're not down with any black causes, you don't eat black foods, you don't respect or associate with black women . . . all you do is shuck and jive with 'em while your hand is busy digging in their wallets."

And what in the world was there to like about being black?

Damn right I'm in their wallets, I thought as the mall opened and customers began pushing through the doors. I shook my head and called out to a big-booty sister who had on a pair of leopard-skin pants that hugged her many curves. Damn! Could she have left some of that weave in the Chinese store so the next sister could get some? Didn't matter. She was good to drop at least a bill each payday, so she got much charm. On top of that, she brought in new customers every couple of months, so you know she was all right with me. I thought about the strand of freshwater pearls I planned to buy Becky Ann, then put on my ghetto game face. "Hey, Keisha!" I waved her wide hips over with a big sexy grin. "My sistah! Bring your fine self over here. What you know good today, gurlfriend?"

CHAPTER 7

KEVIN

*You're Gonna Make Me
Love Somebody Else*

*F*ancy didn't come home last night.

She claimed Sparkle was too upset to stay by herself so she decided to chill with her for the night. I'd blown up Fancy's cell phone almost every hour on the hour, and each time we talked she claimed they were cooking and cleaning for the Fourth of July dinner Sparkle was having later on this evening. When I whined and bitched about being left alone, my wife suggested I amuse myself for the day, then meet her over at Sparkle's after the guests and family arrived.

So I did my usual Saturday-morning thing. I got up at nine and ran three miles, then came home and masturbated in the shower. I considered going up to the academy and checking on the soldiers who were doing remedial training, but I'd been in Iraq for a full month and I wasn't trying to knock anybody's neck out of joint. I wanted to ease back into my position a little bit at a time; plus, it was an unwritten rule that the weekend duty sergeant got to run things his own way.

After my shower I dried myself off with a soft towel I found hanging on a rack. Fancy was good like that. Good about making sure I had everything I needed. She should have brought her ass home last night. She knew I didn't like having so much time alone. Big snatches of empty time allowed me to slip into my fantasies and indulge in what I called my stinkin' thinkin'. Made me want to love somebody else.

I got dressed in our bedroom, putting on a casual shirt and a pair of linen shorts. I didn't bother with my boxers. Instead, I bare-balled it and let the old toolie hang free. After wolfing down a big bowl of Raisin Bran I grabbed a brew and headed for the guest bedroom that I sometimes used as a wood shop.

I was working on a double step for Fancy. I'd bought her a lush, high-profile bed, and I wanted to make it easier for her to climb up on it. I was just an amateur carpenter, but there was something about the solitude of woodworking that calmed me and kept my mind easy. I finished off three beers while I completed my cuts, then used a belt sander to smooth out the wood. I managed to stay in the zone for over five hours before my thoughts barged in. After all, I rationalized, the weather was nice and the hardware store was very far away. A can of cherry stain and two brass ornaments were required to finish the job, so Saturday evening found me cruising down High Street and checking out the sights.

I had my drop-top down and the radio up high. The sun was setting but the temperature was still in the eighties and people were out on the streets. I stayed on High Street long after I should have turned off for the hardware store. The business district faded into the background as I crossed the tracks to the other side of town.

I turned right onto a major cross street, then pulled into

the parking lot of a small store and looked up at the marquee.
BAYSHORE BROWSERS. SPECIALIZING IN ADULT BOOKS AND VIDEOS.
I'd found this place through the Internet and although I'd visited several times before at night, I'd never gone in during the
day.

I stepped inside and the air-conditioning hit me at the door.
The store was pretty big and there were a number of customers hanging around, some browsing through various books,
others checking out the rows of videos. There were a few
women present, to my surprise, and I made a mental note to
bring Fancy with me the next time I came.

I choose two erotica anthologies that were written by black
authors. One was called *Sistergirls.com* and the other was
Brown Sugar 3: When Opposites Attract. I wasn't much of a
reader on my own, but I liked to let Fancy pick out hot scenes
and read them out loud while we played in bed. There was
something about hearing nasty words come out of her mouth
that really turned me on.

Just the act of buying the books and anticipating her reading them had turned me on. My tool was hard and sticking
straight up in my pants, and on the drive back home I let my
mind wander into fantasyland. I knew I had a problem, but at
times like this it was easy to justify my jonesing. Strip joints
and titty bars were filled to capacity and somebody had to
keep them in business, right?

But my control was slipping. More and more I found myself acting out on my thoughts instead of just having them.
This was dangerous to my military reputation—after all, I
was a senior NCO, a first sergeant, which was why I usually
tried to lay low and let Fancy bring the poon-poon home to
Papa.

Fuck it, I thought, and before I knew it I found myself cruising some cheesy neighborhood with my hammer in my hand, in an area where I would have never gone during the day when someone might see me.

Brothers were selling drugs from almost every corner, and even though I saw a couple of police cruisers they seemed to be minding their business and leaving everybody else's alone. With my pants unzipped and my hammer hitting my navel, I went up and down the side streets until I found what I was looking for. I wasn't planning to cheat on Fancy, at least not technically, but I was on a serious high. Like I'd smoked a whole bag of weed. My sexual energy was just that potent.

She was thin and light-skinned and wore a yellow mini-skirt. Even in the fading light I could tell it was dirty. She leaned into my open window and her breath smelled like a fart.

"You wanna have some fun?" she asked.

She was trash. Downright nasty. I nodded and showed her the present I was stroking in my lap. Her eyes got big and she licked her lips, then ran around to the passenger side and climbed in.

"Big boy, huh. Just my type."

Truthfully, she was the kind of woman I wouldn't even sit next to on a bus. I slipped her a twenty and she told me to go down a few blocks to a small park, but I refused. I pulled up just a few paces ahead, outside a house where the lights were on. Maybe somebody would come out and see us. That would make it even better.

She went to work like she really enjoyed her job. Girl mighta been a pro, but she wasn't as good as my wife. She couldn't do that thing with my nuts that Fancy did.

With my hands gripping her dirty hair, I slammed her head down and, thrusting my hips, I pounded her mouth like it was Fancy's stuff. I yelled out loud on my last stroke, and then leaned back in my seat as she sucked and slurped and struggled to get the last drop. Two seconds later I pushed her away and told her to get the hell out of my car. The sight of her was making me nauseous and her scent was seeping into my clothes.

I couldn't get home fast enough to wash her off me. It was always like that. The moment I nutted I had to get away from them. They made me sick. I made me sick. Just thinking about it made me sweat. Made me wanna see my wife and slide up in some sweet, clean trim. I squeezed the head of my toolie twice. Fancy was beautiful. I needed her so badly. She was everything to me. I hit speed dial on my cell phone and called her.

CHAPTER 8

SPARKLE

Helluva Helluva

When I was a kid people used to say that I looked like my aunt Vivian and that I acted like her too. I took that as a high compliment because Aunt Viv was the classiest, sexiest woman I knew. She lived in a big-ass house up in Westchester and kept a stable of handsome kneegrows hanging around who treated her like she was some kind of black goddess. She was my mother's younger sister, and even though she was pushing fifty she was still finer than a whole lot of young birds out there, especially some of those tack heads you see walking around in military uniforms. I could never understand it. If you knew your hair was gonna get all nappy after running for physical training, then why run?

Aunt Viv had helped Nana raise me after my mother died, and she was the one who taught me how to go for whatever it was I wanted. "Get yours, Sparkle," she used to tell me. "And don't pay them jealous bitches out there no mind, either.

There'll always be ugly, funny-shaped women in the world who try to put you down. But you"—her eyes would get all misty—"you're just like me and your crazy-ass mama. You've got exactly what men want, so don't be shy about using it."

The only time I ever saw Aunt Viv get emotional was when she talked about my mother. I was only six when my mother fell to her death, but even before that I remember her being such a beautiful and fragile person that I was almost scared to touch her at times.

"Fell, hell," Aunt Viv would say whenever my Nana brought up my mother's "accident." "Why in the world she was up on that woman's roof in the first place gets past me. She should have let that evil bitch have Walter's black ass. He wasn't much to look at anyway, and I know for a fact his dick was so little he couldn't fuck his way out of a paper bag! And to have your *baby*—your little girl—sitting in that car watching you hit the ground, then lay out there and bleed to death in all that snow . . ." She'd wipe her eyes and shake her head, then hug me to her breasts and run her hands through my hair. "Ain't *no* dick worth all that. Listen, Sparkle, don't you never love no man more than he loves you. And you sure better not love him more than you love yourself. Be like your Aunt Viv, honey. Love 'em and leave 'em. And in between, never let 'em forget who the queen is."

I'd invited Aunt Viv and Nana to come to a Fourth of July barbecue at my house, and wouldn't you know they had to go and invite some of my cousins and their bad-behind kids too. They were all coming down from Brooklyn in a rented van, and were scheduled to arrive in just about an hour.

"I don't stay under no other woman's roof," Aunt Viv said

when I offered to give up my bedroom for her and Nana. "Make me and Nana a reservation at a five-star hotel, darling."

I was looking forward to seeing my crazy family, although I still felt pretty low behind Gary's mess. After all, Miss Sparkle wasn't used to being tossed *anywhere,* let alone publicly humiliated. It almost brought me down a peg, but I was glad my girl Fancy had come to the rescue and even stayed the night with me. Now if that damn husband of hers would just stop sweating her. He'd called three times this afternoon and after the last call Fancy had booted up my computer to check her e-mail account, then asked if she could wear my short black Ecko Red skirt. I let her wear it because she's my girl and all and I love her, but damn if he wasn't bugging her again. I just don't know how she did it. Put up with all that e-mail and cell phone drama. I liked Kevin and yes the man was fine, but give me a break. Separation anxiety was not sexy, and I should know. I'd had more insecure men sweat me than I knew what to do with. Maybe that was why Fancy was such a club freak. Maybe she played with other men because her husband played her too close. That didn't make her wrong, though. In my opinion, it made Kevin small.

I had a thing for men who were bigger than me, and not just in size. It seemed as though I could only respect and truly appreciate a man if he brought it to me large. You know, a man who was swollen with power and self-confidence and knew how to set boundaries and handle his business. Most men took one look at my perfect smile and phat ass and were lost. Plain sprung. Just mesmerized by my entire package. That was all well and good, and Lord knows I gave them something to worship, but every once in a while I stumbled over my own heart when I ran up on a helluva helluva. A brother who just wasn't taking any shorts, especially from me.

The first helluva helluva to knock me off my pedestal hurt me so bad I still can't say his name. He did me so wrong that no matter what Aunt Viv said, I was convinced I was ugly and worthless. Me! Fine-ass *me*! Can you imagine that? Come to think of it, he was the reason I ran off and joined the army. Men, men, and more men. Men with jobs and dental benefits. Men with big bones and money to spend. Men at my disposal, to be used at my whim. Men to help me forget the helluva loving he'd put on my young ass.

Killer was the next helluva helluva to turn me inside out, but in his case he almost killed me with his love. Killer was an older guy, a colonel. Looking back, he needed his ass whipped for messing with me in the first place since I was just a lil old private first class and he was my battalion commander. And talk about bone control? When I first met him I was ready to bust out the Fixodent and Buckley's back cream, but the difference in our ages proved to be no big thang because Killer showed me that in some cases, skill and technique came with age.

Unfortunately, back then I was a hoochie. A fly-ass hoochie. Hooching was my specialty and I had it down to a tee. But Killer almost changed all of that. He put such a dick-whipping on me I ended up fixing breakfast for him on the weekends wearing nothing but his shirt. My panties still get wet thinking about his firm body, moving like a piston filling me up while I worked my booty like there was no tomorrow. I mean, I worshiped that bone. Sucked it like it was the last one I'd ever suck. Bowed down to its magnificent power, blossomed like a flower under his long, powerful strokes.

But then I fucked up. That little witch that lives inside of me took over with her greedy, selfish-ass self. In spite of all Killer was giving me, sexually, financially, and emotionally, little Miss Sparkle still wasn't satisfied. He turned his back on me when he found out I was baking cookies for the battalion's command sergeant major, and no matter what I said, how much I begged, he wouldn't take me back. I really couldn't blame him, but trust me when I tell you: It was my loss.

Now, the most recent helluva helluva was Lonnie Jackson, and boy did I have it bad for this guy. I knew I was hooked on a brothah if I was scared to take him home to meet Aunt Viv, and you better believe I tried to make sure there was a body of water between Lonnie Jackson and my aunt. In fact, I never even talked about him in her presence because Aunt Viv was so sharp she'd pick up on my weakness just by the way I said his name.

Lonnie was an army F-16 pilot who was assigned to McGuire Air Force Base in New Jersey. I'd met him during my short tour in Puerto Rico, and I fed him home-baked cookies for almost eighteen months while he kept my legs in the air and my head in the clouds. Of course he was tall and fine and had perfect teeth—all that went without saying. Would Miss Sparkle settle for anything less? But there was more. Lonnie knocked me out of position. The man had more charisma in his little toe than I had in my whole body. I've never seen a dude who was so smooth he could just glide into and out of situations at will. He was smart, educated, and best of all he was a field-grade officer who was just about to divorce his wife.

"Close your mouth," Fancy had said, elbowing me one afternoon as we watched him eat lunch in the brand-new dining room of the officers' club in Puerto Rico. I'd tagged along with her as she took a few freelance photos for the opening ceremony, and now we were hiding behind a large column checking out the brother's chew. "You look like a sick fish. Trying to reel in his words before they can fall from his lips. C'mon, girl. Let's get out of here before you stare the taste out of the man's food!"

Fancy could go straight to hell. She had no idea what Lonnie was laying on me. He was like a horse trainer. He handled my body expertly, like he'd been schooling thoroughbreds all his life. Fancy didn't know it, but Lonnie was the reason I got stationed at Fort Dix, which just happened to sit side by side with McGuire Air Force Base. She was all flattered when she found out I was being assigned to the NCO Academy. Thought I loved her so much that I had schemed to get to Fort Dix just to be near her. Humph. Did that sound like a Sparkle move? If I was gonna follow someone halfway around the world you can best believe it would be somebody who could knock my boots. Sorry, Fancy girl. You just ain't my type.

———

HOLIDAY traffic was heavy and my family didn't arrive until almost six. That was fine by me because I'd burned the ribs on my patio grill and had to run to four different Acme supermarkets before I could find some more. You know I paid three times more than they were worth, but that's what you get when you shop for last-minute stuff on a holiday.

Nana and Aunt Viv were sitting outside on the patio that opened up onto a small playground. I had insisted on a ground-floor apartment when I moved here, and now I was glad because my cousin Glodean's bad-behind twins, Dayjonay and Dahjonay (I called them Man'naise and Mustard), were out there taking each other up on the swings and having a ball.

I went into the kitchen and took the pan of ribs from the oven where they'd been simmering in spicy sauce. I dipped my finger into Nana's special barbecue recipe and then licked it and grinned. Yeah. Just the right amount of zing and the right amount of zang! I opened the fridge and made sure we were set. There was plenty of juice for the kids and beer for the adults, and the deviled eggs and macaroni salad were already outside on the dining table.

I glanced over at Fancy, who was leaning over the countertop mixing a large bowl of supposed-to-be potato salad and bracing her cell phone between her ear and her shoulder. I made a mental note to push that nasty-looking mess toward the way-back of the fridge when she wasn't looking. My girl was sweet, but she had no kitchen skills. She should have stuck to grilling the franks and toasting the buns. As it was, she'd cut the potatoes way too big and in too many crazy shapes, and to top it off they were underboiled and there was so much mayo in the bowl the whole thing was pure white. What happened to adding a little mustard and sweet relish and a bunch of hard-boiled eggs? Aunt Viv was sure to take one look at that mess and turn up her nose, refusing to touch it.

"Kevin's on his way," Fancy said, shifting the phone and handing me the bowl. There was no way I could stash it away while she was watching, so I went ahead and put it on the dining room table with the rest of the food.

After making sure there were a ton of plastic forks and napkins available, I called everyone inside to eat. I stood back watching my people as Nana blessed the food and everyone began fixing plates. Aside from my uncle Buster, who had been too drunk to travel, and Deebo, Aunt Viv's current flavor of the month, there really weren't many men in our family. Nana had left my grandfather shortly after her only son was born, and Aunt Viv had never married. My own father, Walter Gumble, had been a low-down fucker whose empty promises had led my mother to a cold rooftop on a snowy Christmas day.

We'd lived in a one-bedroom project apartment in Brooklyn, and for seven years Mama had believed Walter when he told her all his money went to take care of his sick mother who lived up in the Bronx. I guess you could imagine how Mama felt when her helluva helluva failed to show up for Christmas dinner. How empty she must have been as we sat parked outside of Walter's mama's brick-style ranch house on a nice tree-lined street glowing with Christmas lights. I remember being cold as hell in that raggedy car he'd bought us, but Mama didn't even look at me when I told her my feet were getting numb.

We watched them come home. Him, his woman, and a little girl who looked like she was about my age. She had on a furry white swing coat and the same kind of earmuffs that Walter had recently bought for me. Mama cried as he got out of that spanking-new Oldsmobile and held the woman's door open, then got between the two of them and walked down the driveway holding their hands and swinging their arms. He unlocked the door and ushered them in, and I could tell there was probably a fireplace and lots of hot chocolate and Christmas cake waiting in a house like that.

I thought about the tiny stuffed turkey that Mama had stayed up all night basting in our sometimey oven. The candied yams she wouldn't even let me taste until he got there. And the collard greens. The bunches and bunches she'd cut and washed and rinsed until her hands were raw, then put them in a plastic bag and hung them outside our project window to keep cold until morning because our fridge was way too small.

"Damn," Mama kept muttering over and over even after their front door had closed. "I guess I must not be shit then, huh? You and me, we must not be shit!"

We were much more than shit, Mama. We were more than Walter fuckin' Gumble ever deserved, and I wish I could have told her that. Still, when he was in that VA hospital out in Bay Ridge, laying on his deathbed and shriveled up with hepatitis, I took four days of military leave and went to see him. I was hoping that somehow he'd finally be able to look at me and say, *Sparkle. Baby, I made a mistake and I was wrong. You and your mama were worth more than gold. More than life.* But instead, as I sat there breathing in his funky, diseased air, that helluva nigger stared back at me with my own damn eyes. *You ain't shit,* his gaze seemed to say, and I saw myself six years old again and doing as my mama had said. Waiting until she waved at me from his rooftop, then ringing his doorbell and running back to the car before he answered.

She landed at his feet, and even though she had on a thick wool coat I swore I heard her bones breaking. Walter had looked down at my mama, who had been dying to be loved and was now dying of it, and then met my eyes through the car window. *You wasn't shit then, little Miss Sparkle,* his dying eyes told me, *and you still ain't shit now.*

Fuck you, Walter, I thought as I watched Nana take out her false teeth and skin a barbecue rib with her gums. *And everybody who looks like you.*

CHAPTER 9

FANCY

Strictly Dickly

Sparkle had gotten it honest. Her family was crazy with a capital C. They were just the opposite of my strict, ultra-religious relatives who fasted twice a month and went to church six days a week. Sparkle's people were loud and sensual and between their heated card games and their love of loud music, they sure knew how to party.

The meat had just come off the grill and we were sitting down to eat when Kevin arrived. "Sugar, put that fork down and fix your man a plate," Nana commanded loudly after I'd made the introductions.

Sparkle's cousin Glodean, the mother of the twins they called Man'naise and Mustard, had stopped eating and was staring at Kevin with her fork in the air. Glodean was cute, but she wasn't Kevin's type. Not enough breasts to fill a training bra. She'd have to come much better than that if she hoped to hook my man. She'd given me a deep, longing look earlier in the evening, and I thought she might be bisexual.

And now her eyes were crawling all over my husband, although he didn't seem to have given her a second glance.

"Dayum!" She laughed and nudged her sister. "She betta watch him! That's one fine-looking muh-fuh!"

Kevin had that effect on most women and I'd grown accustomed to their reactions. He never openly eyeballed them back, and for that I was grateful. Don't get me wrong. I had learned to swallow my pride years earlier, so that wasn't it. How much pride could you possess when you went out in the streets to solicit sexual partners for your own husband? No, once I began giving in to Kevin's needs and demands, my pride had been the first thing to go.

Yet as much as I enjoyed sex, and as depraved as Kevin's love games could become, there were still certain things that I just wouldn't do no matter how much he begged. Sleeping with another woman was one of them. Sure, I'd brought women home to please my husband. I knew what he liked so I picked out the sexiest sisters I could find. The ones whose body types were similar to mine: all breasts and behinds. But I drew the line when it came to touching them or being touched by them. Having two women working him over is probably every man's fantasy, and I could certainly indulge Kevin in that, but there had been one occasion when things went too far and I almost lost it.

Somehow the girl had read me wrong. During our love play she'd taken one of my breasts into her mouth, and while Kevin watched us and lightly stroked my thighs, she brought me to an orgasm just by sucking my nipples.

I was mortified afterward. There was nothing gay or bisexual about me. I was strictly dickly and a part of me felt like I'd been set up. Like she and Kevin had planned the whole thing. Of course he denied it when I asked him. Then he said, "But that's the hardest I've ever seen you come, baby."

I stared at Glodean until she looked away. I didn't know what her problem was, but after that incident I was super suspicious of some women. And don't ask me how I got so lost in that moment that I came. I was still ashamed about that. And now I had a gay girl radar up that made me cautious of any woman who looked at me twice.

We were watching CNN as we ate, with the Kobe Bryant rape coverage bombarding us every five minutes. "Turn that mess off," Zebulon said. She was Glodean's younger sister. "Who gives a damn about his stupid ass? That's what he gets for being such a sellout. Prickly-head fucker. Him, O.J., and Charles Barkley can all kiss my big black ass."

"Leave it on!" Aunt Viv commanded, and Sparkle, who had just picked up the remote, quickly put it back down. "Even though weak men like Kobe have managed to screw the black family almost into oblivion, you can learn a lesson from everything."

Glodean sucked her teeth. "What could a man like him teach me? His wife should have thrown some lye on his ass for barebacking and leaving his DNA up in some dumb white chick he'd never even seen before. With all that money couldn't he afford a pack of rubbers?" She crossed her legs and looked at Kobe's image on the screen, disgusted. "I'm scared of other people's body fluids."

"He can show you"—Aunt Viv set her plate on the floor and took a pack of cigarettes from her designer purse—"the kind of man you don't want to raise them two knucklehead boys of yours to be. Hell, the kind of man you don't want fouling up your own damn life. And you two—" She glanced at Nana, then pointed to Zebulon and Glodean. "—need to watch your nasty mouths in the presence of my mother. I don't care if she is half deaf and y'all are all grown. Both of you cuss like sailors, and Sparkle, you ain't too far behind them. You all ought to learn to"—she turned and smiled at me—"to speak nicely like Fancy here, with her sweet self. Like a little lady."

I got all embarrassed and of course Sparkle laughed her ass off.

"Seriously, though." Aunt Viv lit a cigarette and went on. "What kind of man do you think Kobe is? How much could he possibly love and respect his mama if his idea of a prize is a piece of nobody video trash? It's a shame that when black men get any kind of money or position they think they have to cap it off by having a white woman, or any woman other than a black one, on their arm."

Aunt Viv was running right up Sparkle's alley.

"I know!" Sparkle exclaimed. "And they get the shabbiest, run-down, no-shaped heffahs they can find too! Men like that make me sick! You should see how many of them are in the military, Aunt Viv. Crazy brothers who marry white but still wanna swerve black. They love to come sniffing around sisters when it's time to get their groove on, but when it's time to make a commitment they think being seen in public with a white girl gives them some kind of clout."

Sparkle stood up and grinned. "No offense, Kevin, 'cause I know your brother is a self-hating sellout to his heart, but Aunt Viv, you should see how I treat 'em. Oh, so they wanna push up on all this prime tail when they know they're paying bills for some washed-out no-ass white girl they got waiting at home?" She turned around real slow, treating us to a luscious view of her round booty. "First I let 'em get a real good look at it. Just so they know exactly what it is they're missing. Then I put my hands on my hips"—she tooted out her rump and gyrated her pelvis—"and let my backbone slip. By the time I'm done with them they wish they hadda honored that strong black woman who stayed alive on that stinking slave ship just to make sure their ungrateful asses got born." She sat back down. "I just can't help it. A sister like me, I am my brother's keeper, and I don't care how bad it gets, I'm loving on the blackhand side or I'm not loving at all."

Aunt Viv was beaming with pride and the cousins looked like they were ready to start clapping. I kept quiet out of love and respect for my husband. Kevin wasn't into white girls at all, thank God, but I knew how much he loved Emile, even though I also knew that Emile despised black women, especially me.

"All righty then." I stood up and patted my stomach. It was time to change the subject. "That was good, even though I ate too much." The food really had been wonderful, although there didn't seem to be much interest in my potato salad. I didn't know how to take that, but when I offered Kevin a second serving he licked his lips and told me to go ahead and pile a bunch on his plate. He'd been sweet and super attentive the entire evening, and considering the e-mail he'd sent me I wasn't surprised.

"You get my uniforms from the cleaners today?" he asked as he cornered me in the kitchen, where I'd gone to pop some popcorn and get more ice. Man'naise and Mustard had gone outside to play with the kids next door, and the rest of Sparkle's crew had moved into the living room and were preparing to watch *Love & Basketball*. When Kevin had called earlier I'd asked him to pick up a copy at Blockbuster, which had scored him a hit since everyone in the house wanted to see it.

I shook my head and let him kiss my neck, then put two bags of popcorn into the microwave and set it for five minutes. "Didn't have a chance. Been helping Sparkle cook and clean up all day."

He dipped his head lower and I felt his tongue probing the tops of my breasts. He slid both hands under the skirt I'd borrowed from Sparkle and cupped my bare flesh. "Hmm . . . I see you checked your e-mail."

"Yeah." I kissed him back and pressed myself to him. "And I was a good little soldier and followed your orders." Okay, so this was the second e-mail he'd sent in as many days, but at least this was the kind of game I liked to play. A me-and-him game. Sex when it involved only the two of us could be so passionate. So intimate.

Bracing my back against Sparkle's refrigerator, I pretended to struggle as my husband slipped two fingers into my vagina and moved them slowly in and out. I bit down on my lip as he massaged my clit with his thumb. Sparkle would kill me if she knew I had my butt hanging out in her kitchen. Around all her food. I prayed nobody decided to come looking for me as I nibbled on my husband's lips and opened my legs wider. Three fingers. Four. Wet, sloshing sounds. The smell of buttered popcorn. Deep thrusting. I couldn't take it anymore. Muffling my moans in his neck, I came quickly, my body shivering at his expert touch.

The microwave sounded and moments later Kevin asked, "You okay?"

I nodded, not yet able to speak.

He kissed my cheek and smoothed my skirt. "That was just an appetizer." He looked at me pointedly and licked his fingers. "I'm saving the rest for later."

"Hey, what-cha-ma-call-it!" Glodean yelled from the living room, ruining my orgasm afterglow. "Just what kind of bootleg DVD is this? This shit won't even play!"

As Kevin went into the living room to help get the movie started and I slipped down the hall to the bathroom to clean myself up before serving the popcorn, I couldn't help having a nasty thought. *Yeah, Glodean. You flat-chested little floozy. Go ahead and get up in my husband's face if you want to. Trust me, the only thing you're likely to get is a good whiff of my pussy!*

———

THE movie was wonderful. Sweet, honest, and very tender. I was sitting on the floor between Kevin's legs, resting my head in his lap and wondering if anyone's life ever turned out that well.

"Now that's the kind of movie I like to see," Aunt Viv said. She stood and turned on the lights as the credits rolled. "One where a black man comes to his damn senses and remembers who the queen is—not that she should have ever let him forget."

Zebulon agreed. "And that girl Sanaa Lathan is really pretty. She kinda favors you, Fancy."

"Me?" I shook my head and picked at a few unpopped kernels at the bottom of my bowl. "I don't think so. Anybody want some more popcorn?"

"I'll fix some," Sparkle answered. " 'Cause I'm gonna tidy up the kitchen while I'm in there."

Leaving Kevin chatting with Nana, Zebulon and I went into the dining room and began rewrapping the food that remained on the table. With our arms stacked with trays and pans, we headed into the kitchen just as Sparkle came running out, a trail of acrid smoke following her. "I burned the damn popcorn!" she shouted. I peered into the kitchen and saw two unrecognizable lumps smoldering in the sink. "Help me open up some windows before that scorched smell gets in my hair!"

I rushed into the kitchen and, holding my breath, set the food on the table, then unlocked and raised the window near the stove. But Sparkle's place was so tiny and the burning smell was so pervasive, by the time I returned to the living room everyone else had already taken refuge outside on the front patio.

I joined them, grateful for the fresh air. I was just about to sit down in an empty chair beside Aunt Viv when Kevin came over and squeezed my shoulder. "Let's go over there."

I followed him a few paces over to the swing set. The grass was crunchy under my bare feet and the air was very warm for early September. Kevin sat down on the middle swing, then pulled me toward him. "Sit on my lap," he said, but when I turned around to oblige him I felt his hand against my back. "Uh-uh," he whispered, and gently turned me toward him. "Face this way."

I watched that familiar mask come over his face, then straddled his lap like he'd asked. He lifted the back of my skirt until it was up around my waist and my entire ass was exposed. Then he fumbled in his lap and took out his penis.

Sparkle and her family were only paces away and I could hear their conversations clearly. I glanced at them and hoped to God that since the patio lights were on them and not on us, that I was less visible to them than they were to me.

With my husband's help, I propped one foot up on the swing. Grasping him firmly, I helped him enter me, then eased myself down until I was completely impaled on his penis. I moaned as we took off sailing into the air, Kevin's strong legs pushing off the ground as the swing caught momentum. He held a mound of my ass in each hand and gently raised and lowered me up and down. The experience was unbelievably erotic. Our bodies cutting through the breeze, the dizzying pendulum of the swing, the impact of his dick hitting the apex of my vagina.

I must admit I got lost in the moment. As Kevin sucked my nipples through the material of my blouse and inserted one finger into the rim of my anus, I pulled his head into my breasts and bit down on the moans that were spilling from my lips.

Nasty Fancy.

He bounced me on his penis with short hard strokes, and as Aunt Viv imparted more of her queenly wisdom and Sparkle's laughter cut into the night air, I came and came until I fell limply against my husband, my head lolling against his shoulder.

A minute inched past and I opened my eyes. The breeze was cooling our bodies and Kevin's hands were still on my butt. I looked up and saw that Aunt Viv was busy talking, gesturing heatedly with her hands. The rest of them seemed to be absorbing her words like apt pupils.

Except for Glodean. She'd pulled her chair forward to the edge of the patio and sat with her legs crossed, swinging her top leg back and forth, enjoying the show, and I don't mean the fireworks that had begun rising in the distance and exploding overhead.

Our eyes met in the darkness. Glodean's lips curved into a sardonic smile, then she stuck out her tongue and slowly licked them. Suddenly there was a chill in the night air, and as Kevin's penis shriveled inside of me and his fluids pooled from my body, all I wanted to do was go home.

CHAPTER 10

EMILE

Sergeant Sister Ass-Almighty

It was oh dark thirty on Monday morning when I pulled into my reserved parking space in front of the NCO Academy. The sight of the Academy's unit crest, complete with polished brass and sparkling glass doors, always did something for my mood. Yes, most grunts in my ROTC year group were leading infantry companies out there on the battleground, but despite their dire predictions about my commanding a training company, preparing troops for leadership was nothing to sneeze at. After all, wasn't training our soldiers to fight and win what the army was all about?

As I entered the building the charge of quarters rose from his chair and clicked his heels together. "Company!" he bellowed. "Atten-*tion*!"

I paused for a moment and made sure that every single soldier gave me my proper respect by snapping to attention. "Carry on," I finally said, and walked down the highly buffed floors, nodding at soldiers as I passed.

I neared the hall that led to my office and ran into two of the black females who worked in my arms room. Both of them were proficient in maintaining the unit's cache of M16s and nine-millimeters, but that's where their intelligence seemed to end.

I nodded as I went by. "Specialist Gaines, Specialist Vance." They fell in beside me, singing their daily song.

"Not slap-back, not jump-back, not get-back, but—" Vance tweaked the spare flesh on my back, right above my beltline. *"—Pinchback!"* Then they burst out laughing. "Good morning, sir. How you doing?" That was Gaines. Her mouth was rotating a mile a minute.

"I'm doing fine, soldier. But how many times do I have to tell you about chewing gum while you're in uniform? Right after this morning's physical training test I want you to ask your supervisor to get you a copy of Army Regulation 670-1. Read what it says about chewing gum in uniform and report back to me at the end of the duty day."

I indulged Vance and Gaines not because they were black, of course, but because they were useful. It was the same principle I used with the women who shopped at my kiosk at the mall, and it worked. Whenever I needed to know the lowdown, get deep into the scuttlebutt of the unit, Vance and Gaines were my men. Or my women, I should say.

Continuing on, I nodded at various members of my cadre staff and one or two trainees. The sun wouldn't rise for at least another two hours, but my cadre and student-soldiers were already alert, dressed in physical training clothes, and ready for the end-of-cycle PT test that consisted of two minutes of push-ups, sit-ups, and a timed two-mile run.

Well, most of my cadre, I should say. I walked into my

outer office to find Staff Sergeant Henderson, dressed in BDUs and chatting with Sergeant Daphne Clifton, the unit administrator. I sighed. Sham central. Staff Sergeant Henderson was giving off a cloud of perfume that stunk up the whole office and was sure to irk my migraines. I greeted my secretary, but looked Henderson up and down without speaking. I couldn't stand her. She was serving as one of my graders for the PT test this morning, but I'd had a long argument with Kevin over that one because Staff Sergeant Henderson had a no-exercise physical profile long enough to wipe your ass with.

My foot! My ankle! My back!

Just a bunch of excuses she used to get out of running, when truthfully she could have stood to lose a few inches off those hips. How she managed to finagle those sick-call doctors into indulging her drama I didn't understand, but I had a fix for that. Since she was too broke-down to run I put her in charge of the rest of the sick, lame, and lazy platoon.

Every morning any soldier who could not physically train was required to report for duty at 0500 hours and fall in for PT formation along with the rest of the company. The difference was, when we fell out on the parade field to begin our daily exercises, they fell out on the barracks with mops, brooms, and green scrubbing pads.

And my standards were high too. I wouldn't tolerate a speck of dirt on the baseboards, a smear of wax on the floor, or a streak of dirt on the company mirrors. I even insisted that Staff Sergeant Henderson clean my personal latrine. I didn't give a fart how cutesy-cutesy she looked or how perfect her nails were, I made that wench scrub toilets like she was Aunt Jemima on the pancake box!

But aside from all the bitching she did under her breath, it didn't stop her from riding sick call. That should tell you what kind of soldier she was. How many women do you know who would rather scrub stains out of somebody else's toilet than train to get physically fit? I didn't understand it. She was ate all the hell up.

Seated at my desk, I stared at a color photo of Becky Ann. She was the senior barmaid at the All-Ranks Club, and I'd snapped the picture during the first overnight trip we'd taken together to Hilton Head, South Carolina. Even now I trembled as I thought about the loving we'd made. The contrast our skin had created as I inhaled the sweetness of her hair, traced the outline of her narrow lips, licked the rosy buds of her nipples.

I'd blown half a paycheck in two days, but man was it worth it. We'd sipped the finest champagne and eaten lobster until we nearly burst. I'd indulged myself by dipping chunks of it in melted butter, and when I spilled a few drops onto my lap, my princess had put her head down there and cleaned it up real nice for me.

I was sorry I couldn't do the same for her, even though I swear that was the only thing I wouldn't do for my lady. I mean, I'd take her wherever she wanted to go. Dress her in the most elegant clothing she could imagine. Indulge her, spoil her, love her, respect her. Someday I even planned to get on my knees and ask to marry her, but baby! I pleaded as she stared at me with her beautiful blue eyes. Baby, you have to understand! Most black men won't even lick a stamp, and shopping downtown is something we just don't naturally do!

I tried hard to make it up to her, though. I put my back out giving it to her deep and hard, just the way she liked it. She seemed satisfied and told me not to worry about doing that other stuff, but I worried anyway. And no, despite what you're thinking, no, I didn't think a woman's spot was nasty, and of course I'd tried it before. I'd even come close enough to touch it with the tip of my tongue in a moment or two of drunken vigor. But there was something about the dampness of it, the cave-like quality that appealed to my manhood but not to my mouth. Let's face it. Going down on a woman just wasn't something I could acquire a taste for, and no matter how much my princess yearned to feel my tongue swirling between her legs, if she put that stuff in my face I'd probably throw up in it and pass out cold.

Giving Becky Ann's photo a final glance, I popped a sugar-free mint into my mouth and logged on to my military AKO e-mail account. I had a message from my career manager at the officer personnel management branch, and as soon as I saw the subject my heart jumped.

Iraq.

They were looking for infantry officers to volunteer for combat duty in Southwest Asia, and my branch manager wanted to know if I was interested. Heck no. Not me. I was hard charging and gung-ho, but leaving my Becky Ann to go on a one-year deployment was out of the question. Besides, I knew better than to volunteer for anything, and if they really needed me they'd cut me a set of orders soon enough. I did fire off a response asking him to check with enlisted branch and see if there were any supply positions that needed to be filled, though. I'd ship Staff Sergeant Henderson off before she could say "I broke my fingernail."

I gazed out my window as the soldiers organized themselves by platoons and squads and lined up for the morning's accountability formation. The squad leaders made sure their soldiers were on line, the platoon sergeants took reports from the squad leaders, and then Kevin stepped up and received the platoon sergeants' reports. I liked that. The orderly way one echelon was always responsible for the lower element and accountable to the higher.

I turned to the stack of papers Sergeant Clifton had left in my in-box on Friday afternoon. Rating schemes, duty rosters, training slides—being a company commander involved accepting total responsibility for the training and welfare of your soldiers because the big bosses would hold your feet to the fire for the slightest infraction that happened on your watch.

Speaking of big bosses, I glanced at my day planner and saw that even though today was payday, all of the officers in the battalion were scheduled for an ODP—an Officer Development Program meeting with Colonel Bonita Turner, the commandant of the NCO Academy. Lord, what a trip that would be. I reminded myself that I had a date with Becky Ann later in the evening, and after dealing with Colonel Turner, making love to Becky Ann was sure to be a much-needed consolation.

Outside, a hush fell over the milling soldiers, and at the sound of Kevin's deep voice commanding the company to fall in at the position of attention I stood and retied my sneakers, then strolled outside just in time to take over the formation.

"Sir," Kevin saluted me and said. "Headquarters company all present and accounted for."

It felt odd to face my brother in a commander–first sergeant capacity, and if Fancy hadn't opened her big mouth to Staff Sergeant Henderson, no one would've even known we'd been raised together as brothers. I returned Kevin's salute, gave the soldiers a short but sincere speech about the importance of giving their absolute best effort on the PT test, posted the guidon bearer, and minutes later we were marching toward the parade field where the testing would be conducted.

As luck would have it I ended up standing next to Staff Sergeant Henderson as testing lanes were established. Each grader had between ten and twelve soldiers in their lane, and we sat on milk crates to observe each event.

"Get ready," Kevin called out over a bullhorn, and the soldiers at the front of the lines got down on the ground on their hands and knees.

"Get set." Poised over mats, they balanced their bodies on their hands and the tips of their toes, bodies in line from head to heel.

"Go!" The clock began counting and the soldiers alternately lowered their upper bodies until the backs of their arms were parallel to the ground and level with their shoulder blades, then raised themselves upright by fully extending their arms.

"One," I counted for the male soldier pushing up at my feet. "Two . . ." The young man had great upper-body strength and managed to crank out seventy-five legal push-ups before the two-minute timer buzzed and they were commanded to stop.

I was busy recording his score when I looked down at the next soldier in my lane. Sister was short and thick, and on the command of "get set" she extended her arms and went up on her toes and it was all I could do not to throw up.

Ass everywhere.

Sticking straight up in the air like a gigantic round pillow.

"Hey!" I said and frowned. "Keep it G-rated, please. Tuck that thing in, and let's keep it G-rated."

I was grading the next soldier when Staff Sergeant Henderson decided to start acting black. A pretty white soldier was pushing up in her lane and Staff Sergeant Henderson seemed mad as hell.

"Twelve," she counted at the top of her lungs, glaring at me the whole time. "Twelve! Twelve! *Twelve!*" No matter how many additional repetitions the girl did, Staff Sergeant Henderson threw them out and held her at twelve.

I was having a hard time trying to observe my own soldier and simultaneously figure out what wild hair Staff Sergeant Henderson had up her ass. The two-minute buzzer rang and the soldiers climbed to their feet.

"Twelve." Sergeant Henderson signed off on her soldier's PT card and flung it to the bottom of her pile. Then, muttering so that I was sure to hear her, she hissed, "That's what you get for flunking that sister!"

I had no idea what she was bitching about. I shuffled through the PT cards in my stack until I found the one belonging to Sergeant Sister Ass-Almighty. Sure enough I'd flunked her, but how could I not have? She had barely bent her arms at all, hadn't even come close to breaking the plane as required, and her form was horrible. She'd looked like an upside-down *U,* with her head and feet down and her behind stuck all up in the clouds. Wasn't my fault she had that hump at the bottom of her back and couldn't do push-ups. Maybe she should have done more push-aways from the table.

I looked down the line where the soldiers were preparing to do sit-ups, which was the next event. The slim white girl with the pretty blond hair looked like she wanted to cry. She sorta put me in the mind of a young Becky Ann, and immediately my heart went out to her. Damn that Staff Sergeant Henderson. She knew how important it was for our students to pass their PT tests the first time around. But I'd fix it. On retesting day you'd better believe I'd pull the blonde's card and put her in my lane. I'd look out for her and make sure that the next time she was kneeling her pretty little self on the push-up mat, the only person she'd have to satisfy with her performance was me.

———

THE Officer Development Program meeting with the commandant turned into one of the biggest come-to-Jesus sessions I've ever seen. Colonel Bonita Turner was a touchy broad if there ever was one, and placing her in charge of a bunch of hoo-rah grunts didn't help much. True, she was athletic and could outrun most of the male soldiers in the battalion, but really, what did that prove? Don't ask, don't tell was in full effect, and the way Colonel Turner wore her hair in that butch-boy haircut and that mean bop she had when she walked the battalion area sent the rumors flying.

Colonel Turner had never been married, didn't have any children, and as far as any of the guys could tell she wasn't involved with anything that was swinging a pair of balls. Some swore she was sexless or androgynous, but I told the guys she was probably one of those confused feminist chicks who suffered from penis envy. Wished she had one and was mad as hell at everyone who really did!

Colonel Turner and I were the only black officers in the command, and from the moment she came on board I'd felt some sort of low-level aggression thing against her that made me swell up like I had something to prove. Of course I gave her the respect her position demanded, but I let it be known that it was only a requirement of the uniform and not because of the woman wearing it.

It was about 10:00 A.M. and we were gathered in the command conference room listening as Colonel Turner belabored over some insignificant detail in the army's mandatory sensitivity training program. I'd chosen a seat toward the back of the room, between John Ottenbach, who called himself a ladies' man but was getting a terrible three-block evaluation for bolo'ing at the weapons range, and Bill Jones, the battalion supply officer, who hailed from Ann Arbor, Michigan. None of us had much respect for Colonel Turner, and after taking out my memo pad and pretending to take notes, I'd doodled a series of wide-nosed, big-lipped, big-butt caricatures of her that had Bill and John choking back laughter.

She stood before us in a starched uniform and spit-shined boots, droning on and on, sounding like Charlie Brown's mother. *Waa-waa, waa-womp waa-waa-waa-womp!* Yes, we were to be cognizant of and sensitive to the differences inherent in the soldiers under our command. Yes, we were supposed to exhibit religious tolerance and create environments that were free from sexual harassment and discrimination. Yes, we were entrusted to ensure that the personal rights and freedoms of our soldiers were acknowledged and respected, but this was stuff that we already knew, so what was the sense in sitting around harping on it? Besides, if I could overcome the obstacles of my past, why couldn't a few professional soldiers hold it together for a measly fourteen weeks of training?

I mean, check it. I was the poster child for intolerance and harassment. Remember, I'd been pretty fat as a kid, and even after working hard to lose all the weight my basic body structure had not changed. As much as I exercised and dieted, instead of looking manly my ass was still much too wide, and even though I could feel my six-pack when I poked myself in the gut, there was a still a nice layer of fat padding my midsection. My predicament was frustrating to say the least, and I admit that there were a few times when I considered sneaking off to some private hospital for liposuction and body resculpting.

But I'm a warrior and a chameleon, and I've learned how to even up the odds. To make up for my lack of physique I made sure I out-PT'd every officer in the academy. Not one of those guys could outrun me, and I could do push-ups long after they collapsed from muscle failure.

And it paid off too. They respected me and accepted me into their circle just like I was a regular joe. I fished with Ted Greenwich at least once a month, hunted deer with the executive officer during the season, and had been invited to their barbecues and baby christenings just like the other white officers. During the spring and summer months you could find me out on the golf course hitting balls with my buddies, and I've even gone out dirt biking and motorcycle racing with them on occasion. Heck, I chewed their tobacco and chugged their brew, spoke their English, and even loved their women.

What was there not to like about me? Sensitivity training my foot. These young soldiers had better learn to buck up. Who had ever been sensitive toward me?

I was fidgeting in my seat: annoyed, bored, and anxious to get the whole drill over with. My soldiers had been authorized an extended lunch hour for payday activities, and I needed to make a quick trip to the black mall and pick up yesterday's receipts from Ali. He was a cool guy and an excellent salesman, but you never could tell how brothers were copping these days. I wanted to get my cash out of his hands and into the bank because I didn't really trust him to hold on to my money for two days straight. Right after work I planned to run home and shower, then hop over to the All-Ranks Club and scoop up Becky Ann for our dinner date.

I guess my impatience and aggravation showed on my face or maybe in my posture, because Colonel Turner's tone changed abruptly and I saw a familiar look enter her eyes. You know, the kind of look sisters get when they want to let you know you're fucking up something terrible.

"I'm certain that each of you understands the importance of internalizing the spirit of these policies and modeling the behavior you want your soldiers to emulate. Remember, good leadership begins at the top, and it is your command posture that will determine the climate of diversity in your units."

She addressed the entire room but I knew she was secretly referring to me. Staff Sergeant Henderson had probably been up here bitching and complaining and brownnosing like she usually did. I scribbled on my notepad, then slid it over to Bill. "Check it, Chief. She must be on the rag. Somebody should use it to gag her ass and shut her up."

Bill waited until Colonel Turner looked toward the other

side of the room, then grinned, gave me a thumbs-up, and pursed his lips in imitation of the colonel. John Ottenbach craned to get a look at what I'd written and laughed out loud, much louder than he had to. I tried to slip the pad into my binder, but it was too late.

"Captain Pinchback, is there a problem you'd like to address with the group?"

I slouched in my chair and mumbled, "No, ma'am."

"Then maybe you'd like to share your talents with the rest of us. You know, the notes you've been sharing with Captain Jones and Captain Ottenbach. Why don't you pass them up front."

Dyke. Did she think this was kindergarten? I sighed loudly and shifted my weight to the other side of the chair. "No, ma'am," I repeated. "I would not."

"Would not what?" She stood holding her hand out, waiting.

The room had gone silent and I looked over at John Ottenbach, hoping to share a knowing grin and collectively shrug her off. But Ottenbach wasn't even studying me. He'd suddenly gotten busy examining the regulation that had been passed out at the beginning of the class.

"Ma'am, I would not like to share my notes with the rest of you."

"Well." She exhaled and I could have sworn I saw her neck getting ready to swivel. "It was not a request, Captain." Her hands were on her hips and she took a few steps toward me. "It was an order."

"This pad is my personal property, ma'am. With all due respect I'd like to keep it that way."

I could hear those buddies of mine as they sucked their

breath in with one collective gasp. Their awe empowered me and I knew I'd just scored two points and earned big respect. Insubordination, disrespect to a senior officer, a three-block on my officer evaluation report, yes, all of these things flew through my mind. But hey, somebody had to stand up to this ball-buster, and she'd picked the right man on the right day.

"Soldier, are you challenging my authority?"

She was really fired up now. I'd been reduced to a simple "soldier," my name totally obliterated in order to put me in my place and remind me of the military pecking order.

"No, ma'am. Just exercising my right to retain my personal property."

She was standing over me. "Get up," she said through her teeth. "On your feet!"

I stood and faced her, my eyes steady.

"Lock up!"

I snapped to the position of attention.

"Up here."

She marched me up to the front of the room, and as I stood before my fellow officers I saw the *oh shit* reflected in their eyes. It was nothing compared to what I saw in Colonel Turner's. I stood there locked up at the position of attention feeling like a dummy as she ate me up one side and down the other.

"Do you know who the hell I am?" she asked, raging but controlled. "Soldier, you'd better make this the last time you attempt to lock horns with me! If I tell you to strip down to your boxers and do the funky chicken in the battalion square, then all I'd better hear is, 'Yes, ma'am, yes, ma'am, three bags full!' "

She marched around me attacking from all angles, chastising me like I was a child and chewing my ass down to a nub. ". . . And since you can't behave in a manner befitting a professional military officer I'll give you a little remedial training to remind you of why I wear this full bird insignia on my collar and you wear those two little bars on yours. Front leaning rest position. Move!"

Yes, she did. That black bitch humiliated me in the worst way. Put me in the push-up position in front of every white officer in the battalion. Like I was a brand-new private who held no rank at all.

"Knock 'em out!" she ordered, returning to her briefing charts like I wasn't down on the floor doing push-ups at her feet. Once again she was perfectly calm and professional while I was on the ground beating my face and looking like a damn fool. "Now. As I was saying before I was so rudely interrupted, sensitivity training is paramount for the good order of your commands and the welfare of your troops . . ."

SPARKLE

What Does That Make You?

I was steamed with Captain Pinchback for flunking that sister, and every soldier in my supply shop knew it, so by the time I was done grading for the physical training test they'd completed all of their weekly requisitions and had even started on this month's inventory in an effort to lift my mood.

Hey, my troops knew me. Life was short and I was usually a happy-go-lucky sister, but every now and then a girl had to drop all the frivolous shit in life, like partying and getting her eyebrows plucked, and stand up and be counted.

Somehow I made it through the morning without giving Pinchback a piece of my Brooklyn mind, and by the time I looked up lunchtime had rolled around. Since it was a mid-month payday I ordered two soldiers to man the supply cage and another to answer the phones in the orderly room. Then I thanked everybody else for their hard work and told them to take a long lunch and enjoy their payday activities.

"Remember, you have until fourteen thirty hours," I

warned and pointed to the clock as they all scrambled to get out the door at once. "It's twelve hundred hours now, so that gives you two and a half hours to run some errands and pay your damn bills. Be back on time!"

I hit the door right behind them because I was planning to swing by the black mall and buy this bad leather jacket I'd seen. That would cheer me up! It was a deep chocolate brown and made of soft butter leather. Check this: Miss Sparkle had her some fly-ass brown leather thigh-high boots that would match the jacket to a tee, and I couldn't wait until the weather got a little cooler so I could suit up and profile with class and style.

I wished Fancy was around, but she worked as the community health coordinator up at Fort Monmouth, and even though she sometimes came home for lunch, she usually spent that time with Kevin. I reached for my cell phone, intending to call her and ask if she wanted me to pick her up a jacket too, but then I put it right back in my purse.

I was a little bit pissed with Fancy girl, that sneaky little heffah. I didn't know whether my cousin Glodean was lying or not, but she'd sworn up and down that Fancy and Kevin had been fucking on my swing set during my family barbecue. I'd hurried up and marched my booty out there and sprayed some Lysol all over the damn thing just to be safe. People's kids played out there!

I climbed the stairs to the main floor of the academy and poked my head into the orderly room. "Hey." I smiled at Sergeant Daphne Clifton, the personnel services clerk who worked directly for the company commander. "Where's your boss?"

She waved toward his office. "Gone, girl. Got a phone call

and ran up out of here. He's probably at Colonel Turner's ODP with the rest of the officers."

Good riddance.

The door to his office was open and I could see a thick wooden nameplate that read CPT EMILE PINCHBACK on his desk. Right next to it was her smiling photo, and I swear I just couldn't help myself. I scurried into the orderly room, ran around Daphne's desk, then jetted into his office and frowned. Skinny white heffah. And him sitting there gazing at her all day like she was his savior or something. I couldn't stand him!

Captain Pinchback was just another self-hating white woman–loving Lonnie Jackson in my book. And yeah, Lonnie had pulled the okey-doke on Miss Sparkle and it still hurt. All that time I'd been loving him and supporting him through his divorce, that scrub had been secretly planning a wedding with some white chick. You should have seen how your sister performed. Turned that motherfucker out! I got so drunk I could hardly walk, then made Fancy drive me into Medford to their slamming little church wedding and got up in there and showed my natural black ass.

I don't hardly remember all the details because I didn't come down off my drunk until way after I'd been arrested, fingerprinted, and booked. Thank God I was released on my own recognizance and neither Lonnie nor his precious little bride had wanted to press charges. The whole affair was a huge embarrassment and a tremendous blow to my ego, seeing that they lived right next door on McGuire Air Force Base. So watching fat-butt Captain Pinchback with his stretch-marky arms bowing down to some blond beast always made me wanna start swinging on somebody.

I snatched her picture off the desk and flung it into the trash can. I grinned at Daphne as I ran out of his office and back around to her desk. "He's gonna swear all-out that you did it!"

She wasn't the least bit fazed. "Nah, honey, he's gonna *know* it was you!"

Daphne was cool and I really liked her. Something about her reminded me of my girl Sandie Coffee, and I made a mental note to call and check on her and her basketball team of kids as soon as I got home.

"We're taking payday activities and I've got a private coming up here for phone watch. You wanna go check out the black mall?"

She nodded. Daphne was a decent-looking sister. Not gorgeous like me or anything, but she had some pretty black skin and a really nice smile. I didn't usually get along with the women in my units. You know, bitches can be jealous. Besides, I only needed one or two girlfriends to step out with and the rest of them could kiss my ass. You'd never find me strolling around with no whole gaggle of women. Sparkle liked to *shine,* and when it was time to claim a kneegrow I didn't want nobody tripping me up or throwing salt in my game.

The mall was packed with a lunchtime crowd, and even though we were in military uniforms brothers were trying to get with me left and right. "Hey, light-skin! Damn! GI Jo-Neequa! Look who they got holding the fort down!"

I ignored them 'cause Miss Sparkle didn't cotton to no broke-ass man. How employed could they be if they were hanging out at a mall in the middle of the day?

"Now, right there's a slim-goody." Daphne elbowed me and nodded toward a tall lanky thing who looked young enough to still be in high school. He was strolling through the mall with his hands in the pockets of his baggy jeans, and I was ready to bet my last tube of lipstick that his hands were the only things his pockets were packing. Get a job!

"Chocolate gumdrop," Daphne said, swiveling her narrow-ass hips. "Long piece of shiny black licorice."

I just shrugged. "Not my type," I said, watching him duck into a video arcade. "Jailbait. Rudy-poot little fish like him need to be thrown back in."

She laughed. "Well, your girl sure likes 'em young. I see her in the club on the weekends. Checking wet Pampers and warming up baby bottles."

I stopped and put my hands on my hips. "And who might my girl be?"

"Your girl, you know. Top's wife. What's her name, Francine?"

"Fancy," I hissed, patting my foot. "Her name is Fancy, and she's married. To your first sergeant, remember?"

Daphne shrugged. "Yeah, I guess she is married. She's gorgeous too. I'm just saying she likes young guys. Or at least it looks that way whenever I run into her at the club."

I took a deep breath and let some steam out. Daphne was harmless. She wasn't trying to slander my girl. Anyway, Fancy and I hardly ever partied together because I couldn't stand the All-Ranks Club. Besides, she needed to keep her ass at home on the weekends, and I was surprised Kevin hadn't checked her about that.

"Whatever," I said, striding onward. "Fancy's her own

woman, but she's also my best friend. Every time I turn around somebody has something nasty to say about her, and even though I don't give a damn what people say, I still don't want to hear it."

Daphne smiled. "Chill, girl. Everything is cool."

I felt much better after stepping into Wilson's to try on my leather jacket.

"Looks good on you," Daphne said, lifting my mood, and of course she was right. I modeled that bad boy in the mirror, imagining how it would look once I put on my hip-hugger jeans. Satisfied, I paid for the jacket and threw in a pair of Thinsulate gloves as a treat to myself. I was happy as shit, swinging my shopping bag and leading Daphne toward the food court, when I spotted the perfect handbag dangling from a display.

"Girl, look." I pointed. It was a beautiful shade of brown, an exact match for the jacket I'd just purchased. Best of all, it was an Isabella Fiore and I just had to have it.

Daphne and I trucked over to the kiosk, where a crowd of women were scrambling to buy purses and bags that had just come in. Some young brother with wavy hair and a name tag that read ALI was unpacking tons of merchandise from a huge box and trying to take payments at the same time.

Damn! There were some aggressive sisters up in this mall! They were elbowing me and stepping all over my spit-shined boots like I wasn't even there! Daphne nudged me and pointed to a sign. "They're on sale today only, Sparkle. Twenty percent off."

Now, you know Miss Sparkle loves herself a sale. I elbowed those skanky sisters aside and snatched that perfect little Isabella Fiore from the top of the hook and tucked it in the crook of my arm like it was a football. Just let one of them try to get it away from me. Shit would be on and popping!

I'd just set my Wilson's bag on the floor between my feet so I could dig into my purse for some cash, and when I looked up I couldn't believe my lying eyes.

There he was in the flesh. Jive talking and bullshit walking. Chatting up a bunch of black women like it was something he did on the regular. Son of a gun! He was standing there in that green pickle suit taking money and making change like he owned the joint. Fancy had told me he'd gotten himself a second job to support his white woman jones, but I didn't know he was taking care of that stringy-haired heffah with the hard-earned dollars of black women like me! The fat-head, wide-hipped *pimp*!

I crossed my arms and stared him down.

"Chill, Sparkle," Daphne said, tugging on my arm. "Remember, he's our boss."

I shook her off. This was between Emily and me. I watched for long minutes as he played the I-love-sistahs game, gazing all into their eyes and hanging off their loose bra straps. I would have sworn he knew these women personally. He called them each by name, winked, grinned, flirted his ass off, and made their money disappear like a good little magician.

And you should have heard their dumb behinds. My sisters had fallen for him panties, bras, and wallets. Easy this and Easy that. Yep! He had them so souped up they thought his name was Easy!

"Uhm," I yelled loudly. "Can I get some service over here?"

Heads swung toward me, then back to Captain Pinchback. Okay, yeah, we were both in our military uniforms, but I'd come too far to stop now.

His smile fell off as soon as our eyes met and he looked like he wanted to hit me.

"As you can see," he smirked, "there's a line. Stand on it and wait your turn."

I'm gonna kick this fool right in his nuts!

"Oh. 'Scuse me. I'm sorry, *Emily*. I thought I was talking to a *black* man!"

He waved his hand and pasted that dollar-sign smile back on his face. "You're not much of a woman as far as I can see. Black or otherwise." Then he reached out to ring up the next sister's merchandise and muttered, "Fake-ass black bitch."

Well, he started it, so you *know* Miss Sparkle went ahead and finished it!

"Oh, no, you *didn't*," I screamed on him. "You fronting-ass sellout! That's okay, though. You ain't gotta respect me or none of these other sisters here either! We ain't nobody important to you. We're only your mama, your sister, and your goddamn *auntie*!"

I pushed past a bunch of dropped jaws and indignant titties until I was up in his face. A few of his customers had un-assed the stuff they'd been waiting to purchase and were stuffing their money back inside their designer purses.

"My sisters!" I turned and stared into their eyes. I was gonna bring it to them straight, and by the looks on their faces I knew they'd be able to feel me. "Emily Pinchback here ain't no real brother. And he sure as hell doesn't respect black women, even though weak kneegrows like him come out of our asses and we don't come out of theirs. He's nothing but a self-hating, sister-hating Oreo who's taking your money and spending it on some scraggly-ass white woman! His name is *Emily* not Easy, and this kneegrow is faking the funk and trying to pull off a fraud! He doesn't even *speak* to black women outside of this mall. And y'all heard him just now, no respect for me as his sister. Did he have a problem calling me a bitch right in front of your faces? Hell no! And if he had enough nuts to call me a black bitch, when we wear the same uniform and march in the same boots . . . my sisters who love him and support his booming business with the dollars he turns around and spends on Miss Ann, tell me just what kind of *bitch* does that make you?"

CHAPTER 12

KEVIN

How Far Would You Go?

*Y*ou could fool some of the people some of the time, but Fancy had never fooled me at all. Freaks can smell other freaks, and my wife was a genuine cumming machine.

The year we got married I had organized one hell of a birthday surprise for her. About a week before her birthday, we'd been up hitting skins for nearly half the night when I looked over at Fancy and popped the million-dollar question.

"You're the best, baby," I told her, brushing a few strands of hair back from her honey-colored face. "Really the best. But I wanna ask you something . . ."

"Sure," she said, smiling through her eight-orgasm afterglow. "What?"

"How far would you go, Fancy, you know, to make sure I was satisfied with our sex life?"

She laughed. "I just rode you to the moon and back, Kevin. Would you like to shoot for Mars?"

"For real, though. I love having sex, and I know you love having sex—"

"Making love," she corrected me gently. "I used to love to have sex, Kevin, but not anymore. Nowadays I'm making love. Giving my all to my husband and making sweet, precious married love."

I saw exactly where she was heading and I jerked that wheel hard to the left.

"Yeah, baby. We do make some wonderful love, and I enjoy every bit of it. But sometimes a man just wants some sex, you know? Variety is the spice of life, Fancy, and every now and then a brother just needs a good fuck. Don't you?"

"Well," she stammered. "Uhm, yeah. Of course I like it when we do it rough and raw too. I'm down for adding a little variety as long as I'm doing it with you."

"I like doing it with you too, Fancy, but like most men, one of my fantasies involves getting it on with two girls. Would you be okay with something like that?"

She went quiet for a minute. I could feel her brain working and I gave her time to think. Women killed me. They were fuck-a-holics the whole time they were trying to hook you, and once they got that ring on their finger they joined some secret sect of holy virgins. But Fancy couldn't front. When I first met her she was giving lap dances by the dozens, so there went any claims she might have to being a sexual prude.

"I don't think that would be right, Kevin," she said finally with a little hurt in her voice. Why all the damn drama? I wanted to know. Why pretend to be all modest when the first night I laid eyes on her she'd just about sucked the skin off my dick in a sleazy little spot called Jugz?

I kept at it, hitting her hard.

"You know what kind of man I am, Fancy. You knew I had a lot of needs when you met me."

"Yeah," she shot back. "But you said all you needed was *me*!"

I threw my hands in the air. "I do need you. But shit, if I had wanted some shy little virgin I would have married me one, baby! I thought you were open-minded and sexually free."

She sniffled, hugging her pillow. "I am. I mean—I was. I just—"

"Look, Fancy. I'ma just say it straight out. I want you to find a couple of sistahs who might be interested in having a ménage à trois with us."

She looked horrified. "I don't have any friends who I'd ask to do that!"

"They don't have to be people you know, baby. A stranger would be fine. A lot of women work for call services like that. Find one. Just as long as she's clean and fine and stacked in all the right places."

Her eyes got all big and shit like, *Who me? Couldn't be!* She started crying and wailing and running me a bunch of, but I don't wannas, married people don't get down like that, your dick should be all mine, it should only go up in me . . . so much high-strung bull. But she wouldn't budge. Her no meant no.

So I chilled and went on the devious tip.

I called my man Dink. We'd just gotten to Puerto Rico and I looked him up through the post locator service. Dink was a real smooth niggah. I mean his shit was tight. A pretty boy with swollen muscles that bulged through his uniform, Dink had honeys lined up from here to Tennessee. Drill Sergeant of the Year, Recruiter of the Year, graduated at the top of his class at the Sergeant Major's Academy. Dink was just one of those guys who excelled in everything and looked good doing it.

Dink and I had met when we were brand-new privates and both fucking our squad leader's wife. It wasn't long before she wanted us to do her together, and while I knew I'd been blessed below the belt, that night I discovered that Dink had been blessed too. He had me beat by a full inch. Over the years me and Dink had kept in touch, and whenever we were stationed together we'd each do the other a solid by engaging in a threesome to fulfill some chick's fantasy.

Man, me and Dink fucked the shit out of Fancy.

Turned her out like you wouldn't believe. I rented this grand hotel suite for her birthday and e-mailed Fancy with my instructions:

1. Pick up a room key at the front desk.
2. Come into the room and take the blindfold from the doorknob and tie it over your eyes.
3. Get undressed.
4. Slip under the covers from the bottom of the bed.
5. Climb on the horsey and go for a ride.

Everything went according to plan. Fancy came in and tied the scarf over her eyes, then stripped. Dink was in the bed under the covers, laying on his back and stroking his foot-long toolie. I stood watching from the bathroom as my wife did exactly what I'd told her to do. She patted around for a moment, then lifted the bottom of the sheets and crawled in the bed, then climbed on top of Dink and started moaning.

I could tell by the way she made those little whimpering noises in her throat that Dink wasn't a disappointment. He threw off those covers and gave it to my baby good. Stuck one finger up her ass and made her come almost immediately. By the time Dink pulled off her blindfold Fancy was heading toward another explosion, too far gone to stop.

"Wait . . . wait . . . wait," she protested weakly when she saw his face, then came again. Hard. Dink flipped her over onto her back, giving me my cue. I moved over to the bed and stood naked above her, holding my rock-hard hammer in my hand.

"Happy birthday, baby." I grinned as her face contorted with surprised pleasure. Dink was on the j-o-b. Going to town in that stuff. Fancy reached out and grabbed my hammer with both hands, smiling as she took me in her mouth.

Dink and I switched positions several times that night, our longtime routine choreographed to a tee. Both of us gave Fancy everything we had, her screams and moans and multiple orgasms confirming that she was being pleased to the max the whole time. "Like this?" we'd ask. "Deeper over here? How about like that? Yeah, baby. That shit feels good right?"

Later Fancy told me that it was the wildest birthday party she'd ever had and it made me happy that I was able to get her to not only let go of her reservations, but enjoy it so much too.

After that, it was easy. Fancy just gave in and fell in line. Over the years me and my baby had enjoyed us quite a few more Dinks. We lived on base most of the time, so we had to be careful, though. Military regulations would have me wearing private's stripes if it got out that I was committing adultery on the regular, so we made sure that it was Fancy who picked up our playmates. Fancy who hit the clubs at night and solicited the kind of men who gave off the same freak scent that I did. Fancy who snuck them into the house before I came home for lunch and warmed them up for our midday snack.

And what was good for the lady was even better for the gent. There was no denying that being fucked by two men turned my wife on to the highest heights. Yeah, I know it shamed her, but the orgasms that ripped through her body proved she was born for it.

It wasn't long before I got her to agree to my original request, and once she put her mind to it Fancy brought home some of the sexiest sisters in the universe. She'd hip the girls to what I liked, and together they'd work me over until my nuts were shriveled and my toes were curled.

Yeah, my baby was a freak for sure, but raising the stakes was the only thing that kept my pot going on hot, and trust me when I tell you that what I had planned next was gonna freak her out some more.

CHAPTER 13

FANCY

Hey, Ho!

*M*y phone rang. I'd been waiting to hear from a client I'd been trying to reach, a reserve soldier who had tested positive for HIV and needed to be brought in for diagnosis and counseling, and when I snatched up the receiver and was greeted by Sparkle's voice I was quite surprised.

"Hey, ho! What you doing after work?"

I looked down at my desk calendar and shrugged. "Nothing, actually. Dr. Bledsoe had me waiting for a phone call all day, but if it doesn't come through in the next thirty minutes or so, I'm leaving."

"That'll work," she said, then quickly added, "because I need to get a few things from the outlet mall near Six Flags. Can you meet me there?"

I thought for a moment. Dr. Bledsoe was at an infectious disease control meeting and my client hadn't called yet, but I could always forward my office calls to my cell phone. Besides, I felt my shopping jones coming down too, and there was absolutely nobody in the world I would rather shop with than Sparkle.

"Sure," I answered, already straightening papers on my desk in preparation to leave. "I'm already halfway out the door. It'll take you at least thirty minutes to get up here. I'll meet you outside the food court."

———

I was sitting in a window seat sipping a Diet Coke when Sparkle drove up in her black Nissan Z. I knew it was her the moment she pulled into the parking lot entrance, gunning her motor, swerving around parked cars, her gas foot heavy and her music blasting on extra loud. My girl was too wild.

I ditched my soft drink and went outside to meet her.

"Hey, ho!" I called out, waving from the curb as she parked in an empty spot. Of course she didn't hear me; her music was too loud. I stood there in my pale gray mid-thigh skirt suit with my hand on my hip, waiting for her to notice me.

Sparkle finally cut off her engine and slid from the car.

"Well, damn!" she exclaimed, grinning and slinking toward me in a pair of stonewashed jeans that accentuated her round hips and small waist. Her blond hair hung past her shoulders in tight spiral curls. She was wearing a clingy white belly shirt without a bra, and showing off her gold belly ring and the brilliant tattoo of the sun encircling her navel that was identical to mine.

"You standing on that curb like you trying to *catch* something with your long-legged self. Does your husband know how short that damn skirt is?"

I laughed. "At least I have on underwear!"

Sparkle looked down at her full jiggling breasts and grinned. "And so do I," she said, turning around to flash me the white thong that peeked from the low-cut waistband of her jeans.

"Girl, please," I said, dismissing her with one hand. "I ain't trying to see all that. You know your butt is too big for a thong anyway."

"Oh, yeah." She slapped her hip. "Take a picture of it. Big and round and juicy booty! Just the way the fellas like 'em!"

I smiled inside. I liked being with Sparkle. She was loud and sometimes ghetto, but at least she was real about her needs and what she wanted out of life, and that was more than I could say about my perpetrating ass.

"Let's hit Old Navy first," Sparkle ordered. "There's a jacket in there I want to buy, but not unless they've marked it down."

For the next hour and a half we shopped like two fiends. Even though we wore the same size in everything except shoes, we had very different tastes, and most of the clothing Sparkle tried on and purchased was inappropriate for me to wear to the office.

"Come with me," I told her as we passed a Gap store that had a huge display of cute clothes for kids in the window. "One of the girls on my job is giving a sixth-birthday party for her daughter next weekend and I might as well get her a gift right now."

"I don't wanna go in there," Sparkle protested. "I don't even like kids."

"Come on, Sparkle," I said, schmoozing up to her and playing to her ego. "You know you have the bomb tastes. Help me pick out something cute for the little girl."

We were in the store all of two minutes when my girl began acting ugly.

"Look behind you. Two o'clock."

I turned around slowly, clutching a SpongeBob SquarePants denim jumper in my hands. There were quite a few people in the store and I didn't notice anything out of the ordinary.

"What?"

"Your doggish brother. And his little mutts. As black as he is, is that the best he could do?"

I sighed. Sparkle was referring to a black man who was shopping with two children who were obviously mixed. "Sparkle, please. Cut that mess out. I can think of worse things the man could be doing than taking his children out for a day of shopping."

"But just look at them," she insisted. "He's a blue-black brother, but he still didn't have enough black in his blood to make his kids look anything like him."

I turned away and muttered, "They look a little bit like him to me."

"Yeah, right. Those kids could be the milkman's or the mailman's or the iceman's. Line them up next to any man in this mall and that brother would be the last one you'd accuse of being their daddy. Like I said, as black as he is, he couldn't even make babies that remotely look like they came from his nuts."

I shook my head at the senselessness of it all, but Sparkle was dead serious.

"I think they're kinda cute."

"Get real, Fancy. Just because they're mixed don't hardly mean they're cute. Black kids are cute. Those kids look Arab. Or Hawaiian. Or Puerto Rican. Anything but black."

That was it. I'd heard enough. "Come on, Evilene." I hung the jumper back on the rack. "I don't know why you have to trip like this. Those kids are sweet, innocent, beautiful children."

She shrugged and pointed at the jumper. "Whatever. Aren't you gonna buy that?"

"No." I shook my head and slung my purse over my shoulder. I was done. "I'll just put some money in a birthday card and call it a day."

I hustled Sparkle through the store and out of the door as quickly as I could, actually pushing her once or twice as she stared at the brother with the mixed children in deep disgust.

An hour and a half later we were back at the food court. I'd purchased a pair of designer slippers for Kevin and a new watch for myself. Sparkle had gone berserk. She had so many bags and packages that I had to help her carry them to her car and then cram them in her little tiny trunk.

There were a ton of people in the food court and the lines were long at nearly every vendor. As usual, Sparkle and I were drawing attention. Men eyed us behind their wives' backs, and women looked at us with open envy. Sparkle was way more than pretty, and sure, I knew I was considered attractive, but I hadn't been comfortable under that kind of glare since I got married and left my stripping days behind. But Sparkle ate it up. Moving like she was on a runway, throwing her round ass around in her tight jeans, and showing her teeth to every male over the age of five.

"Girl, stop," I muttered, walking behind her as a freckle-faced brother with a mouth full of food almost got slapped for following her hips with his eyes. His wife had been busy wiping ketchup from the faces of her toddlers and breaking up a mini food fight between her two older kids. She'd looked up just in time to catch her man chewing slowly, mesmerized by the sight of Sparkle's ass sauntering past, and nearly lost her mind.

"Hee-hee," Sparkle laughed over her shoulder, leading me toward a deli stand as the sister started screaming on her man. "If you got it, flaunt it, baby."

I was shaking my head when dude stepped in front of me.

"Oh, so you just gonna act like you don't know me?"

I looked up and faced a good-looking young man. Tall, muscular, and definitely under twenty-five. "Excuse me?"

He grinned, sliding his hands into his front pockets, and I tried to recall his name as an entire portfolio of faces ran through my mind in a split second. "You were really good that night, sweetie. Your man is a little whack for letting me crawl up in his sandbox and play around with his toys, but you were great. Can we do it again?"

I frowned as Sparkle positioned herself until she was standing slightly in front of me. He'd looked a little older under the club lights, but his dimples were just as deep as I remembered. And if my memory was all the way correct, he'd gone pretty deep too.

"I'm sorry," I said coldly. "You must be mistaking me for someone else."

He grinned. "How could I be? Your crib, great wine, mellow music, soft bearskin rug . . . I remember it like it was last night. In fact, I relive it almost every night in my dreams."

"Niggah, *please*!" Sparkle hissed. "Don't you see grown folks talking? She *said* she don't *know* you, so why don't you just care your little young ass on over there"—she pointed— "to Mickey Dee's and get yourself a Happy Meal?"

He looked from me to Sparkle, and then back to me. I continued to stare him down, warning him with my eyes not to push the issue. Of course I'd run into a few ex-playthings before, but most of them had enough sense to nod or smile their remembrance and keep it moving. This one was apparently too young to know any better.

I sighed out loud as he turned and walked away.

"Minnow!" Sparkle giggled at his retreating back. "Perch! Guppie!" Then we looked at each other and shrieked at the same time, *"Crab!"*

Still laughing, we ordered salads from the deli stand and found some empty seats. I kicked off my shoes as I sat down at a metal table across from Sparkle. I'd just finished cutting up the grilled chicken atop my salad greens when the tone of her voice bit into the air.

"Look at that shit," Sparkle sneered, shaking her head.

I paused with a packet of blue cheese dressing in my hand. "What? Look at what shit?"

She indicated with her chin. "Over there. Your brother and his Barbie doll, with her anorexic-looking baloney-smelling self."

Not again, I prayed. I followed her gaze over to a mixed-race couple that was standing in a pizza line. The brother looked sporty in his FUBU shirt and jeans, and his white woman wore a pair of Lycra pants and a spandex top.

"She's tiny, all right," I agreed, tearing the packet of salad dressing open with my teeth.

Sparkle sucked her teeth. "Tiny, hell. Look at her little narrow behind. It's about that"—she held her pointer fingers about six inches apart—"wide."

I looked again. It was true. She was a stick. Straight up and down.

Sparkle laughed out loud. "I bet he wouldn't even know what to do with all this backfield I'm packing." She got up from her seat. "I'll be right back. I need some salt."

I shook my head. "Go ahead and show him what he's missing, girl."

She put a little extra swing in her step as she headed in their direction. "You damn right I will."

CHAPTER 14

KEVIN

So Much More to Give

I'd found her.

She was discreet, fine, and best of all she was down.

Her name was Mica and I'd met her in Wife Watchers, an online chat room for swingers. Her screen name was Swap-WithMe2, and after downloading her photos and getting her telephone number, we decided to meet at a local hotel two weeks from Friday. I didn't get to speak to her husband, but so what? Mica said they were experienced, even with reluctant partners, and after I told her exactly what I wanted she said fulfilling my fantasy wouldn't be a problem at all.

That hadn't given me much time to work on Fancy so you know I acted fast. Right after Sparkle's Labor Day barbecue I put my plan into action. I started acting real cold toward Fancy. I stopped saying good morning and wouldn't even kiss her goodbye when I left for work. I cut out all the phone calls and slept on the edge of the bed at night, refusing to snuggle with her. I masturbated several times a day to keep from begging her for pussy, and turned her down cold when she approached me in bed. "No thank you" was what she got when she offered to iron my uniforms, and I picked over the meals she'd spent hours preparing, then told her I was going for a drive and hit the nearest Burger King or McDonald's.

In a matter of days she was starving for affection and I knew my plan was working. "What's wrong with you, Kevin?" she'd wailed. "What the hell did I do?"

"Nothing," I'd say stiffly. "It's not you, it's me."

Then I'd grab my keys and slam out the door, her cries of frustration ringing out behind me.

Of course I felt terrible about my behavior. I loved my wife and I didn't enjoy hurting her in any way. It's just that I had to break down her defenses. Demolish them in small increments. Get her to a point where there wasn't anything she wouldn't do for me. Where there were no inhibitions and nothing her man wanted was considered taboo. Wasn't that what true love was about?

Fancy responded just the way I wanted her to. Like a little puppy who was eager to please. She bent over backward trying to be nice, and asked for my opinion and input on everything under the sun just to get a little attention. Called me at work every morning and offered to drive in from Fort Monmouth and meet me for lunch. She was close to panic mode and desperate to get back on my good side, so I tested that ass. Just to be sure I had her.

We were taking a group of Primary Leadership Development Course soldiers to the field for bivouac training, and they'd set up fifty pup tents for the troops and a single-frame tent that six NCOs would share. We were only scheduled to be out there for three nights and four days, but that was plenty of time. Fancy hated bugs and she hated the woods, so I knew this would be the perfect opportunity to snatch her out of her comfort zone and see how much juice I really had.

I sent her an e-mail two days before we rolled out. Asked her to put on a raincoat and one of those sexy thongs and sneak out to the field site and give me some pussy.

"You don't have to if it's too much trouble," I told her the morning I left. She was on her way to a photography seminar, packing a camera bag and stuffing it with cases of extra film, and even though I knew she was distracted I purposely kept my voice even and my face blank.

Just like I'd predicted, she jumped right on the hook.

"No, no!" she said, forgetting all about her camera. "It won't be any trouble at all, baby. Actually it sounds like a lot of fun."

You better believe she showed up right on time. I'd given her directions to our training area, which was on the far side of the base, and told her to park behind a line of military vehicles, then look for the largest tent inside the perimeter.

"What if somebody sees me?" she'd asked nervously.

"I'll talk to the fire guards and the roving patrols. They'll issue you a challenge and you just give them the password that I text message to you."

I was laying in my sleeping bag when I saw the tent flaps move. The moon was streaming in from the outlet flap on the roof, and I could see the nervousness in her movements right away. It had rained during the day, and if I wasn't so excited I would have laughed as she clutched her raincoat to her chest and wobbled toward me in those red high heels that had her ankles sinking into the mud.

It was after three in the morning and the other NCOs—her girl Sparkle, three white dudes, and a brother—had been snoring for hours. Earlier I'd made sure that my cot was positioned right next to Sparkle's. I wanted to be able to sex Fancy and look at Sparkle at the same time.

I unzipped my sleeping bag as Fancy approached, pressing my finger to my lips and cautioning her to be quiet. I reached out for her hand as she drew near, and when we touched she squeezed my fingers gratefully.

"Take that off," I whispered.

Fancy unbuttoned the shiny black raincoat and I gasped out loud at the sight of her naked breasts, proud and erect. When I opened my arms to her, she settled down on top of me and I covered her with the sleeping bag. Pushing her thong to one side, I entered her, and as she rode me without protest in the darkness of a tent full of sleeping men and her own best friend, I gripped her by the waist and pretended she was Sparkle until we both came.

Phase One had been a success. It was time to implement Phase Two.

————

I asked Fancy to get her nipples pierced.

Nipple rings were the in thing right now, and I wanted my wife to have them. I was still giving her the distant treatment. Withholding the hammer and most of my affection. After the field episode she'd expected us to fall back into our old lovey-dovey patterns, but I had a surprise for her. I'd walked her out of the field site and made sure she got into the car okay, but I didn't even get close enough to kiss her goodbye, and I turned off my cell phone so she couldn't call me all night either. As soon as I got back to the tent I stroked my tool up again and stared at Sparkle as she slept, until I came once more.

When I first asked Fancy to do the nipple piercing she'd looked at me like I was crazy, but once I shrugged and said no problem, she readily agreed.

I wasn't totally heartless, though. I told her that I would prefer it if she got both nipples done, but if it hurt her too badly she could stop at one.

We had a few drinks before heading out for the piercing parlor, which was about ten miles away. The place was clean and well lit, and I watched the young white boy whose name was Jake take his piercing tools out of a sealed plastic bag.

"Uhm, can you take off your shirt and bra and lie back on the table?"

Fancy was nervous. I could tell by the way she lay there squeezing my hand. I was turned on like crazy, my toolie uncomfortably hard in my pants.

"It's okay, baby," I soothed her.

"Just one?" she asked in a small voice.

"Yeah." I nodded. "Just one."

But something weird happened when dude stuck that sharp tip through her nipple. Fancy arched her back and squeezed my hand as a low moan slid from her lips. "Go ahead," she whispered a moment later, her eyes squeezed shut as she nodded him onward. "Go ahead and do the other one."

"You know we have clit rings as well," Jake joked after both of Fancy's nipples were pierced. She was still laying on the table breathing deeply with her beautiful breasts pointing toward the ceiling, her nipples a bit red, but powerfully erect with tiny barbells passing through them.

She rose up on her elbows and looked at me. Sweat covered her top lip and her face was flushed. "You want me to go for it?"

I shrugged, taken aback. I hadn't even considered sticking the clit, but hell, if she was game, why not?"

Jake instructed Fancy to take off her jeans and panties and pull her feet as far back as she could. I stood beside him looking down at my wife's glistening wet pussy, amazed at the thick juices that were leaking from her sexy slit.

Opening a new pack of ornaments, Jake selected a tiny one and inserted it in a little thing that looked like a staple gun. He put on a pair of disposable gloves and spread Fancy's lips with his fingers while positioning the gun on the skin near the top of her clit.

Jake clamped down until the gun clicked.

I sucked in my breath and clenched my teeth.

Fancy moaned, cried out, and came, ejaculating all over the table.

My baby was a freak indeed.

————

I was pushing Fancy's limits and I knew it. You would have thought I was suggesting she sleep with her own sister the way she went off whenever I mentioned pairing her up with another girl. If she didn't trust me to keep her passions safe the way I trusted her with mine, then what kind of relationship did we really have?

I knew I'd have to inch her into my fantasy, but today I

wanted to try something different and I wanted to make sure she was soft enough to be open to it. Honestly, I know I sound like some no-good asshole who doesn't give a damn about his woman, but that's not it at all. I keep telling you that I love my wife and I hope you believe me. It's just that Fancy needs to know who calls the shots when it comes to our sex life. Hey, a man does have his needs, doesn't he?

It was time to put Phase Two of my plan into motion.

"You been a bad girl," I told her one morning as she was getting ready for work. Fancy had just come out of the shower, and after rubbing scented cream into her firm light brown body, she stepped into a teddy and a pair of white lace panties, then sat down at her vanity table to put on her makeup.

It was a training holiday for the military and I was laying in bed with my hands under the covers. Even though Fancy worked at a military hospital, civilians did not get to take off on military training holidays.

I'd taken my belt from my pants and wrapped it around my hand while she was in the shower, and now I rose from the bed naked and hard, and as our eyes met in the mirror I saw her nipples grow tense and tent the fabric of her teddy.

"Lay on the bed," I said. My voice was low and dangerous and from the look on her face I could tell she was scared and excited at the same time.

She got up from her stool and started to lay back on the bed when I checked her.

"No!" I barked and she froze. "Turn over."

She turned onto her stomach and my nuts got tight. Fancy was really something to behold. She had the tiniest waist and the most exquisitely shaped ass I had ever seen. It was round and firm and the color of creamy caramel. I wanted to drop to my knees and lick her out, asshole and all, but I reminded myself of the bigger goal at hand.

"You know that Ray Johnson who used to work in my office, right?"

Her voice was a trembling whisper. "Yes."

I raised the belt over my head. "That motherfucker had him some of my stuff, didn't he?"

She turned her head and looked at me. "Kevin, what are you doing with that damn belt?"

I swung the strap in an arc, connecting with the crown of her rump. Not hard enough to really hurt her, but with just enough sting that she clenched her cheeks and yelped.

"I asked you a question, Fancy." I let the belt fly again, this time a little harder.

She moaned and tucked her pelvis down into the bed. She knew the deal. This was a love game, yeah. But Daddy was about to take it to a whole 'nother level.

"Tell Daddy what Ray did, baby."

"Ray made me, Kevin."

"Made you what?" The belt snaked out and bit her again, and this time she shuddered and rolled her hips in a slow circle.

"He made me take off my clothes."

"And what else?"

"He put his mouth on my breasts." *Tap*. The belt stroked her.

"Then what?"

"He licked me down there."

"You let that lousy son-of-a-gun get down there to my stuff?" *Tap!*

She squirmed in heat. "I didn't mean to, Daddy! I tried to fight him off. I swear I did. I knew you would be mad if I let him. But he was so damn big and strong. When he licked me out it felt like the Devil's tongue. I tried not to like it but he made me. He pinned me down and did it to me, baby. His back was strong, all those muscles . . ." Fancy's hands were in her panties and I knew she wanted to come.

I began to sweat above her as I stroked myself with one hand and let the belt fly with the other. "You didn't let him put his tool in there, did you?"

"No," she whimpered, her ass high in the air begging for another lick. "Not in there. No baby. Never in there."

I let the strap fly again. "Then where?"

"Oh, Daddy! I can't say it. You're gonna get upset if I do."

Tap! "Then show me, Fancy." I ripped her panties off with one motion and she bit down into the blanket, muffling her scream. "Show Daddy where that big nasty Ray Johnson put his dick. I wanna see just what he did to my woman while I was gone."

Fancy raised herself onto her knees and using two hands, spread her cheeks and showed me her beautifully tight asshole.

"Uh-huh," I whispered. "Then Daddy's gonna do just what Ray did, baby." I threw the belt down and eased on top of her, searching for my target. I wet the head in that dripping softness between her thighs, then withdrew and aimed straight for the back door. "Daddy's gonna give you exactly what that big nasty Ray gave you," I told her. "Except Daddy's got so much more of it to give."

CHAPTER 15

EMILE

Keisha, Laquita, Nay-Nay

*W*e were chilling naked in bed when she brought it up.

It had been a rough week, but just holding my princess in my arms had put all thoughts of Colonel Turner and that mob-like drama at the black mall on the shelf. Becky Ann had just finished taking herself a serious ride. She liked to be on top and I liked seeing her up there as I held her slim waist and lifted her up and down. Just watching my monster as it disappeared into her tight pink cave was hypnotic. Something about that color contrast just did it for me.

Reaching for her, I pushed my nose into her hair and felt myself getting hard again, turned on by her fresh scent. I traced the rosy circle of her nipples with my finger, then cupped her small breast and kissed her on the lips.

I knew Becky Ann dated other guys occasionally, although I wasn't happy about it. I'd never actually seen her with anyone else, but a couple of times her cell phone had rung while we were out and she'd excuse herself to have a brief, whispered conversation. There'd also been a few times when we were interrupted right in the middle of sex, and she'd leave me laying there with a wet erection while she went into the kitchen or the bathroom to take the call.

You know I imagined all kinds of big black niggers on the line trying to talk my girl away from me, and I made sure when she did get back in the bed I put my rock-hard monster back inside her and pounded her pinkness so thoroughly that there wasn't any room in her head to think about another man.

I looked over at her and smiled. I felt bad when she said she wasn't ready to settle down with one man, but hey. I loved this girl and adored every little thing about her. Becky Ann was real slim and pretty, and looking at her skin just amazed me. Not just the milky whiteness of it, but how smooth and textured it was too. None of that pigmented mess that had turned my body five different shades of black. It was crazy how my face was one color, my neck three shades blacker, my chest about eight shades lighter, and then those crusty black patches on my knees and elbows and neck and the black half-moons that connected the back of my thighs to the bottom of my ass.

"Whew . . ." I turned onto my side and rubbed my eyes. "Thanks, baby. You were great. It was the perfect ending to a shitty week."

"You seem to be having a lot of those lately."

I shrugged. "Look at the kind of people I have to deal with on a daily basis. That dyke Colonel Turner at the battalion, that simple-behind Staff Sergeant Henderson at the company . . . I don't know why they let women like them join the army anyway."

"Emile." Becky Ann sat up and leaned back against the pillows. My hand was resting on her thigh and I felt so damn lucky to be here sharing this moment with her that I could have cried. "Emile, you and Kevin had it tough as kids, and I really understand that. But you're awfully hard on black women. Don't you think?"

"Hard on black women?" I gave a short laugh and snuggled closer to her, closing my eyes. "They're hard on themselves, baby. Just trifling. That's why I have you."

She scooted over in a way that left me cold. I opened my eyes and saw that my hand had fallen from her thigh to the bed. It looked big and black on the pale pink designer sheets I'd recently gotten her from Nordstrom.

"I'm serious," she said, searching for the T-shirt I'd peeled off her just an hour earlier. "The way you demean some women really bothers me. I mean, I understand about that lady, Sue—"

"*Dirty* Sue," I corrected, shuddering into the pillow.

She sighed. "Okay, Dirty Sue, or whatever you kids called her. So she was one negative influence in your life. Does that mean that all women in your life have to suffer for her wrongdoings?"

I sat up. I felt a migraine jumping up into my temples and glanced toward the scented candle on Becky's dresser. I was sensitive to strong smells and hated it when she burned that thing.

"No, baby." I put my arm around her and marveled at the vivid contrast our naked thighs made pressed side by side. "Every woman in my life doesn't suffer. I don't hear you complaining"—I tweaked her nipple, trying to lighten things up—"so I must be doing something right." I sure hoped that was true. Months ago I'd hinted around about wanting to be introduced to her parents, and I was hoping that she'd invite me to their family home on the Eastern Shore of Maryland for Thanksgiving dinner.

She moved again and my arm slipped from her shoulder. "There are a lot of things you do right, Emile. But after what happened with that colonel at your job and then that whole thing that came close to a riot with those women at the mall . . ."

"That's different, Becky Ann," I said quickly. "Colonel Turner singled me out to rag on. You can ask Bill or John or any of the guys and they'll tell you the same thing. Plus, you have no idea how dyke military women think. Bitches like her always have something to prove."

"And what about that other woman? Sergeant Henderson. That pretty girl you're always ranting about. Oh, I forgot. She's a dyke too, right?"

"Staff Sergeant Henderson?" I scoffed. "Pretty my foot. You can hardly call her a woman, so I guess she would qualify as a dyke. I mean, she's not nearly a lady the way you are." I reached out and touched her hand. "She's street trash, princess, so don't worry about her. She doesn't even count."

"But she does count, Emile! She counts as a human being!" Becky turned toward me and I saw something fierce in her eyes. "Besides. She must count to some degree. You said all of your customers took her side against you."

They *sure* did, and that shit had pissed me off too. If I hadn't been in uniform I would've taken it to the head with quite a few of those scallywags! Do you know how clannish sisters can get when they're ganging up on a brother? *Who you calling a black bitch?* That Sparkle Henderson had stirred up a big funk pot, then stepped back to see how it smelled. Keisha, Laquita, Nay-Nay, now she had all of them tripping hard and refusing to buy my goods. As if she'd never been called out of her name before! But I knew what to do. While those chicks were hollering smack about picketing my kiosk and getting my vendor's license revoked, I walked dead away from their loud asses and told Ali to give them back their money. Phony bunch of bitches! Making all that noise and knowing full well that come next payday they'd be right back up in my face begging for a discount and hoping for a date.

"My customers aren't going anywhere," I reassured Becky. "That was just a bunch of black female hysteria, so don't believe the hype. Next week this time those scavengers will have picked my cart bone-clean. Won't be anything left except the cash register and the framed picture I'm going to place up there of you."

"Which they'll probably throw darts at."

I balked. "They know better than to try that."

"You don't get it, do you?"

I sighed and almost got lost in her beautiful blue eyes. "What is there to get, hon? I do what I have to do to make it in this world. I didn't set this stage, I was born into it. All I can do now is play the role that was assigned to me."

She shook her head. "But you're disrespectful to black women, Emile. That's something that you do control. And if you can speak to black women in that manner, maybe one day you'll treat me the same way."

"No, princess, no." I jumped to my feet to set her straight. "You're all class and style. Hardly any of them are on your level."

"I'm a bartender, Emile. I never even finished high school.

And I know Colonel Turner. She's a real lady. She talks like she has a good education and she treats everyone nicely."

"Yeah, that's what you think, but I can see right through women like her. Colonel Turner is acting. She's got a chip on her shoulder like you wouldn't believe. Besides, you may not have her kind of education, but I like being seen with you because you don't carry yourself the way some of these black women out here do."

She laughed, but there was bitterness in her voice. "Oh, so it's not really me who's important then, huh? It's more like you need to get back at the women in your life and I'm one way of doing that, right?"

I shrugged and shook my head. Fluffing the pillow, I lay back down because the last thing I wanted to do was argue. I was looking forward to having Thanksgiving dinner with her family and I didn't want to say anything that might mess that up.

I spoke over my shoulder. "Becky Ann, I really care about you. My feelings for you run very deep and I want you to be a major part of my life."

"I like you too, Emile. But we're not restricting ourselves from seeing other people, remember?"

I sighed and closed my eyes. She'd agreed to that shit, not me, and I'd been working overtime to prove that no other man could love her as good as I did. The only man Becky Ann needed in her life was me, and as soon as I met her family and threw the charm on them, she'd be able to see that.

CHAPTER 16

FANCY

The Penthouse

Damn, girl." Kevin let out his breath as I came down the steps. He was waiting in the foyer and broke into a smile at the sight of my strapless indigo dress that was so sheer I might as well have been naked. Of course, he'd picked it out. Yes, I had an attractive body, but still, as a married woman I would never have purchased anything like that for myself.

Kevin pressed his lips to mine and stepped back, still admiring me from head to toe. "You're beautiful, Fancy. The most beautiful thing in my life. Thank you, baby."

I smiled slightly. "Thank me for what?"

"For loving me enough to understand my needs. C'mon." He took my arm and led me out the door. "Tonight is going to be special. I promise."

We drove toward Philadelphia with smooth jazz playing in the background and Kevin's hand caressing my thigh. I was so nervous I was shaking, but he was relaxed and easy and didn't seem to feel my legs quivering under his touch.

I couldn't believe I'd let him talk me into this. After what had gone down with that gay chick I'd sworn I'd never climb in bed with another woman unless her sole purpose for being there was for my husband's pleasure.

And here I was, committing to some craziness once again.

I took a few deep breaths to calm my nerves. This was to be a private affair, Kevin had said. Apparently, the other couple was well connected and had money to throw around. They'd managed to get a premium suite in one of Philadelphia's best hotels, which was something we probably couldn't afford.

"What kind of people are these?" I asked Kevin for the hundredth time. I might have been a preacher's-daughter-turned-ex-club-stripper, but I was still human. I knew from experience that whatever limits I tried to impose on my husband in the bedroom, his fantasies went far beyond that.

"Relax, baby." He sighed and patted my leg. "These are professional, married adults. Just like us. And like us, they know that their marriage stays strong because they keep things fresh and interesting where it counts. They're not vampires or hippies or goth, or any other weird type of crazy madness you might be thinking of. I've seen their photos and they both look good. You'll like them. I promise."

Unfortunately, Kevin's promise meant little to me. I knew what kind of indulgences he required to get off. Part of me also knew how weak-minded I must be to keep going along with this shit, but since my erotic nature had never made any sense to me, and my traitorous crotch was throbbing even now, I crossed my legs and sat quietly throughout the rest of the trip.

The hotel was beautiful and packed with all kinds of people. The valet took our car and Kevin led me through the lobby with his hand at the small of my back.

"Wait right here," he told me as we approached the elevator bank. He ran over to the registration counter and a few moments later he was back holding a key.

"The key to paradise." He grinned. "Nobody gets up to the top unless they have special privileges." I watched as he inserted the key into a slot on the elevator panel that read PENTHOUSE, my stomach dropping as we rose farther and farther into the air.

To my surprise, the elevator opened right into the suite.

"Kevin?"

The most delicious-looking brother I'd ever seen stepped out from behind a small bar with his hand extended. His skin was brown and smooth and his features were simply perfect.

"Hey," Kevin said, shaking his hand. "Derek, right?"

Derek reached for my hand and our eyes locked. The instant our fingers met I melted like hot butter, squeezing my thighs together to stop the puddle that threatened to drip down my legs.

"And this must be Fancy, your lovely, beautiful wife."

Derek handed us drinks and ushered us in. I wondered where his wife was, and what kind of woman she could be for allowing her sexy hunk of a man to swing with another chick, but then I checked myself. Kevin was considered a prime catch in every department and I'd been bringing home bed partners for him for years. What kind of woman did that make me?

We toured the suite and I had to admit that it was impressive. Indoor garden, sauna, Jacuzzi, and a balcony that led to a private garden twenty-one stories in the air.

Derek led us out onto the balcony, and there sat a stunning sister with sweet wide eyes and a gorgeous smile. I couldn't help thinking of how well she'd photograph. "Fancy, Kevin," Derek said, beaming proudly, "this is my wife, Mica Bates. Mica, this is Kevin and Fancy Lawson." We smiled politely and said hello, just like our husbands weren't gonna trade places and be knee-deep in our pussies in just a few minutes.

Mica didn't seem nervous at all, and neither did her husband. I wondered how long they'd been swinging and how often they got together with other couples like this. Their relaxed air certainly made things easier, I admitted to myself. If I were hosting this party it would have been a bust from the moment they stepped off the elevator.

We went back inside the penthouse, where Derek turned up the music and kept the drinks rolling. "Hot tub?" he asked, and Kevin readily agreed.

"I didn't bring a swimsuit," I mumbled, but Mica just laughed.

"No problem, honey. We're about the same size, and I brought plenty."

I followed her into a bedroom, checking her out as her hips swayed beneath her aqua slacks. She had a magnificent build. Curves everywhere. Hips, ass, breasts. Just perfectly toned and proportioned. She opened a closet and showed me an assortment of bathing suits in a rainbow of colors.

"You can change in here," she said, pointing toward the bathroom with a comforting smile. Despite the situation she seemed nice and I liked her. I knew how hard it was to love a man who had peculiar appetites, and life couldn't be any easier for her than it was for me.

I stepped into the plush bathroom and marveled at the size and décor. I'd danced naked in nightclubs that were smaller. There were several hangers on hooks behind the door, and I hung my clothes up neatly before pulling on the stark white string bikini I had chosen. At least it covered most of my behind. Most of the other suits had been thong-bottomed, and I wasn't anxious to deal with that whole dental floss effect they caused.

With a towel wrapped awkwardly around me, I left the bathroom and walked barefoot through the indoor garden and to the Jacuzzi, where Kevin and Derek were busy talking sports, and Mica had changed into a stunning two-piece red swimsuit that accentuated the curves I'd admired through her clothing.

"C'mere," Kevin said, smiling. He gently tugged at my towel and handed me another drink as I stood before the three of them in all my bikinied glory. "Damn," my husband breathed. "Isn't she fine, y'all?"

I swallowed my drink in three long gulps, and reached for another. Mica smiled at me as our husbands pulled us into the swirling water. I sat between her and Kevin, the nervousness leaving me as the alcohol flowed through my body and the heat of the water soothed my nerves.

The four of us talked and chatted and sipped drinks like we were regular couples. A while later Derek climbed out of the Jacuzzi and came back with a silver tray. I saw half a dozen joints and several lines of coke laid out on it.

I glanced at Kevin. He was in the military and Uncle Sam didn't play that. If he indulged in illegal drugs and then got called for a random urinalysis, he'd get busted for sure. Kevin noticed my expression and grinned. "Don't worry, baby," he said, drying his hands on a thick towel held out by Mica. "I got this."

Kevin snorted from the tray and then urged me on. I could try and blame it on the liquor, but that would be a lie. I lowered my face and snorted my share of powder too, and then surprised myself by accepting the lit joint that Derek was offering.

I toked three joints with my husband as the warm water caressed our bodies. On the third one, Kevin laughed, then stuck the lit end of the joint into his mouth, and putting his lips close to mine, blew a thick cloud of smoke directly down my throat, giving me a shotgun. I choked and started coughing and gagging, struggling to catch my breath. We ended up laughing so hard I had to pee, and climbing out of the sucking pool of hot water I pinched him on the shoulder. "You almost killed me, man."

Kevin just grinned and slapped me playfully on the ass. The combination of herb and liquor was doing its job, and as I walked from the room I was conscious of the eyes that were digging on my body, but I no longer cared. I didn't bother to dry off or cover up with a towel. In fact, as the water dripped from my glistening skin I shook my hips for erotic effect, giving them all a good look at my best feature.

I used the bathroom and washed my hands. High, I stopped to grin at myself in the huge vanity mirror. My eyes were tiny and red from the weed and the liquor had a nice buzz going in my head. I sloshed my mouth with a few handfuls of cold water, then stepped out of the bathroom. As I rounded the corner to enter the indoor garden, Mica was there, standing in the narrow walkway that led to the Jacuzzi room.

Now, I'm not gay, but I am a photographer and I knew beautiful when I saw it on a woman.

"Oops." I grinned stupidly. "You scared me. I thought you guys were still in the Jacuzzi." With my nose enthralled by her perfume, I stepped toward her and our damp bodies brushed together slightly as I tried to slip past.

She moved quickly, and before I knew it she had grabbed my arm and pressed herself against me, her tongue darting hotly into my mouth before diving lower to latch onto my nipple through the moist fabric of my bikini top.

I was so stunned that for a moment I didn't move. And then I couldn't move. I was paralyzed. The most exquisite sensations were shooting through my body as she raked her teeth back and forth across my nipple. The heat coming from her mouth combined with the weed in my blood, and that indirect contact thing she had going on with my breast and nipple ring was simply erotic to the tenth degree.

I tried to protest but I was too weak. And then I surprised the heck out of myself. Not by the hot moans that were escaping my lips, but by failing to resist as she palmed my ass with both hands and grinded against me. I gazed at the pinkness of her tongue as it swirled along the white material of my bikini top, my nipple hard as a rock and protruding prominently through the fabric.

Please stop. Don't stop. Oh, please stop. Oh shit. Please don't stop!

Mica crushed our mounds together, rotating hers in slow circles as I stood there helpless and filled with heat. Thoughts of Kevin and Derek flashed through my mind and I tried to push her away, but she held tight to my bottom with one hand and slipped two fingers under the crotch of my bikini bottom with the other.

I panted as she entered me, her probing gentle but exacting. She plunged two, then three fingers deeper inside me as her thumb pleased my clit and her other hand massaged my sensitive ass cheeks.

"The other one," I moaned, pushing her face toward my right breast. "Oh, my goodness. Suck the other one."

I wanted to scream as she reached behind me and unhooked my top, then covered my bare nipple with her soft hot lips. Moments later I surrendered completely as she backed me gently toward the cushioned lounge chair and lay me down. I was ashamed of myself and wondered where my husband was, but that didn't stop me from spreading my legs when she lay on top of me and covered me with her amazing heat.

Mica was an expert and brought my nipples to the hardest peaks imaginable. She sucked my breasts better than any man had ever sucked them. All I could do was lie there and moan as she moved on top of me, the meat of her thigh lodged between my legs. I almost screamed when she slid down my body and peeled off my bikini bottom. She swirled her tongue in the crevice of my navel, her teeth clicking against my belly ring, then parted my lower lips with gentle fingers. The moment her tongue entered my wetness I shuddered and convulsed, coming twice, back to back, as she drank from my juices.

Somehow we were both naked and Mica's lips were once again on mine. The sweetness of myself on her tongue stoked me and I was hot and desperate. I marveled at the thought of our full breasts crushed between us, sensitive nipples surging with the foreign sensations I was experiencing. Never had my sex swelled with such intense pleasure. Mica turned her body slightly to the side, and we held each other as our crotches met, hers just as wet as mine. I threw my head back and opened my legs wider as she rubbed her swollen clit against me.

I was in the throes of my fourth or fifth orgasm when Mica's weight settled deeply upon me and something hard and hot touched my lips. I opened my eyes and behind her I saw Kevin, my husband, pull back on Mica's hips and enter her deeply as Derek pushed himself into my mouth. I accepted Derek's offering as Kevin hammered away behind Mica, sending her soft body pounding into mine and propelling me over a climactic cliff once more.

Nasty Fancy.

I shut my eyes again and thrust myself up to meet Mica's rhythm as my tongue swirled along the rim of her husband's penis.

Freak Nasty Fancy.

Freak nasty, indeed.

CHAPTER 17

SPARKLE

M-e-t-h-o-d-o-f-l-o-v-e

*O*h *no the hell he didn't,* was my first thought, and *yuck!* was my second. Fancy and I were in my kitchen steaming snow crab legs and broiling lobster tails when the telephone rang.

"Can you get that?" I yelled as Fancy headed toward the dining room and I took a ceramic dish of melted butter from the microwave and hooked that bad boy up with some Old Bay seafood seasoning, minced garlic, and black pepper. I dipped my finger into the dish for a sample, and from the corner of my eye saw smoke coming from the bottom of the stove.

Damn! I grabbed a pot holder and pulled open the broiler tray. I was forever burning something up. The shells on the lobster tails were a little crisp around the edges, but the meat looked juicy and scrumptious. I had set them on the counter and was opening the window when Fancy came back into the kitchen.

"Sparkle . . . it's for you," she sang in a singsong little voice. My heart automatically jumped. Lonnie? No. *Hell,* no. Fancy would have been cursing instead of grinning.

Who is it? I mouthed.

"Phil!"

"Phil? Phil *who?*"

She covered the mouthpiece with her hand. "Phil, Phil. You know, the white guy who helped you get off Gary's balcony when those brothers were playing gynecologist and trying to look up your cooch. And don't be acting all funky neither. If it wasn't for Phil those dudes would have run a choo-choo on you right on that basketball court."

"*White boy* Phil?" *Eeeeeuuu.* No he didn't! I aimed one finger inside my mouth like I wanted to throw up. "How the hell did he get my number?"

"Girl, please." Fancy tried to push the telephone into my hand. "I gave it to him. I ran into him downtown as I was leaving a photography seminar and he asked about you."

"Asked about me? For *what*? Tell him I ain't home."

Wait, what was that line that white girls always used?

"Tell him I'm washing my hair!"

"I'm not telling lies for you just because you're too crazy to explore something different. Just talk to the guy, Sparkle, damn! What's the big deal?"

"The big deal is," I said loud enough for him to hear me as I pushed that damn phone right back at her, "I don't mess with white boys. Never have, never will. I don't live nowhere near the plantation, so there ain't shit me and Phil need to talk about unless he's willing to call up some of his mafia homeys and have them bust Gary in the kneecaps or yank out his teeth without numbing him up."

Fancy looked all wounded. "Oh, so what I did for you wasn't good enough? Hooking you up with that info and putting my job on the line was a small thing? I'm the community health coordinator, Sparkle! Dr. Bledsoe could have fired me for writing you that damn letter!"

Yeah, yeah, yeah, I yawned. Fancy had written an official letter to Gary's wife informing her that her husband had tested positive for syphilis and urging her to get tested immediately. Gary's play-niece had called Fancy's office cursing up a storm about the ass-whipping she planned to put on her creeping husband with his little dick self. We'd gotten a good laugh out of that one, and yeah, I'd felt somewhat vindicated for the way he'd left me out there naked and mad, but still. Fancy could kill all that noise. Miss Sparkle wasn't swinging nowhere with a white boy. He'd have to promise me some rare diamonds or a brand-new convertible sports car or something to get me tripping straight to the left like that.

"Sparkle, please." She was still offering me the telephone. "There's no harm in talking to him. C'mon. You're gonna make me look bad. I gave him your number and told him you'd be happy to hear from him. Don't do me like that, girl."

"Don't trip, Fancy! I'm always there for you."

"Yes." She smiled. "You always are, and that's why I love you. So be there for me this time too, Sparkle. Just talk to the brother—I mean the man. Talk to the man and keep an open mind. Hey, it's on his dime so it doesn't cost you a thing."

Fancy made me sick. Always trying to act all logical and sweet when she wanted me to do something I didn't want to do. I didn't even remember what Phil looked like. I just knew he was white. I wondered how much money he made and if what they said about shriveled little white pee-pees was true. I almost laughed at that one, because as black as Gary was, he'd had the dick of a baby midget.

"All right." I looked down at my seafood that was getting cold and the butter that was threatening to thicken up. "I'll yell at him for a second. But"—I pointed to my food—"I got a plate of crab legs waiting on me and that's my priority. If Phil really wants to talk to me, tell him to call back later, after I eat."

———

OKAY, so you know the deal. I spoke to the guy. Twice. No, I'm lying. Three times. Shocked the shit out of myself too. Phil didn't have any rap to speak of, but he did have a nice conversation about him. He was a homeboy too—from the Bronx.

His name was Phillip Mercorella and he was thirty-two years old. Never married, no babies, and he swore he wasn't gay or on the downlow.

We clicked like a Bic when I found out that, just like me, he loved potato knishes with mustard and ketchup and ate franks with red onions from the dirty man on the corner under the big Sabrett umbrella. Phil was also in the army, which was almost as bad as him being white, but when I told him how I felt about dating servicemen he didn't seem fazed at all.

"No problem" was what he said. "We don't have to date. I'd just like to get to know you better, that's all."

Yeah, right. If I had a dollar for every time I'd heard that line my fine ass would be rolling around in a beachfront mansion on some Caribbean island. Of course he wanted to date me. All men did. I had a nose for the game of chase, but since Phil wanted to pretend like he wasn't a cat, I'd go along and act like I wasn't a mouse.

We'd been talking by phone for a couple of weeks when I determined that Italian or not, Phil must have had some black in him. Boyfriend said he loved backgammon, and was forever talking about going up to the Bronx to get an Italian icee and some dirty Chinese food from the take-out store on the avenue.

"Nah, nah, nah!" I shouted. "How about a turkey and cheese hero with everything on it? I'm talking lettuce, tomato, onions, oil and vinegar, salt and pepper—"

"Yeah, baby! I like it when they make them longer than my arm. And what about a bagel? You like toasted bagels with butter, baby?"

I let that *baby* thing slide because Phil had said he was into old-school music too. The Doobie Brothers, Four Tops, Michael McDonald, the Dells. He always had some slamming music playing in the background whenever we talked on the phone, and he even knew all the words to the songs. He'd invited me over to his house to listen to some of his tracks, but I didn't trust myself to get too close to Gary's apartment without kicking the door in.

"Why don't you bring your CDs over here instead?"

I knew I was crazy as soon as the words came out of my mouth. I never invited men to my crib. That's why I was over at Gary's house in the first place. I loved getting my swerve on, but why would I want some transient kneegrow rolling his half-washed rusty ass around in my two-hundred-dollar sheets? Leaving toe jam and pubic hair in my princess bed?

He hesitated. "Look, Sparkle, if you're worried about running into your friend next door, don't be. He moved out a couple of weeks ago. "

"Who, Gary? I'm not even thinking about that fool."

"Well, good," he said. "But I'm accepting your invitation anyway. I'd like to see you, so yeah, I'll come over with my music."

Now, remember, the only time I'd seen Phil was the night that I had gotten played out of position. I'd been so focused on getting back at Gary, the dickless wonder, that I barely remembered what Phil looked like. Fancy claimed he wore glasses but had dark hair and was nicely built, but then again Fancy thought Brad Pitt was fine, so what does that tell you? No, I'd decide for myself if I liked what I saw in Mister Phil. And hey—if I didn't like it, who said I had to open my door and let him in?

We set it up for Friday night and I didn't do anything special to get ready for him either. I mean, I looked good all the time, but why go through all the drama of putting on extra makeup and whatnot just to entertain a man like Phil?

At precisely two minutes before seven on Friday evening a white Jeep Grand Cherokee pulled up in front of my apartment. Ol' Phil was prompt. Two points for him. I watched him get out of his ride and approach my door, and in the space of thirty seconds I inspected him from head to toe. Before he could ring my doorbell good I'd already scoped him out and knew a whole lot about him.

For instance, Fancy was right. Phil looked strong. He was tall with beautiful jet-black hair and had a sturdy, muscled build. His teeth were really nice and he must have ditched the glasses and gotten a pair of contacts because I loved the intensity in his blue eyes. I was a bit surprised, though, by his taste in clothes. Phil showed up wearing a starched pair of jeans and a white polo shirt. His hair was parted on the side and looked fresh and clean, and he had a nice pair of Timberland boots on his feet. I was puzzled. Weren't white boys in the army supposed to run around chewing tobacco and wearing dusty Levi's and run-over shitkickers?

I let him into my apartment and took his jacket.

"Hi," he said, handing me a box of Krispy Kreme dough-nuts. Ladies, your sister was slipping. I'd been so busy check-ing out his clothes and his body, I had totally missed the box he was carrying in his hand. "I thought you might like some-thing sweet."

Gone, boy! I thought, smiling inside. Trying to get on my good side already. I could eat about eight Krispy Kremes all by myself, and that wouldn't leave very many for him.

"Thanks," I said. "You can have a seat in the living room and make yourself comfortable."

I put the doughnuts on the kitchen table and got my backgammon board out of the hall closet. When I went back into the living room Phil was sitting on the floor with his back against my couch and looking through his case of CDs.

"You want to hear anything in particular?"

I shook my head. "Whatever you've got is good."

While he searched for some music, I pulled out my little mahogany folding table and set up the backgammon board, assigning him the white pieces and keeping the black ones for myself. My foot got to tapping when I heard the Hall and Oates cut he'd selected. *M-e-t-h-o-d-o-f-l-o-v-e . . . it's a method of modern love . . .*

"That's the cut," I said, swaying my hips and noticing that

he was actually nodding to the right beat. Two more points for him!

"Yeah, I like it too. Those two white boys know how to jam."

I laughed my ass off. I liked Phil already. He had a good sense of humor and didn't take himself too seriously and that was refreshing.

"You know," I said after a moment, "I never really thanked you for helping a sistah out that night at Gary's. I mean that fool pulled some dirty mess, and if it wasn't for you I probably would have had to slide down that sheet like it was a fire pole!"

I laughed my ass off again. Just to show him that I wasn't touchy about the whole incident and he didn't have to be worried about hurting my feelings or nothing if it ever came up again.

"Don't mention it," Phil said. "I would have helped anybody in that situation. I'm just glad I was there to help you."

He actually beat me in two games of backgammon before I got mad and quit, and then I ordered a pizza, which Phil paid for, and we drank a couple of wine coolers and just sat back and enjoyed the sounds. Phil told me about his parents and two sisters who still lived in the Bronx, and I shared a few tidbits about my people in Brooklyn with him.

We had such a good time that night that Phil started coming over with his CDs on the regular. Sometimes I had to pinch myself or pull out a few strands of my hair to make sure I wasn't walking and talking in my sleep. I was chilling with a real live white boy! Me! Fine-ass Sparkle Shawnte Henderson spending quality time with a white boy!

But white boy or not, Phil had heart. And stamina. The first few times he came over I thought he was trying to keep his distance and front like he wasn't interested in just sexing me, not that I'd ever let him.

I'd given him the brief tour of my tiny apartment, even my bedroom. I liked nice stuff, so I spent my money wisely and never purchased slum. I was proud to show off all the quality merchandise I'd chosen to surround myself with and display my skills in making the utmost of the little bit of space I had.

"Have you ever dated a black girl before?" I asked him one night as we chilled on my sofa listening to some jazz. We were sitting really close to each other and it seemed natural when I rested my head on his shoulder.

Phil nodded. "Yes, I have."

"How many?"

"Two. One in college, the other right after I joined the army."

"And?" I turned toward him. "What happened with them?"

He took my hand and rubbed it. "Nothing happened. They were good relationships, but things just didn't work out, although I'm still friends with both of them."

You should have felt how fried I got inside! So he was still friends with them heffahs, huh?

"So," I pressed on. "You've been attracted to black women for a good minute then, huh? Do you ever date white women?"

"Sparkle," he said, tracing the skin of my palm with his finger. "I'm attracted to good women, period. I don't have a racial preference because I don't look at people in terms of skin color. I measure them by their hearts. But since you asked, yeah. I've dated white women on occasion. And one or two Asians too."

I got quiet for a minute. I had to think about that one. Old boy was an international fucker. A member of the equal opportunity rainbow coochie coalition.

"But if it means anything to you," Phil continued, "I've never dated a woman who moved me the way you do, Sparkle. I know it's too early to forecast our future, but in just this short time I enjoy being with you more than I've ever enjoyed being with any other woman. Black, white, or otherwise."

I nodded and put my head on his shoulder again, letting the music fill my heart. I wasn't about to admit it, but I liked being with him too. Even better than I'd liked being with Lonnie. That long-headed fool.

It wasn't long before Phil and I were spending almost all of our free time at my place, just talking and listening to music. Of course I teased him. My name *is* Sparkle, and who could resist all of this phat ass? I wore skimpy shorts and shook it like a milk shake all up in his face. Phil never once stared at my body. Instead, he acted like I was some skinny little flat-chested size three–four or something. Yeah, I'd been with men who could hold out before, but eventually all roads led to the prize between my thighs, no matter how much they tried to act like they weren't sniffing me.

But not Phil. He never even tried to kiss me. Maybe he was gay, I told Fancy. Or maybe he thought all black women were sex fiends and was waiting for me to make the first move.

"Maybe the motherscruncher *respects* you!" Fancy screamed on me when I called her on the phone.

"Damn right he does." I laughed. "But I bet the minute he

leaves my house he runs straight home to wax that little white willie!"

Fancy got mad. "I gotta go, Sparkle." Click.

"Uh-oh," Phil said one Friday night as we sat munching Snickers bars on my sofa and watching *Forensic Files*. "I think I'm having a New York moment. I have a taste for some Chinese spareribs with duck sauce all over them. You game?"

"Oh yeah." I grinned, jumping to my feet and doing a little dance. The baby-blue short shorts I was wearing had PLAY-GIRL written in big white letters across the ass, and I busted him eyeing my buttery thighs as the shorts rode up my curvy hips. "I feel an egg roll jones coming down. There's a menu on the fridge," I told him. "We can order in."

"Actually, I know a great place near the Victory Mall. The place is really small, but they make a combination fried rice that tastes like it's straight off Fordham Road. My treat."

I panicked. Okay, you know Miss Sparkle is out to get hers, and a free meal is a free meal no matter who's sitting across the table from you. But what the hell would I look like going out to dinner with some white guy? And at a joint right near the black mall? I started racking my brain trying to think of a restaurant that was at least fifty miles out. Preferably in another state.

"C'mon," he said. "We order in all the time. Plus, it's a Mandarin restaurant. Not that much different from Chinese, and I guarantee you'll like it."

Like it my foot, I thought. Yeah, Phil was cool and all, but there was no way in hell I'd be caught dead with a white boy within ten miles of the black mall. It just wasn't happening.

"You know what, Phil?" I raised my arms in the air and

yawned, exposing the tattoo that surrounded my navel. "Let me take a rain check on that, okay? It's getting a little late and I need to get myself together for tomorrow. I promised to ride with Fancy to Philly in the morning and we're leaving pretty early."

"Philadelphia?" he said, showing interest, but I could hear the disappointment in his voice. "I love that city."

"Yeah, it's not New York or anything," I said, "but it'll do. Somehow Fancy got the hook-up to show some of her work at a photography conference. Supposedly there'll be all kinds of highfalutin talent scouts from big-shot magazines like *National Geographic* and whatnot, sniffing around looking for new meat."

Phil smiled, then stood and picked up our Snickers wrappers from the coffee table, crushing them into a ball in his fist. "You've got a way with words, Sparkle. Talking to you always puts me right back in New York, where I have the best memories. But anyway, the conference sounds like a great opportunity for Fancy and I really hope her work gets noticed."

He'd taken to leaving some of my favorite of his CDs at my house, you know, to keep from carting them back and forth and stuff, so after taking his jacket from a hook he headed toward the front door.

He turned to me. "As usual, I had a great time. See ya soon?"

"Yeah." I smiled, but deep inside I was pissed at myself because Miss Sparkle was truly sorry to see him go. I eyed his muscles as he slipped into his jacket and found myself wondering what he'd look like naked. "Give me a call in a day or so and we'll hook up for some Chinese next weekend, okay?"

"Bet," he said, then touched my cheek and left.

———

I must have changed my mind a million times before the next weekend rolled around. "I ain't going," I told Fancy as we drove toward Philadelphia the next morning. She looked distracted, deep in thought, and I was stretched out in the passenger seat, reclining to the max and trying hard to sort through my inner conflicts. "Hell no, I ain't going. In my family, we don't roll like that with white people. And how stupid would I look *anyway* walking down the street with a white boy? Brothers'll be grilling me and calling me a sellout. Nope, I ain't going."

Two days later I had changed my tune. I called Fancy at work. "Lunch can't hurt, can it? Phil is really chill. He doesn't act like a white boy at all. You know how the ones in the army do, spitting tobacco and digging all up their asses and shit. Phil acts just like a regular guy who likes the same kinda stuff that I like. He's got mad jokes and the air is easy around him."

"Then give him a chance, Sparkle." Fancy sighed into the phone, sounding exhausted. "It's not fair that you're holding back on him just because he's not black. It's not your job to make sure the entire black race stays pure."

"It's not? Okay, okay. I'm not saying that it is. But damn, couldn't he at least be Puerto Rican or Dominican or something? Anything with a little bit of color in him would be better than him being white."

"Look," Fancy said. "I'm tired of you. You're steadily making this an issue when it doesn't have to be one. Why don't you cut through all the bullshit and see this thing for what it is? He's a man, you're a woman. It's obvious that there's some sort of mutual attraction or you wouldn't be ringing my phone off the hook and burning a hole in my ear."

Heffah called herself reading me!

"I don't be ringing your damn phone off the hook!"

"Just go have dinner with the man, Sparkle. Hell, have breakfast, lunch, and dinner with him if you enjoy his company. And if any brothers look at you funny, tell them all to kiss your striped ass. This is the new millennium. They don't have a monopoly on dating outside the race."

Fancy's words were starting to make sense, but I still couldn't hardly stand myself for feeling the way I felt. To take my mind off things I treated myself to a shopfest. I took a comp day off from work on Tuesday and drove up to Brooklyn and picked up my girl Pebbles from her brownstone in Fort Greene. Pebbles taught design at Fashion Institute of Technology, and, like me, she was fiendish about her shoes and clothes. Armed with our critical eyes for fashion and wearing jeans and sensible shoes, we shopped like a pair of crack hos hunting for new pipes.

I came back home whipped, my car overflowing with boxes and bags, my eyes blurred and my toes hissing. I looked at my caller ID and saw that Phil had called a few times, but I didn't call him back.

Let him sweat it out for a while, I thought as I modeled my new clothes in the mirror. He might be white, but he was still a man, and like every other guy who was all up in my mug, he'd have to chase Miss Sparkle if he wanted to catch her.

CHAPTER 18

KEVIN

Group Funk

I was checking my voice mail at work when I got a big surprise.

"Er—hello. This call is for Kevin Lawson. Kevin, Derek Bates here. I just wanted to thank you and your lovely wife for having dinner with us last weekend. Mica really enjoyed the company and we'd love to do it again sometime. Peace, Derek."

I wondered how Derek had gotten my job number, but then I remembered that we'd exchanged business cards the night of our foursome. I sat down at my desk and grinned. Damn right Mica had enjoyed it. She was ten times more freak than me and Fancy put together. When Derek had signaled for us to creep into the indoor solarium, I'd nearly tripped out at the sight of her luscious ass as she lay on the couch, fucking my wife.

And there was no way Fancy could lie and say she didn't

enjoy it either. After a ton of all-around orgasms, all four of us had taken a nap in the king-sized bed, and when I woke up about an hour later Fancy and Mica were tangled in the sheets and quietly moaning their way through Round Two.

My secretary knocked on my open door and waited until I looked up.

"Hi, Top. I've got a bunch of stuff for you."

I nodded as Specialist Danbridge deposited a stack of papers in the plastic holder on my desk. My eyes were on her as she turned and walked out of my office, her ass doing wonderful things for the woodland camouflage of her military uniform.

I was straight, though. I hadn't given her or any other woman in my unit more than a passing glance ever since that night I almost got caught in one of my female soldiers' room. I was a platoon sergeant at the time, and this fine little old private with beautiful brown skin could've gotten me kicked out of the army.

She'd been giving me the eye, letting me know exactly what she wanted, and one night while I was pulling overnight staff duty for my battalion, I'd snuck over to the company area to tighten that ass up. Never mind that she had a boyfriend, and he too was one of my soldiers, my third squad leader, to be exact, that Hershey's skin of hers had me so mesmerized I just had to get me a lick.

The company offices were on the first floor of our building, and her room was on the third. I'd chatted with the charge of quarters who was pulling night duty, then signed into the visitors' log and made my way upstairs on a fake security check.

Chocolate has never tasted so sweet as it did that night.

It was the skin on this chick, I'm telling you. Yards of dark brown sugar, I just couldn't get enough of it. Until we realized her man was out there knocking on her door.

We kept right on grooving too, she got hers and I got mine, but even after we were done that young sergeant was still out there knocking. Bitching and cursing. "I know you're in there, Dana!" he screamed, refusing to go away. The bad part was, he knew somebody was in the room with her too. "Send that niggah out," he shouted. "Whoever he is, I'll kill his ass!"

What was a brother to do? To make shit worse, just as I jumped back into my uniform and was tying up my boots, I heard the charge of quarters yelling down the hall. "Hey! What floor is that platoon daddy on? Sergeant Lawson! Sergeant Lawson! You got a phone call in the orderly room. Battalion wants you to get your ass back on duty ASAP!"

My goose was cooked. I ended up hiding in that private's room until four o'clock the next morning, when her boyfriend finally gave up and went away. But since I was stuck in there with no way out, I went on ahead and got me some more of that chocolate, enough to make me sick, and when I finally showed back up at battalion headquarters I told them a big lie about getting really dizzy and passing out in my car.

So Specialist Danbridge was safe with me. Her and every other female soldier under my command. I'd learned a lot that night because my reputation could have been ruined. No way would I let my dick get me in that kind of jam. Not if I could help it. That's what I had Fancy for.

I sat there reveling in my memories for a moment or two longer, then reached into my in-box and got down to business. As a company first sergeant the work was never done.

There were alert rosters that needed revising, lawn-raking details to be coordinated, and a duty roster to be published. I checked my e-mail and saw a message from Emile, giving me a heads-up about a tasking to Iraq.

When I saw who it was he wanted to send, I shook my head. Emile had a thing for Sparkle that was downright unreasonable. I didn't feel this way just because I wanted to bang her or because she was my wife's best friend. I just couldn't see why he hated her so much. Why he hated all black women so much. As far as I was concerned it was an unreasonable waste of energy, not to mention a lack of self-love.

I fired back a message telling him that under no circumstances was I giving up the best damn supply sergeant in the brigade. Training units ranked low on the requisition totem pole, way down the line from infantry and armor and artillery brigades. Sparkle might look like an air-brained hottie, but she was tops when it came to running a supply shop. There were a ton of line commanders in Southwest Asia who would snatch her up in a heartbeat and be glad to have her. But no. I had plans for Sparkle, and she wasn't going to Iraq, Kuwait, or anywhere else.

At sixteen hundred hours I looked up from the training notes I was reading and stretched. The battalion command sergeant major was holding a meeting in thirty minutes and I needed to freshen the shine on my boots and make sure I was ready to take notes.

But first I needed to make a call.

I fished the business card from the back of my wallet and dialed his number.

"DCB Consulting, may I help you?"

I kept my voice low. Specialist Danbridge always got real quiet when I made a call, and she didn't know that I knew she rambled through my desk drawers when I was gone. "Yes, may I speak to Derek Bates?"

"May I ask who's calling?"

"Kevin Lawson."

"One moment please."

Moments later Derek was on the line.

"Hey, bro! How's it going?"

"Good," I said. "Real good. I got your message and wanted to holler at you in return. Fancy and I had a great time as well and we can't wait to have dinner with you and Mica again too."

"Well." Derek's voice boomed. "Mica is out of town for the next couple of weeks. She's in Mexico working on a contract for her firm."

"Really?" I said. "I'm sure Fancy will be disappointed to hear that."

"No doubt. But hey, the two of us can still hang, right? I know a nice club up in New York I'd like you to check out. It's located in the heart of the Village and if you've ever been in that area, you know it's nothing you're likely to ever forget."

We made plans to meet on Thursday night, and then hung up. In the next five minutes I slapped some Kiwi on my boots and gave them a quick brush shine, and then beat feet over to the battalion headquarters where the command sergeant major hated to be kept waiting.

———

NEW York City was wildin'.

The lights, the traffic, the hordes of people, everything.

I sat back as Derek pushed his white Lexus through the jam-packed traffic, amazed at the pulse that beat in the heart of this city.

Derek found an outdoor parking lot that charged something crazy like thirty dollars for four hours, and I shook my head as he paid the attendant without hesitation. I wasn't cheap by any means, but damn. This was a city that never shut down. Let's do the math. Imagine having fifty spots that made thirty dollars every four hours. Beat my little army pay coming and going.

We walked a few blocks and then turned onto a side street. It was dim and desolate in comparison to the main drag that had been exploding with lights and people.

"So what's the name of the place?" I asked, looking around for a sign or a marquee.

"Don't know." Derek shrugged. We passed a boarded-up store, a junkyard, and an elementary school. "Some people call it Club Flex, but I've heard it called a whole lot of other things. Not just by one name in particular."

"Well, where the hell is it?"

"Right here," he said, turning toward a narrow, nondescript doorway. "This is it right here."

Kevin knocked twice and the door was opened by a handsome young man. He looked about twenty-two and was dressed in Rocawear from head to toe.

"Sup?"

"Sup," Kevin responded and handed him something that I couldn't see.

The young guy stepped back and opened the door and the sounds of music rode the scent of weed that drifted out the door.

I peered into the darkness and saw that we were in a loft that had several levels. On the ground floor there was a gym with a few Bowflex exercise machines and a couple of racks of free weights. At nearly midnight on a Thursday brothers were getting their workout on too. I followed Derek through the sweaty room and into an open hall that was lined with large lockers.

"Hey, man." Derek turned to me as his eyes scanned the crowd. "I'm going to stroll for a while. Make yourself comfortable and meet me back out front in a couple of hours."

I nodded, thinking, *What kind of club is this? Where are all the honeys at, my man?* Derek disappeared up a flight of steps, and when two linebacker-looking guys walked past me wearing nothing but towels around their waists, I jetted toward the stairs too, but instead of following Derek up, I headed down.

The music wasn't half as loud down here, and a moment later I saw why. I was in a large dim room. A massive TV screen was showing a porn flick. Niggahs were lounging in slings and on couches, and I grabbed a seat on a beanbag and jumped into the movie. It was one that I hadn't seen before, and some niggah with a tool twice as long as John Holmes's was standing there stroking himself up.

As my eyes adjusted to the darkness I couldn't believe what I thought I saw across the room. Looked like two brothers sprawled on a couch to my left were getting their swerve on.

With each other.

I couldn't help but stare as one of them went down on his knees and buried his head in his partner's lap. "Oh, shit!" I said louder than I meant to as I turned away, repulsed. Okay.

Where the fuck was Derek? I jumped to my feet. It was time to fly.

I climbed the steps two at a time until I was on the second floor. I'd passed through crowds of some of the hardest-looking brothers I'd ever seen. Thugged out with killer looks in their eyes, but there wasn't a woman in sight.

Upstairs the television was tuned to CNN and a few brothers were napping on cots and other sat playing cards and chess, drinking, and smoking blunts.

Derek was nowhere to be found, so I went over to the bar and killed a double shot of gin, then claimed a chair on the edge of the room and pretended to watch the news. Brothers swaggered past me left and right, some disappearing in pairs into the doorways that lined the hall, others coming out. Some of these guys looked like armed robbers. If I didn't know any better I would have sworn they were shooting a rap video up in this joint, just minus all the mandatory titties and ass.

I kept my eyes peeled for signs of Derek, but he was nowhere to be seen. A few minutes later I had pushed through the crowd and was back at the bar ordering myself two more doubles. I swallowed the first one in a single gulp, but had to wait until the fire went out in my chest before tossing back the second.

"Hey, man," I said to the brother seated on the next stool. "Where's the john at in this place?"

He stared at me and then pointed. "Go through that door and take a right. Second door on the left. I'll watch your seat."

I went through the door like he told me, and almost

laughed out loud as I saw two hard-looking men standing against a wall kissing. Them niggahs looked straight as arrows and strong as hell. I would've chosen them to watch my back in a foxhole any day.

I took my leak and hurried back to the bar, determined to get out of here with or without Derek. Why he would bring me to a place like this was beyond me. As fine as his wife was, I had no idea the brother swung that way. Two ashy-ass niggahs with rough feet and sweaty balls wrestling around together in bed? Hell no. I'd kill me a niggah if he tried to suck my tool. If Derek hadn't shown up by the time I finished my last drink, I was just gonna have to wait for him outside.

Back at the bar I tossed down my drink and ordered another one.

I carried the shot glass back to my chair near the television, and noticed that the guy who'd offered to watch my seat at the bar had followed me. He was tall and built like a lot of these dudes. A real John Henry–looking niggah.

"Rondu," he said, and reached for a dap.

"Kevin," I answered but held back on the dap, and he laughed.

"Don't even think it, niggah," he said. "I'm just part of the cleaning crew. I got a girl."

Rondu sat down next to me and lit a joint, then passed it, and even though I wasn't all that much into weed unless I had a girl nearby, hell yeah I toked it. I felt like I deserved it with all the weird shit I was seeing. New York was wild! As soon as I got home I'd drink a quart of goldenseal mixed with a little something-something that I'd learned would hide the drugs in my urine, and I'd be set.

I rubbed my eyes for a quick second, and when I opened them somebody had switched the channel from CNN to BET, and Mary J. Blige was dancing in a video, doing her thing. Except she didn't look like Mary J. She looked like Biggie Smalls in a white miniskirt. I shook my head to clear it, and the fog came down on me even thicker.

For a couple of seconds I felt hot and nauseous, and then I got really cold.

"You all right, man?" Rondu was asking me as I swayed in my chair. "This shit is potent." He laughed. "You gotta have some nuts to handle this."

The next thing I knew I was sitting on a bed in a small room. How I got there who the fuck knew? Who cared? I was higher than I'd ever been in my life.

Time went by in snatches. I felt my hammer getting hard and I laughed. Vanessa del Rio was bobbing between my legs, slobbing me down, giving me the hottest blow job in the world as 2 Live Crew screamed *Just put him in the buck!* She laughed and slid my pants off, then shoved me back on the bed and pushed my legs up high in the air, still chuckling as she climbed on top of me.

My tool was as hard as a bat but I couldn't find her hole. I grabbed myself with two hands and tried to poke my thing through her stomach, but Jennifer Lopez slapped my hands away and said in a deep voice, "Chill, man. Just relax and enjoy the flow."

And then *some* damn body lit a firecracker up my ass.

I bucked and yelled out, but my asshole puckered and the flames grew hotter as the fire moved deeper and deeper through my body, my legs waving in the air like a bitch, the weight on top of me pressing downward, stroking me urgently.

Soon my cries turned into a deep groan and I felt myself explode, my tool jerking in spasms. I didn't understand it. How could there be so much cum on my belly when I was ten inches deep in Fancy's stuff?

I just couldn't call it, and a moment later I didn't want to. The last thing I saw before I welcomed the horrific blackness coming down on me was my new friend, Rondu. Pulling up his pants and slamming out the door.

———

THE next day was Friday, and before the sun was up good I found myself leaving Emile a message with the charge of quarters that I was too sick to come in. I laid in bed staring at the ceiling, and two minutes after Fancy left for work I was out the door right behind her.

Without grabbing so much as a toothbrush, I climbed in my car and drove west nursing a sore asshole for fourteen hours straight, stopping only for gas and water, and arriving on Brunson Hill Road well past ten at night.

Everything looked just like I remembered. The house still wore the last coat of paint that me and Emile had put on it. The porch looked smaller. The third step was broken and somebody had set a wooden plank over it that had been worn down to a few raggedy splinters. The screen door was still there, banging in the night breeze. The frame was rusted out and missing the mesh.

I heard music coming from inside, and the sound of crying babies. Somebody got slapped, and wailed at the top of their lungs. I started up the steps and I was twelve again. I paused to listen at the door, just like I always did. If Dirty Sue was in her cups, her cursing and bitching would sure 'nuff send me around to the back door. Or maybe around to Teesha's window. But if all was calm, then I'd go right in.

And that's what I did.

I twisted the doorknob and it turned like always. Nobody locked their doors on Brunson Hill Road. Nobody had anything that was worth stealing.

The first thing that struck me was the front room. It was overrun with babies and debris. The smell hit me next. Pissy mattresses. Old beer bottles. Teesha's dirty pussy. The funk of my dreams.

"Who dat?" a little boy asked. He was about nine. His shirt was off and his thumb was in his mouth.

The eyes of a thousand dirty children looked up at me and I read them all loud and clear. "Hey, mistah," one little boy asked, eyeing me eagerly. "You branged us any peanut butter?"

A young girl who looked about thirteen walked toward me and stared. If she wasn't Teesha, then I wasn't Kevin.

"Nah, stupid," she answered, her eyes glued to my shoes and my watch, calculating their worth. "He the new rent man." She tossed her little Teesha hips at me and said, "Might as well carry your ass back on outdoors 'cause we ain't got it right now."

I looked beyond the kids and farther into the room, and that's when I saw her. Lil Mama. Sitting on a milk crate.

"That niggah ain't here to collect no damn rent," she said, watching me from narrow eyes. She was smoking a cigarette and nursing a baby from the biggest, longest tit I had ever seen in my life. "That ain't nobody but that old Kevin. Whatchoo doin' here, boy?"

"I-I . . . hey, Lil Mama. How y'all been? Where's Dirty Sue?"

She put her head back and laughed. There couldn't have been more than five teeth in her whole rotten mouth. "Dead and buried with her evil ass. Dead and buried." Then she grinned slyly and looked toward the kitchen. "Teesha!" she hollered, an amused smile playing on her lips. "Teesha! Guess who done come up in here!"

Teesha ambled into the living room and she was even bigger than Lil Mama, if that was possible. The whites of her eyes were yellow, and she wore her hair cut closer than mine. Dressed in a filthy pink housecoat, she pressed her lips into a line. As I stood there staring dumbly, I caught a whiff of her body and my tool leaped in my pants.

"You want you some more," she rasped, her words sounding colder than an empty grave. "Don't you?"

"I won't tell," I whispered.

Two hours later I was on the road again, my manhood restored as I headed for home. Spent. Crying. Confused. Ashamed. And reeking with group funk from head to toe.

CHAPTER 19

SPARKLE

No Baloney

"Hi. I'm Michelle. Can I get you a drink before dinner?"

Hell *yeah,* she could bring me a drink! Matter of fact, she could bring me two. It was a busy Friday night, and for the last ten minutes I'd been sitting in the middle of the crowded room pretending to study the menu, but in reality I was scanning my sector and sneaking looks all around me. There were two black couples in the house, but they weren't seated nearby and both were deep in their own conversations.

But at the sound of the waitress's voice, I almost ducked under the table. What was a sister doing working up in Olive Garden? I'd chosen the restaurant because I figured that unlike a Chinese joint or a rib shack, it wouldn't be swamped with black folks. Yet here was a straight-up dreadlocked African-looking Miss Thang standing over me with big hips and a nice smile.

"I'll take a glass of white wine and a Coke," I mumbled as my eyes dove back to the menu. See, that's why I didn't want to do this shit. My face was hot with embarrassment and I couldn't even look over at Phil.

"Would that be regular, Diet, or Vanilla Coke?"

I glanced up to see if she was being funny, but her smile hadn't changed at all. Sister had applied her makeup like a pro, and I figured if she had blush and brushstroke skills like that she should have been out there making a living as a makeup artist, not slaving her life away up in some Olive Garden.

I was so busy wishing I could disappear that I couldn't even tell you what kind of drink Phil ordered, but when he got up from his chair opposite me and took a seat in the one right beside me, I had no choice but to meet his eyes.

"You okay?" he asked.

God no, I wasn't okay. I was embarrassed and ashamed of myself, but I also liked Phil and didn't want to hurt his feelings so I played it off. "Miss Sparkle is fine." I tried to chuckle. "Haven't you noticed?"

He reached out and rubbed my hand. "All the time, baby. I notice how fine you are all the time."

My face got hot again and my eyes jumped back on the menu. It wasn't like I was unaccustomed to compliments. No, the sweet nothings that fell off of a man's tongue had always come a dime a dozen. Miss Sparkle was a prime specimen and I never got tired of hearing about it. But for some reason compliments seemed extra sincere coming from Phil. As if he were simply admiring me to himself and his thoughts had slipped from his mouth.

"You memorized that thing yet?"

I glanced at him, and then at the menu that was practically

covering my face. "What? Oh! Nah, I'm just trying to choose between the shrimp scampi and the chicken piccata."

"Why don't you just order both?"

See, that's what I'm talking about. Miss Sparkle couldn't stand no cheap man, and here was a man who wanted me to have my cake and eat it too.

Phil ended up ordering two entrées as well, and before I knew it we were laughing and talking and sharing four huge dinners between us. Michelle, our Nubian waitress, checked in periodically, but not too often, and whenever she ventured over it was always with a smile and the polite offer of her service.

Now, you can't tell it by my tiny waistline, but Miss Sparkle knows how to get her eat on. We couldn't finish all four of the main dishes, but we damn sure put a hurting on them, and after asking Michelle for a couple of to-go boxes Phil and I threw down on two slices of fluffy cold lemon cake.

"I know a cool place where we can get some after-dinner drinks," Phil said as he paid the check. I was feeling good and full. Full from all the tasty things I'd eaten, and good from being in the company of a man who I enjoyed. But go with him to a bar? I hesitated. I mean, dinner was one thing, but having drinks with a white man at a bar meant something totally else.

"Please?" Phil smiled, taking my hand as he held the door open for me. "It's still early, Sparkle. Let's go out and have a little fun."

Okay, okay, okay! So I went! Damn! Shit, sue me!

Phil took me to a hip little bar called Jackie's, and to my surprise the music was decent and the crowd was over thirty and mellow. I walked in behind him, holding his hand and letting myself be led. I didn't get a good look around until we were seated in a booth and I was on my third rum and Coke, but when I did take in the scene I immediately relaxed. I wasn't the only sister in the house, but I was close. I saw two other black women and one of them didn't halfway count because she was with a white boy—but then I caught myself.

I was with a white boy too, but that had stopped mattering some time ago, I admitted to myself. Like Fancy had said, this was the new millennium and it was time to throw some of those stale-ass judgments out the window. I decided that since I was out with Phil and he was definitely chill, I was going to enjoy myself to the max.

Besides, nobody else seemed to give two shits who I was out with. Maybe all that sellout drama was strictly in my head, because so far no brothers had stared me down, nobody had called me a nigger, not a soul had given me a shitty look or made a smart-ass comment. In short, nobody had harassed me or behaved toward me the way I usually behaved whenever I saw a mixed-race couple.

"And fuck 'em if they do," I muttered as Phil pulled me out onto the dance floor where a slew of nonrhythmic folks were jacking up an offbeat version of the electric slide. The crowd parted to admit us and I found myself shaking it like a milk shake beside an Asian guy who looked at me and grinned. I did that little lean forward, dip back, real sexy move, and the Asian guy went crazy.

Damn right he liked what he saw! Phil tried to bust a little move and throw his hands in the air as he did a modified version of the two-step. Not a problem. I adjusted my groove and two-stepped right along with him, enjoying the swell of the upbeat crowd surrounding us. I let him pull me closer and rested my cheek lightly on his chest. Nope. He didn't smell like baloney, and nobody seemed to care that I was working it out in mixed company.

Nobody at all. But then again, the night was still young.

CHAPTER 20

EMILE

Hey-Hey-Hay!

*T*hanks again for the lovely dress, Emile. You're always so generous and you have the most incredible knack for choosing the right gifts."

I grinned from ear to ear, basking in Becky Ann's compliments, and I was just glad that she'd taken off work to be with me tonight. Friday nights were always extra busy at the club. She stood there wearing the sweet red Donna Karan original I'd purchased that looked like it had been designed and stitched especially for her. I mean, the hot little number fit her slim body to a tee, and everything about it was sweet and elegant, just like my baby.

"It was my pleasure, princess," I said, still grinning. "You deserve the finest."

And I meant it too. I'd spent the better part of a week's profits on Becky's dress and the butterfly pendant I'd gotten to go along with it, but I didn't care. Money meant nothing if you didn't have someone special to spend it on, and despite the drop in sales that had been plaguing my kiosk at the black mall, just watching the reaction on people's faces when I walked into Gerald's Steakhouse with Becky Ann on my arm was enough to convince me that my money had been well spent.

This was the third weekend I'd invited Becky Ann out for dinner and drinks and only the first time that she'd accepted the offer. Yes, her job required her to work most weekends, but you know how beautiful women can be. They can afford to be choosy about the company they keep, and I'd almost done a cartwheel when she'd finally chosen to spend a Friday night keeping company with me.

I'd told her to pick a restaurant and she'd chosen Gerald's, which was very upscale and classy. Earlier in the day I'd had the dress and the pendant delivered to her apartment with a note requesting that she wear both tonight, and she had graciously obliged.

Although I'd been forced to stare down a sister who had rolled her eyes and sucked her crooked teeth at me as we waited for our table, the night seemed magical as Becky Ann and I laughed and talked through dinner. I'd ordered a grilled chicken Caesar salad with creamed spinach on the side, and Becky had a whole Maine lobster with a baked potato, drawn butter, and a medley of mushrooms, broccoli, and asparagus.

"So how was your week?" I asked. I'd called her several times between Monday and Thursday, but had only talked to her briefly to confirm our date.

"Great," she answered, dipping a crown of broccoli into the melted butter. "We were really busy this week. Payday, you know."

"Yeah." I nodded, looking around. Military paydays always brought out the crowds. In a way waiting for the 1st and the 15th was no different than waiting for a Welfare check.

My eyes settled on a couple seated at a booth across from us and I groaned out loud. The brother had a big dookie Afro and a mouth full of gold fronts, and his date had fingernails that were so long they'd curled over and around in loops like one of those old-fashioned crazy straws. And good grief! Was that a pork chop she was gnawing on?

Becky leaned forward, her eyes following my gaze of disgust. "What?" she asked. "Do you know those people? Are they some of your friends?"

I shuddered and quickly shook my head.

"No, darling. I don't have friends like that."

She took a sip of her flavored water and asked innocently. "Friends like what?"

Oh, no, I thought. She wasn't sucking me into that argument tonight.

"Youngsters," I lied soothingly. "Those kids can't be over what? Twenty? Twenty-two?"

Becky Ann's eyes remained locked on mine for a few seconds, then she nodded and picked up her fork, nibbling at a sliver of lobster. "Yes, they do seem rather young. But you have lots of young people in the company you command, don't you?"

I jumped right on it. "Yes, a lot of my soldiers are very young. It's a shame too, because they're so far away from their families that most of them get homesick quite often. Especially during the holidays." I speared a chunk of chicken with my fork and chewed it quickly. "The single soldiers are the worst. You know, the ones who are alone like me, those who live in the barracks or in tiny off-post apartments. I hear Kevin is spearheading a project right now to find area families to invite a few soldiers into their homes for Thanksgiving dinner."

It was working. I watched her eyes soften as I suppressed a grin.

"It must be awful for them," she said. "Living all over the world, so far away from home all the time. That's a great program Kevin's got going. Bravo for him!"

I nodded rapidly. "Yes, it is great. The only problem is finding enough families to voluntarily open their hearts and their homes. That can be a problem."

She lowered her fork to the table. "Is that right? I'd have thought that tons of people would jump at the chance to share their meal with a soldier, especially since there's a war going on. I hope Kevin doesn't give up on his quest. By the way, what are your Thanksgiving plans?"

Bingo! Here comes the invite!

I shrugged nonchalantly. "Don't have any at the moment. I'm one of the soldiers on Kevin's list who is looking for someplace to eat."

She expressed her surprise. "That's odd. He's your brother, right? Why don't you just get together with him and his wife for the day?"

Me? Eat from the table of that scandalous ass Fancy "Suck Dick" Lawson? Not in a million years. As many men as she had creeping through Kevin's house, there was no telling what kind of cooties that skeezer had on her hands.

"Oh, I would love to spend the day with them," I lied smoothly, "but unfortunately they're going out of town that weekend. My sister-in-law's parents are aging and in nursing homes, so they make the trip back to Kansas to visit them as often as possible."

"I see," Becky Ann said in a small voice. She placed one tender bird-like hand gently on mine and smiled. "I'm sorry to hear that Mrs. Lawson's parents aren't well, but I'm certain everything will work out."

———

BECKY Ann had chosen the restaurant, but I'd chosen the after-spot.

I picked a small bar called Jackie's that was only a few minutes away. I'd stumbled on Jackie's during my first week in New Jersey. It was located east of Fort Dix, heading out toward the Jersey shore, and I liked the scene because there was little to no drama. No young heads in baggy jeans shooting at one another and scaring the womenfolk and blasting P.I.M.P. from car speakers that cost more than their cars.

No, Jackie's was easy and over thirty, and the music was so retro that hardly any black folks congregated there. The bar was in full swing when we arrived and a bunch of people were moving around on the dance floor doing the electric slide.

I led Becky Ann over to the bar and ordered myself a beer and a glass of white Zinfandel for her.

"Would you like to dance?" I yelled into her ear, anxious to get on the floor and show her off in that red dress. Becky nodded, and I led her out there, prouder than a peacock at the prize I held on my arm.

"I never learned this dance," Becky Ann admitted shyly.

I grinned. Even as a fat kid I'd been a great dancer. Light on my feet. But I'd never show my baby up or put her in a situation where she was uncomfortable or embarrassed. "No problem," I assured her. "We'll hang out over here on the edge and just do our own thing."

I danced at a mild pace, grinning at her the whole time. Becky Ann was no dancer, but I liked the way she moved her body nevertheless. In fact, I was in awe of everything this lady did and my heart swelled as I took her hands and danced deliberately to the beat, trying hard to get her off one and three and onto two and four.

"Oops!" she said as she drove her stiletto heel into my big toe. "Sorry!"

"It's okay," I said, pulling her close. Just then the beat changed and a slow jam settled the mood and brought the pace way down. I gathered Becky Ann even closer to me, so close I could feel the tips of her precious breasts grazing my chest as my arms encircled her tiny waist.

Becky Ann did better moving to a slower beat, and I buried my nose in her hair as we swayed gently on the dance floor. I modified my slow grind so that she could easily follow my lead, and I was just drifting into a pleasure zone when I saw her.

She was across from me on the dance floor, her round hips gyrating like a video ho, a short skirt riding up her tail and a yard of yellow weave hanging down her back. I probably wouldn't have even seen her if she hadn't thrown her head back and laughed, but once I heard that loud-ass ghetto donkey bray, I knew exactly who she was.

My blood went to boiling in my veins. As much shit as she talked? What the hell was she doing here? Humping some white guy into oblivion? Talk about the pot playing the dozens with the kettle! Staff Sergeant Henderson was more than a ghetto hoochie. She was a jungle-fever-having hypocrite and that made her even worse.

"What?" Becky Ann craned her neck to look at me. I'd stopped dancing and was standing in place, my nostrils flaring like a bull and sweat beading up on my nose. I wanted to kick that bitch's ass. Up in here skanking with a white guy after all that shit she talked about me at work, calling *me* a sellout and turning my mall customers against me.

"That bitch has some nerve," I muttered and shook my head. I turned away and tried to lead Becky Ann off the dance floor.

"Wait just a minute." She pulled away from me, her eyes following the path of my devil-glare. "Isn't that one of your soldiers? That sweet girl Sparkle who you're always mistreating?"

I nearly blew a gasket. "Me mistreat *her*?" My body shook. "She's the one who's always riding me! You should hear some of the crap she tells people about me!" I screwed up my face, mimicking her. "Emily is a sellout! He spends his black-earned dollars on Miss Ann! Emily can't stand being black so he chases after white women!" I shot some more venom at Staff Sergeant Henderson as the moving crowd bumped against my stationary body. "You should see what she did to that picture I keep of you on my desk. She threw it out with the goddamn trash."

"Well," Becky Ann said slowly. "Is it possible that any of the things she says have any validity?"

I stared down at her as she stood there wearing my entire paycheck, and I bit hard on my tongue. I couldn't unleash my fury on Becky Ann; that would never do. But I was damn sure gonna tell Staff Sergeant Henderson which part of my chunky black ass she could kiss.

Grabbing her hand again, I practically dragged her through the crowd until I was standing yea close to Staff Sergeant Henderson and her blue-eyed date. You should have seen the look on her sweaty face when she recognized me and realized that I'd busted her chilling with her very own snow bunny.

"How's it going, Sergeant Henderson?" is what I said, but the tone of my voice made it sound like *Bitch, what the hell are you doing here?*

She grinned up at her date and tossed her head, slinging her weave. "Hey-hey-*hay*! Whatchoo doin' out here shaking a leg, Captain Pinchback? I didn't know you had it in you. Say hi to my good friend Phil." She made the introductions. "And Phil, this is my company commander and not-so-good friend, Captain Emile Pinchback."

"Oh, so it's Emile tonight? Any other time it's Emily this and Emily that."

Becky Ann jumped in. "Hi. I'm Rebecca Ann Grantley." She held out her hand to Staff Sergeant Henderson. "I've seen you around base quite a bit."

"Sparkle." Staff Sergeant Henderson grinned and shook

Becky Ann's hand. "Yeah, I've seen you a couple of times too. This is Phil." She gestured toward her date, who also shook Becky Ann's hand. "We bogarted a booth over on the other side of the room. You guys wanna join us?"

I clenched my teeth as Becky Ann dropped my hand.

"We'd love to, Sparkle. Just lead the way."

———

DON'T even ask me how I let myself get sucked into this one. Who would have imagined it? Me and my baby sitting in a booth across from Stinkin' Sparkle Henderson and some clean-cut white boy who obviously didn't know he was merely her latest flavor of the week.

"Good to see you out there stompin' shit up, Emile. Like I said, I didn't know you had it in you." Sparkle grinned. "I can call you Emile, right? All that military mess has got to go on the weekends."

Ghetto-Gerta had the nerve to spear the lone cherry floating around in her drink with the tip of her straw, then put it to her lips and suck it loudly into her mouth. I nodded in response, although, like I said, any other time she would have been hollering *Emily* instead of *Emile*. "Yeah, it's after duty hours and we're away from the company so I guess Emile is okay for tonight, Staff Sergeant Henderson."

"Sparkle," she corrected me, giggling. "Sparkle. You know, like that brilliant twinkle you see in my eyes. Sparkle."

I grunted, but kept my mouth closed. I didn't trust my own tongue as it flipped around in my mouth. I looked over at her date and tried to figure him out. He was definitely in the military, but it was hard to tell if he was an officer or an enlisted man. Nah, I decided after studying him for a few moments.

He had to be enlisted, probably a senior NCO. Even though he looked tough and strong, there was no way he could be an officer if he was slumming with a slouch like Sparkle Henderson. No flipping way.

"Nice club," Phil said, looking around.

"Yeah," his dumb date repeated. "Nice club. This is my first time here but I used to bring my girl Fancy up this way to take pictures and stuff. She's a camera freak."

Becky Ann exclaimed, "A photographer? How neat! We have a friend who lives here in New Jersey, but runs a program at New York City's School of Photography. Right, Emile? Godfrey Baker."

I just nodded. I wouldn't wish Fancy on Godfrey if he were my worst enemy.

"Whatever." Sparkle waved her hand in the air. "My girl doesn't take pictures full-time or anything, but she really digs the camera, you know?"

"Still," Becky Ann said. "Godfrey might be able to give her the big break she's been waiting for. Here." I watched in disbelief as she dug into her purse and pulled out a slip of paper. She wrote her name and telephone number on it and slid it over to Sparkle, the half-drunk harlot with the brilliant glint in her eyes. "Tell Fancy to call me. I'll give her Godfrey's number and maybe he can help her in some way."

"K. I'll have her call you tomorrow."

I sat there burning up. Why'd she have to go and give Sparkle her number? What good could come of that?

"A fresh round?" Phil gestured toward me and asked, signaling a waitress as she neared our table.

I glanced over at Becky Ann. "You want anything, dear?"

"Actually, yes. What are you drinking, Sparkle?"

Staff Sergeant Henderson answered, "One fifty-one and Coke." Then whispered, "But check it, gurlfren'. These fools pour a gallon of soda in your cup and then wanna add just one damn drop of likker. But I'm on it." She pointed to her pocketbook, which looked more like a backpack. I couldn't believe it when she partially unzipped it and a twenty-ounce bottle of Coca-Cola peeked out. "Just order the rum, gurlfren', and then you can add your own soda."

"And what if they want to know where you got the cola to put in your drink?" I asked coldly, without even realizing that I'd spoken out loud.

She howled. "Don't even start! I'll just tell 'em that I squeezed it out of my fountain!" she said, staring down at her bulging breasts. "Diet on the left, regular on the right!"

Everybody at the table exploded in laughter. Everybody except me. Phil scooped Sparkle up in his arms and gave her a big squeeze, kissing her wetly on her cheek. Becky Ann laughed so hard that tears came from her eyes.

I stared at that high-maintenance buffoon and saw a Dirty Sue in the making. It was all I could do to look at her. Yeah, Phil was an enlisted man. No self-respecting officer would be caught dead sitting next to the hood rat that he was hugging.

"So, Sparkle." Becky Ann dried her eyes and rested her elbows on the table. "Where are you from, and how long have you been in the army?"

"New York City," she said, grinning proudly. "I'm a city girl to the bone. Brooklyn born and bred."

Well that explained the soda in her purse. She was a regular Project Patty. Low class? No class!

Becky Ann smiled even wider. "Years ago I went to summer camp in New Jersey with a group of girls who were from Brooklyn. Most of them were just like you. Witty, outgoing. We had a blast."

"Get out of town!" Sparkle shouted. "I went to summer camp in Jersey too! It was a Fresh Air Fund type of thang. A bunch of white folks who felt sorry for city kids like me and thought we needed to get away from all that crime and concrete. It was someplace up near Butler. A joint called Camp Vacation."

"Camp Vacation?" Becky shrieked, flinging a loose strand of hair out of her face. "I went to Camp Vacation too!"

Sparkle held her hand out, palm forward. "Girl, stop! Just stop the flippin' madness! Tell me you were *not* a Vacation Kid! Coomelah-coomelah-coomelah vista!"

"Ohhh, no-no-no-nah-nah-vista!"

"Ah, shit now. Eenie-meenie desta-meenie ooh-ah, lah-walla meenie?"

"Exxa-meenie, solla-meenie ooh-ah lah-walla meenie!"

"Beat Billy oaten-doten, bo-bo, bah-deeten dotten shhhh . . ."

"Beat Billy oaten-doten, bo-bo, bah-deeten dotten shhhh . . ."

"Wait, wait!" Phil shouted. "Teach me. Slow down and teach me!"

Becky Ann laughed her ass off, her face flushed. "Okay, okay. Repeat after us. Flea!"

"Flea!"

"Flea-fly!"

"Flea-fly!"

"Flea-fly-floe!"

"Flea-fly-floe!"

"Vista!"

"Vista!"

"Coomelah-coomelah-coomelah vista . . ."

I just sat there listening to their nonsense with my chin in my hand. Fuming.

CHAPTER 21

SPARKLE

All Good

*O*oooh! Pull over right here!" I squealed, sounding more than a little bit tipsy. I pointed toward a late-night Dairy Queen whose front window was all lit up. Another Friday night had rolled around and here I was out barhopping and chilling in public with a white boy two weekends in a row.

We'd gone to a little Irish pub off of High Street, and how I thought Miller draft and Jamaican rum was gonna mix with a strawberry float was way beyond me.

"You want some ice cream?" Phil asked, dutifully sliding up to the curb.

I nodded and belched, tasting rummy beer. "Yep. A strawberry float. I'ma sit out here, though," I told him, sinking farther into my seat. "If that's okay with you."

I watched him walk into the ice cream parlor amazed at the way he looked from the back. Delicious. He didn't have a hint of that tight-ass walk you see on some white boys, or that goofy, loping swagger they displayed either.

Nah, Phil was cool. Had a cool walk, a nice ass, and some nice teeth. Plus, he was sweet to me. Not sweet like a bitch or a flunky or nothing, but sweet because he wanted to be, not because he had to be.

I watched him through the window as he ordered, and when he came back with my float and nothing for himself, I decided to play with him a little bit. As he drove toward my apartment I did my best to tease him, pushing spoonfuls of vanilla ice cream dipped in strawberries into his mouth.

Back at my apartment he lingered outside the door.

"You wanna come in?" I asked, setting my purse on the floor just inside the foyer.

Phil shook his head. "No, I'd better not. It's been a fun night and all, but I think I'll go and let you get some rest."

Niggah please, my liquor screamed. Ain't no man ever worried about my beauty sleep before! When Miss Sparkle invited them inside, inside their asses came!

"I'm fine," I said, tugging on his fingers and running my thumb along the inside of his palm. That rum had me hot. "I've got plenty of energy. I'm not tired at all."

I couldn't believe it when he shook his head again. "I'd better not," he repeated, pulling me close. Close enough to feel what was bulging in his pants. "But I did have a great time with you tonight." He kissed my forehead and ran his hands along my arms, then stepped away from me and smiled. "Good night, Sparkle. If you're not busy tomorrow, then maybe we can get together again. There are a lot of good movies playing this weekend if you feel like checking one out."

I nodded dumbly as he walked back down the path and toward his car. Now, what in the hell had just happened? Had Miss Sparkle just been dismissed? I think not!

Okay, yeah. I did it. I acted a fool. Before he could get to the curb I took off running behind him like a drunken sprinter. At the sound of my lumbering footsteps he whirled around and I leaped into the air, sailing into his arms. Now, Miss Sparkle ain't no frail-ass size three–four. Baby got back, hips, thighs, the whole package. But Phil caught me in his arms like I was a baby bird, and before I knew it our lips were glued together and he was tonguing me down like a pro, murmuring my name over and over again.

I don't even remember him carrying me back to my apartment, but I do remember how hot he made me feel. We barely made it inside and closed the door before I grabbed my purse, snatched out a condom, and then stripped out of my clothes right there in the foyer, glowing under the thrill of Phil's heat.

The first time was hard and fast and desperate, yet he waited for me, let me come twice before he let himself go. We lay there on the bare floor for long minutes afterward, him rubbing and touching and massaging every part of my body and me enjoying the way his hands felt on my skin.

"I'm sorry," he finally breathed beside me. "That wasn't supposed to happen."

My grin stretched a mile wide. Believe it or not, Mister Phil was packing a *pow* for a white boy. My stuff was thumping and aching quite nicely.

"Oh, yeah it was," I told him, reaching for him again. To my surprise he was still hard and I had to admit that even though his skin wasn't brown, he had one of the best-looking bodies I'd ever seen.

He took me again, right there on the floor, and I loved every moment of it.

By the time the sun came up we'd already taken a shower together and Phil had invited me out to breakfast. Screw the food! I got up in that restaurant and behaved like the stereotypical black nymph. I couldn't keep my hands off him! I played with him the entire time we were eating, sitting across from him with my foot in his lap, massaging his erection with my bare toes. This time we didn't even make it back to my house. Parked under some trees on the side of a dark road, we climbed into the backseat of his car and I screamed as loud as I could as he licked my stuff until I almost passed out.

I think I dozed off after that because the next thing I knew we were back at my place and Phil was helping me out of the car.

"Look," he said, pointing toward the sky. "It's a beautiful sunrise, Sparkle. And it's all the more beautiful because I'm seeing it come up with you."

It wasn't yang, y'all, and I knew it. The boy was serious. He really dug me, and if I must admit it, I was feeling him too.

We watched the sun come up from the rocker on my front patio. I lay with my head in Phil's lap as he held me and stroked the side of my face. I don't know what got into Miss Sparkle. Maybe it was the sight of a new sun fighting to be born, or perhaps it was the comfort and security radiating from his arms, but without the slightest hesitation I unzipped Phil's pants and turned my face toward his lap.

I felt him get weak for me, and it made me want to please

him even more. And with my head moving gently to the swaying of the rocker, I did for sweet Phil what he'd already done for me, and sistahs let me tell y'all something: It was all good.

———

BUT all it took was a phone call to bring me back to my senses. At ten after two that afternoon I was dozing in my bed, spread-eagled and loving the way my showered and perfumed body felt on my clean sheets. Phil had gone home at ten, promising to call in the early evening so we could plan the rest of our weekend.

"Hello?" I said, hoping it would be his voice on the other end of the line.

Not.

"Sparkle? This is your Aunt Vivian. I tried to reach you this morning. Don't you return your phone calls?"

My mind went on rewind. I vaguely remembered hearing the telephone ring early this morning, but Phil and I had been snoring on my living room sofa and there was no way I was getting up to answer the phone.

"I must have been knocked out, Aunt Viv. I didn't even hear the phone."

"Well," she went on, "I dreamt about you last night and it wasn't a good dream neither."

I sat up and leaned on one elbow. Aunt Viv was crazy like that. It was almost as if she'd smelled my sins. "Oh really?"

"Yes, really. I didn't dream about teeth or fish or anything like that, so I'm not worried about you dying or being pregnant, but you were wrapped in something that looked like a thick white cloud, and it was spinning out of control and moving farther and farther away from me, and no matter how hard I tried, I just couldn't reach you. Poor Deebo had to hold me down I was thrashing around so hard in my sleep. To tell you the truth, it plain frightened me."

I sat all the way up then. "Um, that's some strange shi— I mean stuff, Aunt Viv. Me wrapped up in clouds and all. I don't even like heights." I coughed and tried to keep the lie from showing in my voice. "Don't worry, though. Miss Sparkle has both feet planted on the ground, Auntie. I'm straight."

"Uh-huh," she said, sounding unconvinced. "I sure hope like hell you are. Just don't be out there doing nothing foolish, girl. This family done had its share of tragedy and you're about the only one of Mama's grandkids who has a lick of sense. You keep making your Aunt Viv proud, you hear?"

"And you know that," I said, keeping my tone upbeat. "I'm cool, Aunt Viv. Miss Sparkle's got it going on, and everything is under control."

Two seconds after I hung up I went searching through my nightstand drawer looking for my little black book. I must have been crazy. I couldn't believe I'd been stupid enough to break my golden rule. Yeah, I had a pang or two of regret over what I was about to do, but there was no way around it. So what if I felt grand chilling in his arms? Good dicks came a dime a dozen, and I had quite a few dollar bills I was willing to spend tonight. I could hear Aunt Viv talking in my ear and you know she was right: The best way to get over an old man is to get yourself a new one. I thumbed through my well-worn address book. Check it. I'd start making calls at the letter *A*, and before I got to the letter *D*, watch and see if I didn't have me a funky date for the night.

And trust me, regardless of the bells I'd heard and the vibes I'd felt last night as I got loose with a white boy who had done to my body what he'd already done to my heart, everything about my date tonight—to include his shoes, his wallet, and his hair—would be blacker than black.

CHAPTER 22

FANCY

But I Am Straight

"Just a minute," I called out as the doorbell rang.

It was the first Monday in November and I was playing hooky from work. I'd just taken a bath in vanilla-scented beads and rubbed vanilla oil into my skin for a full ten minutes. Draping a robe around my shoulders, I ran downstairs and peeked out the window to see if any of my nosy neighbors were lurking outside. Living in government housing meant having absolutely no privacy, and I'd heard a rumor that the stay-at-home wives and mothers who lived on my street had a running list of everyone who came into or out of my house. Especially the men.

"Hi," she said simply when I opened the door.

My face got flushed and embarrassment flooded me. After the things we'd done together, the way she'd made me scream and moan, how was I supposed to greet her? Like a lover or like a sister-friend?

This was our second time meeting without our husbands,

and I felt more than a bit guilty as I stepped back and let her in, trying to control my breathing as she followed me into the living room.

Our apartment was small, but that was to be expected from military housing. I'd spent the morning dusting and vacuuming and burning light incense, but there was nothing I could do to make my home as impressive as the Princeton town house Mica shared with her husband, Derek.

A feeling of utter amazement came over me at the sight of her standing in my living room. Ever since the night Kevin had convinced me to swing with the Bateses my life had been crazy as hell.

For one thing, I'd been forced to acknowledge that Kevin and I were a lot more alike than I wanted to admit when it came to our sexual appetites. For so long I'd fooled myself into thinking that the perversity of our sexcapades was all Kevin's doing, and that I could be satisfied with only having monogamous sex with my husband, but maybe I was wrong. It was obvious that I got off on the kinky and unusual just as much as Kevin did, and after that amazing four-way encounter, it was possible that I enjoyed it even more.

The other thing that worried me so much that I'd lost six pounds, and had considered calling my local Presbyterian pastor for counseling, was the rush of hidden desire that the wife-sharing thing had driven to my surface.

I was hooked on what I'd experienced with Mica that night, and from the moment she touched me I'd been consumed with thoughts of sex with women, driven almost mad with shame and secret desire. I felt deviant and dirty, but also very delicious, which amazed me because even during my stripping days I'd been freethinking sexually and very uninhibited, but never interested in women. And now, engulfed in the erotic desire to feel the heat of a woman's soft wetness throbbing against my own, I was irresistibly compelled to do it again and again.

"So," she said. "How's everything going?"

"Things are good here," I answered evenly, motioning that she should sit on the sofa. She had on a mint-green pantsuit that went really well with her complexion and accented her curvy frame. "How was your trip? Did you enjoy Mexico?"

"As a matter of fact, I did. How'd you know I was out of the country?"

I shrugged. "Kevin told me. He and Derek went out for drinks a couple of weeks ago, you know."

"That's right," she said, crossing one shapely leg over the other. "I remember. They went to some wild club in the city. Some sort of exclusive men's joint where no women are allowed. Did Kevin have a good time?"

"Well." I was puzzled. "I guess so, but I'm not sure."

Did she say New York? As far as I knew, Kevin had taken Derek to the NCO club right here on base. I remembered being worried because he'd come home all wrung out, stumbling through the door and so dizzy that he'd fallen and had to crawl up the stairs. My husband couldn't hold but so much liquor and I figured he'd been out there playing the macho role and drinking way more than he could handle, but when I went to help him take off his clothes and into bed he fought me off, staggering into the bathroom and locking the door, insisting that he could take care of himself just fine. I'd dozed off when I heard him moving around in the shower, and the next morning I was concerned because he said he had a hangover and stayed home from work. I was also a little surprised because the house was empty when I got home from work. He hadn't called, there was no note, and I didn't see my husband again until early the next morning.

"Are you certain they went to New York?"

"Oh, yeah," Mica answered. "Derek is a regular at the clubs in the city. He usually drives up about once a month. In fact, I think I called him on his cellie when they were heading back down to Jersey, and he said Kevin had had so much fun he'd tried some things he'd never tried before. Derek said Kevin had passed out in the passenger seat, so I guess he must have had a blast."

"I guess," I answered, suddenly uneasy. Maybe they *had* gone to New York on Thursday evening, but why would Kevin lie? And where the hell had he gone the next morning and stayed throughout the night?

Mica was still smiling at me, but I didn't know what to say or what move was appropriate to make. While I was learning her body intimately, there was so much I didn't know about who Mica was as a woman, yet getting inside her head was something she just would not permit. The first time she'd called me was the day after our initial encounter and just the sound of her voice stroking me through the telephone line had brought me to a climax.

After I'd composed myself, I tried to make small talk and get to know her, but she schooled me real quick.

"Look, Fancy. I'm sure you're a wonderful person and all that, but we're not in this so we can do barbecues and car pools. We're both married, and the way this thing is done, we get our physical needs met and then we go back home and shop and chitchat with our straight girlfriends."

"But I *am* straight," I'd protested.

Mica had sighed. "Okay, darling. You might enjoy getting with a man on the regular, but just like me, you also enjoy being with a woman, so how about we just focus on that."

She'd invited me over to her house near Princeton, and I'd taken the morning off from work, driven the hour in heavy traffic, and had the greatest sex of my life.

"Next time we meet let's do it at your place," she suggested as we lay in her bed, our legs and arms still entwined. "Let's try and keep it interesting and maybe it'll last a little while."

I'd nodded my agreement readily. Anywhere she wanted it was cool with me. Just as long as I got to feed from her nakedness, to feel her lips on my breasts, her slick mound pulsating and pushing hungrily into mine.

During the next few weeks as I waited for our next encounter I started feeling crazy. Feverish with a profound loss of appetite. I caught myself staring into nothingness, daydreaming of Mica, and wanting her more than I had ever wanted any man. The implications behind that were not lost on me. Could my undeniable love of sex have been masking the fact that I was really gay? Had some sort of repressed twist in my sexuality been laying in wait for me all these years?

I was confused, but I was still hungry. I jonesed for Mica's body so badly that I fantasized about her during sex with Kevin. I masturbated in the shower with thoughts of her magnificent breasts heating my blood.

And now she was in my house, soon to be in my bed. I'd have her all to myself for two whole hours before Kevin came home for lunch.

I rose from the couch and sauntered into the kitchen, taking two chilled glasses from the freezer.

I filled the glasses with ice from the dispenser on the door, then set them on the counter. "Lemon?" I asked over my shoulder, then realized that she was right behind me.

Like always, Mica didn't waste any time.

I was turning with the glasses still in my hands when she slid my robe off my shoulder and I felt her warm breath at the base of my ear.

"Yumm," she whispered, inhaling my scent. "You smell delicious."

I felt weak again and it was all I could do to remain upright. Mica took the glasses from me and set them on the counter, then explored my mouth with her tongue as she slipped the robe completely off my body. Her hands were insistent as they roamed my naked flesh, and for a moment I was immobilized, torn between hot shame and wanting what she had to offer.

Somehow we made it upstairs, where I led her toward Kevin's workroom that doubled as our guest bedroom. It was done up in shades of peach and lavender, and the sheets were freshly washed and misted with lavender extract just for this event.

"Uh-uh," Mica said as I tried to guide her past the master bedroom where Kevin and I slept. She took one look at the vast expanse of ivory and our huge four-poster bed, and urged me in that direction. "I want to do it in there."

What could I say? No? Not hardly.

I felt another twang of apprehension as I followed her into my bedroom. Of all the times we'd shared our passions with others, Kevin and I had never allowed anyone upstairs in our house, and we certainly had never violated our bedroom.

"Undress me," Mica commanded as she stood in the center

of my room. My fingers felt like clumsy sausages as I undid her buttons, pushed her shirt off her shoulders, and unzipped her skirt, exposing her garter belt and thigh-high stockings before letting it all fall to the floor.

Aside from her garter, Mica was naked beneath her clothing, and a gasp caught in my throat at the sight of her firm body. Proud and lovely, and totally feminine in every way.

For the next hour and a half Mica instructed me in the art of making love to a woman. Each of the previous times we'd lain together she had been the aggressor, doing all sorts of exquisite things to my body to please me into a frenzy.

But this time the tables were turned. It was I who cupped her breasts and licked her chocolate nipples. I who slid two fingers deeply inside of her moistness, teasing her clit until she moaned and thrashed beneath me. I who sucked her toes, kissed behind her knees, licked the insides of her thighs, and then finally for the first time in my life, lowered my mouth to the vagina of another woman. Only heaven knew it could taste so sweet.

How long I drank from between Mica's thighs escaped me. All I knew is that I'd found my poison, the elusive nectar I'd been searching for all my life. I was so enraptured with gulping her essence that I didn't hear the door when it was opened downstairs.

As Mica held me by the hair and ground herself into my mouth, I didn't hear the footsteps as they ascended the stairs. Like a starving woman, I licked Mica from the height of her mound all the way to her anus, and I didn't hear my husband's gasp of disbelief as he dropped his hat and keys in wounded surprise.

But I did hear his voice when he finally found it. I heard him scream out my name and curse Mica's perverted life as he grabbed me by the hair, snatching me from the warmth of her naked body and sending me crashing coldly to the hard floor.

KEVIN

Use What You Got

I told you Fancy was a freak!

My wife tonguing out another woman! Who could have imagined that? Of course I pretended to be pissed. I threw Fancy on the floor, stomped my feet around, cussed and screamed, but even while I was raging my thing was on hard. If it had been anybody other than Derek's woman that she was with I would have cheered Fancy on. If it had been her best girlfriend, I would have jumped in the bed, got it on with them, and died a happy man.

But it was Derek's wife, and I'd told Fancy to stay away from both of their asses. Club Flex. I trembled at the thought of it. That joint was nothing more than a faggot bathhouse for straight-looking brothers who were living on the down-low. My memory of that night was still blurry, but enough of it came through to make me sick to my stomach. Me. As many women as I'd run through in my lifetime, somehow I'd ended up getting used even worse.

I was furious that Derek had even put me in a position like that 'cause I for damn sure hadn't given off any gay vibes. Sure, I liked to fuck, but I only touched women. And the fact that I'd been drugged was hardly any consolation. How many times had I heard about soldiers in Korea and Japan and even in the States who went to a club and left their drink on a table, danced for a while, and then came back and downed it? One of my old running partners from California had done that shit and to this day he's not right in the head.

I must have slept with at least twenty sistahs since that night. Some I picked up off the streets, others I dug out of my emergency stash. Booty calls who didn't mind being part of a hit-and-run. I was burying myself in trim. I even went running back to the house of Dirty Sue. I was trying my best to get thoughts of how that nigger had poked me out of my head, but no matter how many boots I knocked, nothing seemed to help.

But my stupidity didn't speak for what Fancy had done, and I was gonna milk her mistake to death. After all these years of me begging her to do this very thing, she ends up getting with old girl behind my back.

I tossed Mica out the door as she tried to jump back into her clothes. There was a group of Tupperware-looking white girls standing around in my neighbor's yard, and you should have seen the looks on their faces as I slung Mica around my yard. "Screwing my wife?" I yelled over and over. "Screwing my goddamn wife?"

But dig. The whole time I was cussing Mica out and calling her a thousand names, I was praying she didn't peep the fat erection that was trying to bust out of my drawers. By the time I got back in the house Fancy had crawled her fine naked ass down the steps and was groveling on the floor. Crying, begging me to forgive her, babbling about how confused she was and how she just couldn't control what she'd been feeling.

Me? I was grinning inside because I was gonna *use* this shit.

Use it to the max. Never again would I accept a "no" from Fancy. All that *I-don't-want-no-woman-to-touch-me* yang was out the window. A blind man coulda seen how much fun she was having munching between that girl's legs.

And in *our* bed!

Yep. From now on my wife was gonna participate and co-operate. With me, and with her fine girlfriend, whose hot firm body was forever haunting me in my dreams. I could see it now. Me getting some from the back, Fancy getting some from the front. It was going to be wild.

———

TUESDAY morning. A new cycle of senior noncommissioned officers was being processed into the academy, but instead of the normal eight-week cycle of training they were mandated, we'd been tasked to push them through in six.

"Can we really do this?" Emile asked, standing over my shoulder and reading the proposed training plan.

The situation had gotten so bad in Iraq that the army was sending every available troop to the region. Training courses were being expedited, the guard and reserve forces were just about tapped out, and recently we'd caught wind of a program designed to take rejects from the navy and air force and make soldiers out of them in four short weeks.

I nodded. "Yeah, man. It'll be tight, but it can be done." I pointed out the specifics. "These are National Guard soldiers who are only mobilized for ninety days before shipping out. They have a ton of other stuff to do and requirements to meet. We'll just have each small group leader consolidate their modules. Combine leadership with battle-focused training. Shift the career specialty tracks back to week five instead of week seven. It'll work."

Emile nodded. "Cool. Make it happen, Top. Keep me in the loop."

"Yes, sir," I said, saluting him from my seat. Emile and I tried our best to keep things professional between us on the job and so far, so good.

Gathering my notes and a few extra copies of the training plan, I headed down the hall to the company dayroom, where my staff and instructors were waiting for me to begin our morning meeting.

I noticed that the door to the supply shop was open so I poked my head in.

"Get moving!" I yelled, trying to smell her perfume above the scent of cleaning oils and field gear. She was notorious for being late, but I wanted me some of that so I forced myself to keep my voice light. "The morning meeting begins in five mikes! I'd better not beat you there!"

"I'm coming, First Sergeant," Staff Sergeant Henderson yelled and I broke out in a sweat. I couldn't even let myself think about her coming until I put my plan into place. As fine as she was, I'd be forced to make a detour to the latrine and beat off at the thought.

I walked briskly down the hall, commanding my toolie to remain at ease.

"Good morning, First Sergeant!"

I grinned. Specialist Gaines and Specialist Vance. Two

young sisters who weren't half as smart as a manila folder, but were always pleasant and upbeat and were fine to boot. They were chewing bubble gum and cleaning the double glass interior doors that guarded the entrance to the NCO academy. Squirting a blue liquid from bottles of glass cleaner, they took turns smearing it around with pieces of dry cloth.

"Young ladies," I said seriously, then corrected myself as they giggled. "I mean, young soldiers. How many highly motivated, finely trained, fit-to-fight soldiers does it take to make a glass door shine?"

Vance answered, her dimples flashing in her pretty face. "Two, Top. One to spray the cleaner and the other to wipe it up!"

Oooh weee, I thought as both of them fell out laughing like she'd said something hip. I hoped Vance had some good trim because even though the lights were on in her head, there wasn't a soul at home. I was turning to walk away when I glanced out the doors at the parade of soldiers disembarking from a blue military shuttle bus.

We were responsible for training senior enlisted combat engineers at the academy, and I watched as the men hoisted their duffel bags on their backs and made their way from the bus to the entrance of the building.

"Make a hole," I said, gesturing Vance and Gaines away as I kept my eyes on the herd of uniforms coming toward me. "Let these soldiers through,"

A second later my blood ran cold. "That's enough shining for now," I said, studying the crowd of men who were heading in my direction. They were pushing through the outer doors, and there was one man in particular who stood out from the rest.

I couldn't believe what I was seeing and I stood there blinking as a wave of rage surged within me. Rage and deep shame. He was so thick I could see his muscles through his uniform. Sick motherfucker. He was talking to a skinny white guy, and had that same mocking grin on his face that he'd worn the last time I'd seen him.

Duncan. The name tag on his uniform read DUNCAN.

He glanced up as they pushed through the inner doors and our eyes met. I saw recognition flitter in his, and I won't even tell you what he saw in mine. He raised his chin in a slight *What's up,* then turned away as a couple of soldiers from the orderly room directed the flow of students into the conference room down the hall. Of course I didn't nod back, but I kept grilling him with my eyes, burning a hole in his back until he was out of my view.

"Specialist Matthews!" I ordered. "Bring me a copy of that student roster!"

Specialist Matthews ran over and handed me his roster, and I quickly scanned the document until I found what I was looking for. Sergeant First Class Duncan. Ronald Duncan, aka Rondu. An eleven-bravo from an NG unit out of Queens, New York. The dick-sucking niggah who had sent me running back to Teesha and them. A low-life John Henry–looking booty bumper from a downlow club in the city.

Use what you got. I forced myself to calm my growing rage as Staff Sergeant Henderson ran her hot little body past me down the hall, grinning and trying her best to get into that meeting before me. *Use what you got.* Yeah, Sergeant First Class Duncan had got him a piece of my ass that night, and there wasn't much I could do to change it. But he was on active duty now and this time I was on top, controlling all the strokes, and if he refused to go along with the program and get down with what I was scheming up, then let's just say his black ass would be mine.

———

I walked up on him in the All-Ranks Club later that night. I'd sent a runner to his barracks room with a note telling him what time to meet me.

"Sup?" he asked. The niggah looked shaky.

"What?" I growled, squeezing my drink in my hand. "Oh, so now you scared? You wasn't scared a couple of weeks ago, motherfucker."

"I don't know what you talking about, Top."

I nodded. "You better fucking not, because didn't nothing happen."

This time he nodded. "You wanted to see me?"

"What was that shit you gave me?"

"What shit?"

I stood up. "If I have to mess you up in this club, I will. Don't fuck with me, Sergeant, because I'm struggling hard not to kill you."

He swallowed. "I don't know the ingredients. It was a cocktail. A super Roofie. I bought it already mixed."

"Well, you're gonna buy some more."

"What?"

I put my drink down and stared at him. "You heard me. You're going to buy some more of that shit. For me. On Thursday. You're gonna make a run up to New York, and you're taking me with you."

CHAPTER 24

EMILE

Bullshit!

"Can I get you anything else?" Becky Ann asked as I sat at the bar nursing a warm beer. Thursday night at the club was right-arm night, and I was catching the tail end of it. Commanders usually brought their most senior NCOs out for a drink to welcome in the close of the workweek, but my right arm had disappeared from his office before I could invite him out.

"No thanks." I shook my head. I was still in uniform so I had to limit how much I drank.

"Not too much longer. We close in less than an hour," Becky Ann reminded me, smiling as she moved farther down the bar. I watched as she chatted with the older male soldiers, command sergeants major and colonels who closed the bar down almost every night. They were ancient and more than ready to retire, but not at all eager to go home early to their wives. Instead, they hung around the bar and struck up easy conversations with my baby, and I could see why. She was soft and pleasant, and not at all hard on the eyes. It had been a long day, and all I wanted to do was hang around until her shift ended, then drive her home and crawl into bed beside her.

An hour or so later Dusty, the manager, had shooed the last customer from the bar and locked the doors. Becky Ann quickly finished counting out the bar receipts and then tidied up her area.

"Well." I stood up and stretched, yawning deeply as she came from behind the bar holding her purse and a fluffy jacket. "Ready to wrap it up?"

"Sure," she said. "Just let me get Dusty to sign off on my time sheet and then we can leave."

She was quiet as we headed toward my car, which was fine with me because I was exhausted. I unlocked my ride and opened her door, then closed it tightly once she was safely buckled into her seat belt.

"Emile," she said as soon as I opened the driver's door and climbed in. "We need to talk."

Not again, I thought, sighing as I turned the key in the ignition and drove out of the empty lot. Whatever was on her mind, I wished she'd wait until tomorrow before sharing it because I was too beat to indulge her.

"What about?" I asked, keeping my eyes on the road.

"Your brother," she said flatly. "We need to talk about your brother."

What a relief. Better about Kevin than about me.

I played it cool. "What about my brother? I didn't know you knew him all that well."

"Actually, I don't," she said. "But apparently Laurie does."

The name didn't ring any bells. "Laurie? Who's that?"

She leaned forward in her seat and turned toward me. "Remember Theresa, that really cute lady whose baby shower I went to earlier this year? The one who was having twins and her husband is in the military police force and always deployed, and since the child care on base is too expensive, she decided to sell Tupperware instead of going back to work after her babies, both boys, were born?"

Of course I didn't remember.

"Yeah. What about her?"

"Well, Theresa is a friend of Stephanie's, who goes to night school with Laurie. Theresa is into body-pampering products now. I mean, how many Tupperware customers can you actually find? Well, last Monday she had a spa party slash get-together. A fruit-and-cheese, forget-about-the-kids, soak-your-feet-and-get-a-free-facial affair. She held it in the morning because that's when most moms are available, especially if they don't work during the day and their kids are in school. I couldn't attend because I had a dentist appointment that morning, or else I would have been there as well, probably just to purchase a product or two. You know, in the interest of supporting her home business."

"Uh-huh."

"Apparently, Theresa has been really busy since the twins were born, and since her husband is always gone she hasn't been the very best housekeeper. She asked Stephanie if she could host the party over at her house since Stephanie is such a neatnik and her youngest daughter is in kindergarten full-time this year."

She paused and I inserted the appropriate response.

"Uh-huh."

"So, as it turns out, Stephanie lives in the same housing

area that your brother and his wife live in. Right next door to him, actually."

"Oh, really?"

"Yes. It seems that the spa party had just ended and the guests were leaving when your brother came home, probably for lunch."

"And?"

"Well, I wasn't actually there, but according to Theresa there was some sort of commotion over at your brother's house, and the next thing they knew he was throwing a woman out on the front lawn."

Yes! I screamed inside. He'd finally gotten rid of that skeezer-ass Fancy! Why hadn't he told me? I'd have taken him out to celebrate.

"Kevin threw a woman out? I guess he's finally fed up with his trifling wife."

She shook her head vigorously. "I don't think so, Emile. Theresa says she'd never seen this woman before, and besides . . . the lady was naked."

"Naked?"

"Yes, naked. Kevin was shouting and swearing and throwing clothes at her as the woman tried to get away from him."

Now I was the one shaking my head. "That's ridiculous, Becky Ann. If a naked woman was in Kevin's house then she was there to see Fancy. That's why I warned you to stay away from her. She's no good, baby. Has the loosest morals I've ever seen on a woman."

"Well, according to Theresa, it's not your sister-in-law who's loose, but your brother."

I laughed. "That's bull. Kevin is a ladies' man, yeah. But it's Fancy who sneaks guys into his house when he's not there. It's

Fancy who picks up slugs off the street and screws them while her husband is out there pulling duty all over the world." I shook my head, disgusted at the bad taste her name left in my mouth. "Fancy's the one who's living foul, princess. Not Kevin."

"I wouldn't be so sure about that if I were you, Emile. Theresa says Kevin uses his wife to bring in their sexual partners, not the other way around. It's just that this time he came home and threw one of them out. Usually your brother hangs around and enjoys the company."

"Bullshit!" I spat. "What? How would Theresa know what goes on in Kevin's house? Is she a peep freak or something? Is she over there listening in through the walls?"

Becky Ann shook her head. "I don't know, but Laurie was there on Monday too. She recognized your brother, Emile. She said he's a swinger who takes his toys home to his wife. Laurie goes to college most nights, but she also works for an escort service on the side. She told Stephanie and Theresa that Kevin and Fancy are regulars at her company, and the reason she knows this is because she's done a couple of threesomes with them herself. She says that Fancy sometimes calls inquiring about the dates, but it's usually Kevin who decides who they actually take home."

I stopped at a traffic light and put on my left blinker. Becky's words were fucking up my head and a moment passed before I trusted myself to speak again.

"These military dependents have way too much time on their hands, especially the enlisted wives. You can't believe too much of anything they say, darling. They're not like you. They don't have your kind of integrity."

She spoke sharply. "Emile, wake up. Your brother is a predator. I didn't want to tell you this, but just a few days ago I saw him with a guy who I know for a fact sleeps with men. They were standing at the bar, deep in conversation. Involved."

Forgetting myself, I turned completely around to face her, astounded.

"Watch the freakin' road!" she shrieked.

"That," I said a few shaky moments later, clearing my throat and gripping the steering wheel, "is a very serious allegation, Becky Ann. A character assassination like that is nothing that you should be tossing around lightly."

"It's true, Emile. In my job I get to see almost every soldier who comes through your NCO academy. A lot of the students you guys get in are also reservists who drill here every single month. Most of them I know by name. People talk, you know. They're away from home, bored, stressed out by this environment, drinking a bit too much." She hunched her shoulders and shrugged. "Like I said, soldiers talk. And sometimes they talk to me."

I made a sarcastic noise deep in my throat. "For your information, hundreds of soldiers come through the academy each year. Kevin is a first sergeant. He's supposed to talk to his troops. What do you think a first sergeant does for a living? He's their daddy. That doesn't make him gay."

She sniffed. "His poor wife."

I threw up my hands, and then just as quickly put them back on the steering wheel. "His poor hell! All of you women are just scarred by this recent downlow drama. Every man out there doesn't have a questionable sexuality, I want you to know. Looka here. Kevin's been knockin' boots since he was ten years old. If he liked men, I would have been one of the first to know about it, okay?"

She was unconvinced. "The guy I saw your brother with is definitely bi. His unit is somewhere in New York, but he comes to Dix for drills. He's a switch-hitter, and from his own mouth I know this to be true. I just think somebody needs to tell Kevin's wife."

I glanced at her, my eyes hard. "Why are you so concerned about Fancy all of a sudden? What is it to you anyway? You don't know the first thing about women like her. That girl has a checkered past. She's a wannabe photographer who takes pictures of naked people! Trust me. She's only one paycheck away from working from somebody's street corner, and I don't mean as a school crossing guard either."

Becky Ann's voice was dry and cutting. "There are diseases out there that cannot be cured, Emile. Women are being infected by their men at an alarming rate. What affects one woman affects us all. Black and white."

I turned onto her street, then pulled into her parking spot and just sat there. I didn't even bother shutting off the ignition because suddenly I had no desire to sleep in her bed. "I already told you, Becky Ann. Kevin is all man. Chief does not bring home hookers, and there isn't a gay bone in his body. But just to shut those bigmouthed gossiping friends of yours up, I'll talk to him, get him to tell me what I already know is true. Just wait. His nosy neighbors will have to find somebody else to launch their verbal grenades at because *my* brother isn't gonna be the one."

She crossed her arms. "Fine."

"And you, Becky Ann"—I pointed in her face—"when I find out that all of this stupidity is nonsense, and it *is* nonsense, you are going to owe my brother a big-time apology."

She unsnapped her seat belt. "Like I said, fine. Get to the

bottom of this and if you can assure me that Kevin's not putting his wife's health in danger I'll put my apology in writing. In fact, I'll put a big fat bow on the 'I'm sorry' card and deliver it to him myself."

"Good!" I practically yelled as she climbed out of my car. "You get ready to do just that, you hear me, Becky Ann? You hear me!"

She stood there holding the car door open and staring at me with cool blue eyes. "I hear you, Emile," she said quietly. "The question is, can you hear yourself?"

CHAPTER 25

KEVIN

'Fess Up

*F*or somebody who doesn't like pork you sure are greasing those sparerib bones." It was soul food week at the mess hall, and Emile looked up from his plate of barbecued ribs, turnip greens, and corn bread and shrugged.

"You're the one who wanted to come here. I hate this kind of food."

I chewed a mouthful of my potato salad. "Tell that to the mess sergeant. Besides, you're the one who didn't want to talk at the office, and since I have a meeting in half an hour, speak niggah. Speak."

Emile sighed and looked at me like he was explaining a difficult geometry concept to a kindergartner. "How many times do I have to tell you that I'm not your niggah? I'm your brother, Chief. Your brother. I'm an educated man and there's not a drop of niggah in me. I wish you could understand that." He winked and kept on chewing.

Grinning, I took a sip of water from the bottle in front of

me. "Nah, for real though," I said. "What do you have to tell me that's so important you were willing to blow your diet to come up in here?"

He put down the rib he was gnawing and wiped his fingers on one of the hundreds of napkins balled up near his plate.

"Nothing much. I just wanted to check on you, man, you know? Make sure everything is straight."

I nodded. "Cool. I'm cool. How 'bout you?"

"Oh, I'm cool," he said quickly. "I'm real cool."

"So?"

"So, how's Fancy? She cool too?"

Emile was nobody's poker player because I peeped his hold card the minute he mentioned my wife's name. "Fancy's doing fine," I said evenly. "Just fine."

"Yeah, you know my girl hooked her up with a photography contact, right?"

I nodded. "I heard. That was good of her, and Fancy's work is really getting a lot of exposure now. Thank Becky Ann for me."

"So y'all are okay?" he asked, shoving a piece of corn bread into his mouth. "I mean, y'all feeling all right and nobody's not sick or anything, right?"

"Y'all who?"

"You and Fancy."

I pushed my chair back. I knew my brother. He never came through the front door when he had something bad to tell me. " 'Fess up, Emile," I demanded. " 'Fess up right the hell now."

He sighed and downed half of the red Kool-Aid in his glass before speaking.

"I've been thinking about this for a while now, man, and it

took me a whole week to decide how to approach you. But there's no easy way for me to say this, Kevin, so I'ma just go ahead and say it straight."

I nodded, waiting.

"I've been hearing some crazy shit and I'm concerned. I'm not saying I believe all that I'm hearing, but I am concerned. Concerned about you and Fancy."

I chuckled. "C'mon, man. Fancy is a fine woman, and people are jealous. They always talk about us. Besides, you don't even like my wife. She's a sister, remember? Why would you be worrying about her?"

He shrugged. "It's no secret how I feel about women like Fancy. You know that, Kevin. And that's not to say I'm knocking your wife or your choices in women either. You do you and I do me, right?"

I held out my hands. "When have you ever given my woman any credit for anything? You can't see past the fact that she's got brown skin and a big ass. You trying to tell me something about my woman that I don't know?"

"Well . . ." He squirmed. "Now that you mention it, maybe I am."

"Like?"

"Like for the longest time I thought the same thing that everybody else on this base probably thinks."

"And what's that?"

He mimicked. " 'Poor Kevin. Married to the biggest skeezer this side of the Atlantic. His wife is such a skank she humps strange men in his bed when he's not at home.' "

I froze. "You don't know what you're talking about, Emile."

He dismissed my 'tude.

"Come on, man. Your wife is humping in the club half naked on Friday nights! She has a lunchtime gig going on out of your crib, Kevin. You can't tell me somebody hasn't tried to pull your coat about her at least a million times."

"What me and my wife got going is nobody else's business."

"But now I'm hearing that maybe it's not really Fancy who's out there, Kevin."

I just looked at him.

"I'm hearing that it's you who's the swinger. That Fancy might just be a victim."

I felt like rushing his ass. "A victim? You accusing me of something?"

He sighed and scooted his chair closer to the table. "Rumor has it," he said quietly, "that you're out there fucking around on your wife."

"And who are you? The fucking morals police?"

"Nah." He shook his head quickly. "Fuck on, baby. Fuck on. I'm just your brother, Chief. If you want to get you some ass on the side, that's your business. The only reasons I'm stepping to you is because I'm worried about your career, and about who you're supposedly getting your ass from."

I pushed my plate back and put both elbows on the table. This fool was gonna make me kick his ass like we were ten years old again. "Listen, Emile. My career is solid, and I don't get in your personal business, so don't you get in mine. You're just mad because Sparkle got your kiosk closed down. Don't take that shit out on Fancy, because she didn't have nothing to do with it."

His voice softened. "Forget that damn cart. I can get another one any day of the week. It's you who I'm worried about. I hear you've been hanging with some questionable brothers, man. Some guys who swing"—he flipped his hand back and forth—"both ways."

I jumped indignant, my mind racing. "What kind of shit is that for you to say? A niggah like me? As much as I love pussy?" I snorted like he was a fool for real. "I probably get more trim in a week than you've had in your whole sorry life. I can't even believe you brought no shit like that to me. You ought to know me better than that."

"I'm not saying what you do or what you don't do, man. But you're in the army, and I love you. I don't know if the rumors are true, but I don't wanna see nothing happen to you, Chief. In or out of uniform. I'm just asking you to protect yourself," he said softly, then added, "And if you're doing what they say you're doing . . . you might want to think about protecting your wife."

"My wife is straight, homes! You don't know a thing about being married or how to make a marriage work. You ain't never worried about Fancy before, and don't start now neither."

Emile nodded and wiped his hands. "You got me there. I don't have a wife. But if I did have one, I doubt if I'd be bringing any stray cats home to fuck her."

I stood up so fast my chair fell over. "I'm gonna forget what you just said, Emile. 'Cause if I don't, brother or no brother, I'ma have to tighten you up."

He had the nerve to smile up at me. "That *Don't ask, don't tell* thing doesn't always work. You might want to wrap that thing up when you leave the house and while you're at it, have a little more respect for yourself as the first sergeant of my company."

"What's with all that *Don't ask, don't tell* shit? Emile, you know me better than that! I am *not* gay. And as for my wife? I do what I wanna do. If I say fuck it, Fancy fucks it. If I say suck it, she sucks it. I got her freaked like that. And she loves it."

Emile grew quiet for a long moment, then asked softly, "Goddamn, Chief. Teesha and Lil Mama fuck you up that bad?"

"You always were on my dick, Emile. You fat, jealous motherfucker."

He stood up and faced me squarely, then picked up his hat. His eyes were sad as he grabbed the last rib off my plate. "Handle your business, brother. Okay? Just handle your business."

CHAPTER 26

FANCY

Evening Ecstasy

*I*t was late Friday afternoon and I was exhausted. I was just about to shut my computer down for the weekend when an e-mail alert flashed across the screen.

It was from Kevin's AKO military e-mail account and the subject line read: EVENING ECSTASY. I shivered before opening it, partly out of dread, and I'll be honest, partly out of excitement too. I clicked on the envelope icon on my screen and waited for it to open. Kevin's e-mails had been coming much more frequently since the morning he'd caught me making love to Mica. And I still couldn't understand his reaction. He'd been trying to get me to fool around with other women for the longest time, and when I finally did and actually found myself liking it, he snapped like a lunatic.

"Why that bitch, Fancy?" he had screamed at me. "Why'd you have to screw around with that perverted-ass bitch?"

All I could do was lay there on the floor and cry. I didn't understand it myself and I didn't have the right words to explain that to him. He was the one who'd picked her out in the first place! Sure, he'd told me he was through swinging with Derek and Mica, but I didn't know there was bad blood between them. I figured he'd simply lost interest in them as a couple and was ready to move on to the next challenge.

I guess the idea that I would actually sleep with someone, male or female, without involving him was too much for my husband to bear. But Kevin made it clear that had it been anyone other than Mica, he wouldn't have been half as angry.

Of course he tormented me for weeks. Rubbed my mistake in my face until I felt lower than a dog. "How did she taste, Fancy? I thought you weren't into women?"

And what could I say in return? How could I deny what I'd done? I simply kept quiet and did my best to appease him as much as I could. I had apologized until I was blue in the face, but Kevin refused to let it go. Instead, he fed my humiliation with a series of back-to-back e-mails, each one proposing a new scenario, each one setting us up with a new woman. A woman my husband had chosen. A woman he expected me to make love to.

"Don't be shy," he'd whispered one night, about a week after catching me with Mica. We were having a candlelit threesome and Kevin was commanding me to do the most intimate things to the strange woman who lay spread-eagle on the rug before me.

"You did it before, so go ahead and do it now."

And I did. Without even asking her name, I made love to her in the most personal of ways as my husband urged me on, watching over my shoulder as he took me from behind.

Okay, I'm sure you want to know. Did I enjoy it? Simply

put, yes. I had three orgasms, the first one ripping through me the moment I tasted her on my lips. Am I proud of it? No. I'm a firm believer that not everything that's good to you is good for you. Just because I've discovered that I can get off on women doesn't mean I'm all of a sudden gay. I get off on men too. The way I figured, I was just a sensual person who had some deep sexual needs, but everything has its limits, and after the shame of getting busted with my head in Mica's lap I probably wouldn't have gone to bed with another woman on my own ever again in life. If it wasn't for Kevin.

His e-mail finally popped open and I began to read:

Sweet Fancy,
You've been such a good girl lately that Daddy wants you to have a little fun tonight. I booked us a room at the DoubleTree Hotel. Be there by seven.

My eyes skimmed the list of instructions he'd provided, and despite the sordid nature of it all, I felt myself growing hot inside.

I printed out his e-mail and shut down my computer. It was going to be a long night. I had planned to spend the evening with Godfrey Baker, Becky Ann's friend. He and his wife, Paula, were the most positive black couple I'd ever met, and under Godfrey's tutelage I was beginning to see the world through a new set of lenses. But of course fulfilling those plans was now out of the question. The hotel Kevin had picked out was way across town, right near the Greyhound bus station. I'd have to take a bath and change clothes in a hurry because he certainly wouldn't appreciate my being late.

Staring at the framed photo of my husband hanging among others I'd taken on my wall, I emptied my water bottle into the pot of the lone plant sitting on my desk, and after gathering my personal belongings I waved goodbye to my co-workers and climbed in my car to begin the long, traffic-filled drive back to Fort Dix.

FANCY

Three Inches More

*S*o how did it go with Phil?" I asked.

Sparkle and I were browsing through Macy's, looking for a dress that I could wear to my art show next weekend. I was excited about the evening and more than grateful to Becky Ann for the photography hookup, but right now life was hectic for me on all fronts.

Over the past couple of weeks there'd been a rash of new HIV cases diagnosed between Fort Monmouth and Fort Dix. The clinic staff attributed it to the fact that there were twice as many soldiers being activated and inprocessed, and since a deployment to Iraq was highly probable for most of them, DNA samples had to be collected and HIV tests performed en masse.

To top it off, I'd been snapping loads of photos for the upcoming show and trying to get them all developed while keeping my husband satisfied in and out of bed. It wasn't surprising that I'd had very little time for socializing and hadn't seen Sparkle in more than two weeks. I stood behind her and watched as she slid dress after dress along the metal rack, frowning as she searched for what she considered just the right look.

"How do you *think* it went?" she snapped over her shoulder, pausing to study a short red number that was cut low in the front and had tiny shoulder straps.

I shrugged. She'd seemed evil and distracted from the moment I picked her up at her apartment. She hadn't said more than three sentences in the car the whole way to the mall, and I could have sworn I smelled beer on her breath even though it was only eleven in the morning. The good thing was, we'd been in the mall for over an hour and she hadn't made a single comment about the brothers and their white women, and we'd seen plenty. I'd been bracing myself for her verbal assault on them and even on their kids, and despite the fact that this was a very diverse mall she hadn't uttered a single negative word.

"Beats me," I finally said and waited for her reply. Her back was to me so I couldn't really see her face, and her voice hadn't betrayed anything either. But I knew Sparkle, and if she had been the least bit pleased by her date with Phil she would have been shouting it from the rooftop.

She didn't respond.

I sighed. Obviously my girl wanted me to pull the info out of her ear, but my own life was falling apart. Who had time for Sparkle's drama?

"Okay, Sparkle. We haven't talked in over a week, and since I wasn't there aiming a flashlight I have no idea how your evening with Phil turned out. Why don't you just tell me?"

I tried to position myself so that I could look into her eyes, but she purposely turned her back on me again.

"I shouldn't have to tell you shit, Fancy. You know me. You know what kind of cookies I like to bake."

"Oh, Lordy. Please tell me you didn't. Tell me you didn't take that nice man home with you and fuck his brains out on your living room floor."

"No." Her voice was cold. "I did not fuck him on the living room floor, Fancy." She picked up another dress. "It was more like the backseat of his car, the lounge chair on the front patio, and twice in the foyer by my front door."

I grabbed her arm and pulled her around until she faced me.

"Girl, are you serious?" A moment later I saw pain flood her eyes and I knew that she was. "Well damn. Was it that bad? Bad enough to make you want to cry? I mean, shit! How weak could it have been if you kept going back for more?"

She studied her manicured nails. "That's just it, Fancy. It wasn't weak. It was great. Powerful. Exciting. It was all that and three inches more. It was probably the best sex I've had in ten years."

I threw up my hands. "So what's the problem, then? You got your head slammed good. I'd have thought you'd be walking around bragging and doing the cabbage patch. So when are you going back for seconds? Or should I say thirds?"

"Never."

"Well then, the dick couldn't have been that good."

"Oh, it was good. But I've had about four other dicks since then. No biggie. They all do just about the same thing."

"What?" My mouth was wide open.

"They all make you come, stupid."

"No, I mean what about you having four other dicks since just last week?"

"Yep."

I blushed and shuddered like I was some virgin.

"Girl, go on back to Phil. Having great sex with one man beats mediocre sex with four any day. Stick with Phil."

She shrugged, tossing her blond curls. "Can't. I cut him off. Told him to lose my phone number and to stay away from my apartment."

I snatched a dress from the rack even though it was ankle-length and mint green. "Sweetie, you're tripping. You like Phil and he's good in the sack. Why in the world would you do that?"

Sparkle frowned. " 'Cause," she whispered.

I stared, clutching the ugly green dress. " 'Cause what?"

She finally looked at me. " 'Cause I like him too much. 'Cause he's a gentleman and the most thoughtful lover I've ever known. 'Cause he's down to earth and a whole lot of fun. 'Cause he's generous and honest and treats me like I'm special. 'Cause he—"

"What, Sparkle?" I demanded, tired of her silliness. I was just waiting for the *W* word to come past her lips. I was gonna let her have it big time. " 'Cause what?"

" 'C-c-cause. . . ," she stuttered, tripping on the bomb that would blow up her lips. " 'Cause . . . 'cause he wants me to meet his family."

I stared at her. "And?"

"And he wants to meet mine too."

I was still staring. "And?"

"And?"

"Yeah. And? You act like he asked you to commit a crime or something."

She mumbled something smart under her breath and swished over to another rack. I followed her, totally confused.

"I can see how he'd want to get to know you better, but I didn't know you guys were so tight that he'd want to meet your people."

"It was more like a dare," she muttered. "He asked me to come to dinner at his house, and then dared me to take him home to my folks. Picture that. Me bringing a white man home to my Aunt Viv. It ain't happening, girl. We don't roll like that in my family."

I couldn't believe what I was hearing. "Oh, so you mean to tell me it's fine for your Aunt Viv to lay up in her fat brownstone and make soup with that fine niggah Deebo, a man young enough to be her grandson, but you can't spend time with a man who respects you and really likes you just because he's not black?"

She looked at me like I had fangs. "You're damn right. Besides, Deebo got lucky. Aunt Viv looks good for her age. Better than most of those stretched-out young girls who blow up after having just one baby. It doesn't really matter whether the bone she's sucking on is young or whether it's sprouting gray hairs. It's still black."

"That shit is too ridiculous," I said, losing my patience. "I'm pro-black too and I really do love my people, but idiots like you and Emile take this race thing to an unhealthy level."

"Don't be comparing me to Emile," Sparkle snapped. "We don't have a damn thing in common."

"Yeah, you do," I said snidely. "Both of you are sad and

confused. You both have race issues and you both date white people."

She practically screamed. "I don't have race issues, Fancy!"

"Then answer me this. Do you really like Phil?"

"Yeah." Without hesitation. "I really do."

"Is he a good man? Is he honest with you and does he treat you with respect?"

"Yeah, hell yeah, and big-time."

I rolled my eyes toward the ceiling in frustration. "Then I don't see what the problem is. Your Aunt Viv doesn't live in your bedroom."

"She doesn't have to. Even with a body of water between us she can still read me like a book. Dig this. Not only did she call me while Phil was there, not two hours after he left my apartment Aunt Viv was ringing my phone off the hook again. Talking about she had some crazy dream about me being wrapped up in a white cloud." Sparkle pressed her hand to her breasts, pained. "That shit freaked me out, Fancy. It was almost like she'd cold busted me in the buck with him. Almost like she knew."

I hated to ask, but I knew she needed to tell me. "So what did you do?"

"I cut him off cold," she said miserably. "I got scared and panicked and called about ten kneegrows. Me and Phil had planned to get together again later on that day, but by the time he called I'd already set up dates with five other men."

"Damn," I said, amazed.

"Damn is right. Because not only did I dig all the way down to the bottom of the skeezer barrel for those cast-off kneegrows I'd picked up after Lonnie got married, it only took me a quick second to realize that as black as they were, not one of them could do justice to the way Phil laid it down. In or out of bed."

I nodded. I could dig it. "Then call him up, Sparkle. Get on the phone and tell him you're sorry and see if you can get back with him."

"Been there, done that."

"And?"

She pursed her lips tight, then said, "And it didn't work. For a white boy, Phil has a lot of heart. He said he adores me, but he still wasn't having it. Told me to either get comfortable enough with our relationship to take him out of the closet to my family and to the rest of the world, or he could settle for us just being friends."

I picked up a slinky wine-colored dress and held it up, admiring the shimmering material and wondering if I had a pair of shoes at home that would match. "Well, girlfriend," I said, trying to sound comforting. "I think you need to make another phone call."

"To Phil?"

I waved my hand. "Nah, nah. Not yet. Don't call him again. Not just yet anyway, because you almost messed that good thing up. Put in a call to your Aunt Viv first, Sparkle. Get her old behind on the line and let her know you're coming over for dinner. Tell her to round up the posse: Deebo, Zebulon, Glodean, and those cute little twins who remind me of gigantic packs of fast-food condiments. Tell your auntie to get in that kitchen and scrap up a meal that will make you wanna slap your Nana. Tell her you're feeling really good and you want to share something wonderful with her over dinner. And don't forget to warn her that you're bringing a friend."

CHAPTER 28

SPARKLE

High Hopes

*O*kay. Y'all know me. I believe in giving people what they want. Well, Phil had asked for it and now he was about to get it. He wanted me to take him out of the closet, fine. I'd snatch him outta that closet and put him on center stage so fast it would make his goddamn hair nap up.

Fancy was right. That mixing-the-race phobia I'd been carrying around all these years belonged to Aunt Viv, not to me. It hadn't truly become mine until Lonnie dumped me for that crackish-looking white girl.

But Phil was one good brother, white or black. He treated Miss Sparkle like the queen she was, but without all that drop-jaw awe that some men seemed to develop in my presence. I mean, yeah. I'm all that, but damn. You just don't know how hard it is to be the only royal somebody in a room full of peons, and if I wasn't attracting men who slobbered at the sound of my name, then I attracted the opposite assholes like Lonnie who had trouble remembering who the queen was even with a cue card.

I called Aunt Viv and told her to expect me and a friend for dinner. You know she tried to be all nosy and get his name out of me over the phone, but I wasn't going there. Everything about Phil was gonna be a big surprise. I just hoped she didn't drop dead the moment she saw him.

I knew Phil was dying to meet my family and for me to meet his, but he still tried to play hard to get when I showed up at his office and asked him if we could talk.

"Sure, Sparkle," he'd said, taking me into his office and closing the door. The army had cracked down on relationships between officers and enlisted personnel who weren't married, so we had to be careful. I stood there admiring his space with all the framed diplomas and certificates on the walls. I admired Phil too. He looked pressed out and handsome in his starched uniform. "You know how much I enjoy talking to you," he reminded me, "but before we take things any further you need to be sure you're ready to have a real relationship with me."

I walked over to the window and looked out at a detail of young soldiers who were raking leaves. "I've been in plenty of relationships, Phil. I think I know what I'm ready for."

"I'm not too sure about that, Sparkle."

I turned around and saw that he was leaning against his desk, his arms crossed.

"Why do you say that?"

"Because you're embarrassed to be seen with me."

I was cold-busted so you know I straight showed out!

"What! Me, embarrassed? Get out of here! How could you

even fix your mouth to say something crazy like that, Phillip?"

He shrugged. "Easy. I don't know any other woman who would rather stay home with me and play backgammon than go out on a date and spend my money."

"We went on a date!" I protested hotly. "I even introduced you to my company commander. We hung out with him and his white girlfriend!"

"See? That's what I mean. Why'd you have to go and mention her race?"

I played it cool. "Get used to it. Black people always notice race. America raised us that way. But black men like my commander deliberately choose women outside of their race, and that burns me up. Any old piece of trailer trash will do, just as long as she's not black. Self-hater!"

"But look how that affects you! Why should his choice in women bother you so much, Sparkle?" he asked gently. "Whether he deliberately stays away from blacks or just happened to fall in love with someone white, your commander's denial of self shouldn't speak to who you are as a black woman, or as a person for that matter."

"So what are you trying to say?"

"I'm saying," he said, calmly crossing the room to where I stood, "that this—" He rubbed the back of his hand against the back of mine. "—is just skin. It's just skin, baby. That's all. Mine shields my muscles and my tissues the same way yours does. If you cut either of us, we'll both bleed."

"That's true," I admitted softly and stepped closer to him. The starch in our uniforms made crinkle noises as I pressed myself against him, loving how I felt in his arms. "But we're still different."

He smacked me on the ass.

"We are!" I laughed, grinding against him and grabbing his crotch. "You have a thing-thing, and I have a thang-thang!"

Laughing with me, Phil allowed me another brief hug and then gently broke the contact. "Seriously, though," he said. "I want to be with you, Sparkle. I really do. But I need you to be totally confident about your feelings for me. I know relationships like ours aren't always easy, but if both of us can get honest, then maybe we can make this work so that it can lead to something more."

"So basically," I said, smirking and putting my hands on my hips, "you just ain't gonna be my undercover plaything no more, huh?"

"Nope. Not gonna be your plaything, baby."

"And you're tired of living in that closet with the rest of my skeleton bones."

"You got it, baby. Open up the closet door and let the bones fall where they may."

———

PHIL and I drove to New York on Saturday evening to have dinner with his family. The only reason I'd agreed to go was because I was sure those Italians were gonna show their behinds real good and bless Phil out for bringing a black girl home. No problem. If they showed their ass I'd show my toe, and that would be the end of that *let's-go-meet-each-other's-family* mess he was stuck on.

You know I went up there as fly as all outdoors. Made up and fragranced to the max. My clothes were perfect, my hair was blow-dried and freshly curled, my legs were slamming, and my smile was about two hundred watts strong.

Phil had been shocked when he came by to pick me up, and for a moment I thought the cat had his tongue.

"You look . . ."

I knew exactly how I looked. Bronzed skin glowing, diamonds sparkling, tailored skirt riding my thighs, and matching sleeveless vest with a low-cut back . . . I waited patiently as his eyes took in the splendor that was me.

"Stunning, baby," he finally said. "You look stunning."

That was the whole idea. Get them to focus on how I looked, and not on how I felt. Of course I had white girlfriends and had been around white people before, but this was different. I was on the arm of one of their own, and even though Phil was relaxed and easy during the turnpike drive, I fought hard not to let my nerves go bad.

Phil's house was smaller than I'd expected, although it was in a very nice area of the Bronx. To my surprise, I got hugs from everyone the minute I hit the door. Everyone except Granny, that is.

"And this is my grandmother," Phil said, leading me toward a wrinkled old lady who was propped up in a wheelchair in front of the television. "Granny is deaf, and she can't see that well either."

That's a lie, I wanted to tell him. Granny had them all bamboozled. She could see good enough to know that I was a black woman, and she didn't like it one bit. She sat there dribbling into her bib and giving me the evil eye, and there was no doubt in my mind that she wanted my black booty out of the big house and back into the fields where she thought I belonged.

Phil's parents, Meg and John Mercorella, were really nice, though, and so were his sisters, Patsy and Lisa. They were all smiles and compliments, and one of his little nieces was so cute she tripped me out.

"Wow," she took her thumb out of her mouth long enough to say. "You're a movie star, aren't you? I think I've seen you on television before."

Yep, Miss Sparkle had them all sprung, and it didn't seem to matter at all that I was black. They made me feel welcome and comfortable, and if the food wasn't so bad it would have been a perfect night. Oh, don't front! Y'all know white folks can't cook! Even the nice ones. Yeah, yeah, yeah. I know Italians can throw down on some ziti and lasagna, and don't even mention the spaghetti and meatballs, but the meal they cooked for me must not have been their specialty because everything on my plate tasted the same! My steak tasted just like my potatoes and just like my corn on the cob. Hard and crunchy. And not a drop of salt or seasoning on anything!

I ate as much of it as I could, but on the way home Phil swung by a pizza shop without me even asking, and we both threw down on two sausage Sicilian slices with extra cheese, so there!

Okay, turnabout *is* fair play, and the following weekend we were scheduled to have dinner with my crew. Of course my day started off messed up from the jump.

We were due at Aunt Viv's place in Westchester at six that evening, so I made a hair appointment with my girl Shonnie in Philly for 10:00 A.M. Now, I know all about making a late entrance 'cause I've made quite a few of them myself. But how about Shonnie's tail wasn't there when I arrived and the girl who was filling in for her didn't show up until after eleven?

If she had parted my hair she'da seen a patch of pisstivity on my scalp!

"Where's Shonnie?" I said as she motioned me toward the chair.

"Oh," she answered, shaking out a plastic smock and chewing a big-ass hunk of Bazooka. I knew it was Bazooka 'cause I could smell it coming all out of her mouth.

"Uhm. Shonnie ain't coming in today 'cause her baby's daddy got stabbed up in a club on the west side where he works part-time as a bouncer. He got another job that he hustles in the mornings down on Chestnut, but some skank got him caught up in a trick bag over some bogus child support charge that don't make no damn sense since he's black as tar and that baby looks just like Eminem, but it was either feed the little yellow crumb snatcher or take his ass to jail, so he got him another hustle on the side but his new baby's mama is one of them real psycho hos who gets a little dick and lets it go to her head, 'cause tricks like her don't just want the money she wanna *be* with a niggah, even though she knew he had a woman when she was going down on him, so now he's laying up in the hospital all stabbed up and Shonnie had to go up there and see 'bout him, so she won't be coming in today and probably not tomorrow neither, but don't worry. I'ma hook you up. Your shit's gonna be butter."

I looked at her ten-inch curled-under roller coaster–looking fingernails and the two square inches of bald scalp around her edges and shook my head.

"Uh-uh, boo." I grabbed my purse and headed toward the door. "I came all the way from Jersey, but nah. I appreciate the offer, but I don't let just anybody play in my hair."

She broke. "*Your* hair? You mean that nappy shit sticking up outta your weave that's only"—somehow she snapped her fingers—"*that* long? You think I ain't good enough to slap a perm on them peas?"

Oh? So she wanted to bring a little 'tude? Well Miss Sparkle hails from Brooklyn and we sling mad 'tude too!

I turned around at the door. "I'm not saying you ain't good enough, boo. But you got some pretty raggedy-looking trees up in your own damn forest. You sure as hell ain't jacking up mine."

"Skank!" she hollered. "You ain't all that, with your fake everything! Take your stuck-up ass on back to Jersey to whoever glued in those wack-ass tracks!"

Okay. So we know I didn't get my hair done, and as ghetto as sister-girl was, she was right. It was way past time for a perm, and my hair was kinking up something awful. Blow-drying those two inches of new growth at the roots just wasn't getting it anymore. Oh, well. My people would be too busy examining Phil to pay too much attention to me. I was going just as I was, naps and all.

But my hair proved to be the last thing I should have been worried about. I jetted over to the lot where I'd parked my Z, and dug in my purse to pay the attendant, and that's when I discovered my car keys were missing.

"Yo, lady," the attendant said, shaking his head as I beat up my purse. He looked young enough to be my son. "Your keys are in your car, yo."

Holding my wallet between my knees and my makeup bag under my chin, I looked up at him, ready to go off. "What?"

"You looking for your keys, right?"

"No, stupid. I'm looking for your tip! Shouldn't you be in school somewhere trying to get a diploma?"

He put his hands in his pocket and grinned. "You fine and you funny too. For real, though. Your car. The keys are inside 'cause you never turned it off. It's still running."

I looked across the lot and felt my heart sink. Stuffing everything back inside my bag, I jetted over to my car and beat my hand on the windshield. "Damn! Damn, damn, damn, damn!"

"Don't worry yourself like that, pretty," he said. "I got a cousin who can stick a hanger down that crack near the window and pop the lock. He works in an indoor garage over by the mall. You want me to call him?"

I whipped out my cell phone and dialed Phil and asked him to call a locksmith. Thirty minutes later I was back in my car. A hundred dollars lighter and with naps still in my hair.

DINNER was a disaster.

By the time we got to Westchester I was even more spazzed out than I had been earlier in the day. I'd lost one of my contact lenses when it fell into the sink, my period started, and with it came two juicy zits on my chin, and to top it off traffic had been really heavy during the drive and my blood pressure went up so high I was ready to get out on the turnpike and beat somebody's ass.

"You gonna be okay?" Phil asked as we sat outside Aunt Viv's house, preparing to go inside. All the way up I'd been raging like a madwoman. Cursing out cars that weren't going fast enough, pissed at people who couldn't stay in their lanes, generally having a high-level case of ultra road rage, and I wasn't even driving. And now Phil laid his hand on my thigh, and just his touch seemed to make me feel better. I inhaled deeply and nodded.

Aunt Viv's house was one of those showpieces where you didn't dare to bring your kids. She had all kinds of expensive, fragile carvings and delicate pieces everywhere, so why she was allowing Man'naise and Mustard to run all over her front parlor like a pair of wild animals was anybody's guess.

I had already hipped Phil to my family as much as I could, but for his sake I prayed that they'd at least treat him nicely, even if they didn't like him. But did any of them respect my choice in a man? Hell naw. You know them heffahs cut up left and right around that table. I busted Glodean sniffing around Phil on the sly. *Move it, bitch!* I wanted to yell. Wasn't no damn baloney up in his hair. And Zebulon almost got her ass whipped for whispering to me during dinner. Getting all up in my business wanting to know if Phil had a little pink dick.

But Aunt Viv was the worst. Bad enough she'd peeped through her peephole when we rang the doorbell and refused to let us in, even after I told her Phil was my friend, that he was the date I'd mentioned. After I finally convinced her that he wasn't a serial killer who had snatched me up outside and wanted to come in and stab up the whole household, she went ahead and told Deebo to unlock the door, but she stared at Phil for the longest time. Looking him up and down, probably wondering what the hell kind of drugs he had hooked me on to make me bring some white boy home.

She kept trying to get me alone all night.

"Sparkle, come in here and watch this chicken for me, baby."

I dragged Phil everywhere. Even made him walk me down the hall to the bathroom when I had to pee.

"You got that mulldoon trained," Zeb said, trying to give me a high five. "Following you around just like a little puppy. Go 'head, girl. Work his ass before he works you."

I just looked at her with her yellow behind. Miss Sparkle was fine, yes, but I would scrap her out in a minute, Aunt Viv or no.

Deebo was the only one who acted like he had any sense. Everybody else would barely open their mouths to speak to Phil, but when I introduced him to Deebo, Phil reached out for a handshake and Deebo ignored the hand, giving Phil a big hug instead, respecting him like the man he was.

The grand finale of the evening came when we were clearing the dinner table. I was bending over scraping my plate into the garbage when Glodean tried to get brand-new.

"Damn, Sparkle, you must be really confused."

I turned around. "About what?"

"Your identity, girl. Not to mention them damn roots of yours. First you sell out on the brothers, and now you letting your shit go. Look at you. Your face done broke out, all the green is gone out your eyes, and I ain't never seen your hair this jacked." She laughed out loud. "Peas and carrots all up in your kitchen!"

I mushed that bitch right in the face. With my dinner plate.

It was on. Westchester was the location, but Brooklyn was in the house. Of course that jealous heffah tried to scratch up my face, but I was ready for that. Heffahs had been going for my face since I was ten.

Now, all that stuff you might have heard about me shamming out of PT is true. I wasn't a runner, okay, but I was damn sure a scrapper. I slapped Glodean's hands away and yoked her around the neck. Before I knew it I was slamming her head into Aunt Viv's stove and slinging her tail around that kitchen like the two-cent ho she was. Zebulon started screaming, but she didn't jump in it. She knew better. I'd taken Zeb down when we were seventeen, and that was the last time she'd tried to run up on me.

Phil and Deebo got in between us and tried to break us up. Glodean took advantage and swung around Deebo and straight at Phil, catching him on the jaw. I charged her ass again, punching her in the face with about four combinations. She pulled away from me and ended up falling to the floor, and that's when I grabbed the back of her shirt, snatching her clean out of it and exposing one of her breasts.

"Goddamnit!" I heard Aunt Viv cussing as Deebo got in between us again. "Don't y'all tear my damn house up! Sparkle, what the hell is wrong with you?"

"Me?" I yelled, huffing and puffing. I pushed my hair back and adjusted my sweater. Glodean was hiding behind Deebo and her sister, talking shit with her sad little titty hanging out, pretending like she wanted to get next to me.

"Move, Zeb," I said, beckoning Glodean on. "Let her go, Deebo. Pay your way over here, Glo. And I guarantee you, I'll pay your way back."

Aunt Viv got all nasty. "Shut up, Sparkle! Ain't nobody doing nothing to nobody up in here. If anybody passes another lick it's gonna be me!"

I looked at Phil, then turned away and sucked my teeth. "I ain't gotta put up with this shit," I muttered under my breath, tucking my weave back into a roll. "Bunch of stupid bitches." I grabbed Phil's hand and stormed out of the kitchen.

"What was that?" Aunt Viv hollered.

"You heard her, Aunt Viv," Zeb quipped now that she was safely out of the slap zone. "She called us all stupid bitches."

"Let's go," I told Phil, taking our jackets out of the front closet.

"Yeah, go!" Glodean yelled from the living room. "And take your funky little white boy with you!"

And then Phil did something that made it all better. Just as I opened my mouth to curse her slam out, Phil pulled me into his arms and kissed me, muffling my curses and showing me with his tenderness that this was a battle that I didn't need to fight.

I sighed when the kiss was over, and suddenly there was no fight left in me. I walked calmly into the kitchen, ignoring Zeb, but keeping my eye on Glodean, who had slunk over to the sink and slid a butcher knife out of the rack. My aunt stood near the window huddled in Deebo's arms, a look of deep pain on her face.

"Thanks for dinner, Aunt Viv," I said, kissing her cheek. "I'm sorry for fighting in your house. Matter of fact, I'm sorry for coming. Good night."

I walked out of the kitchen and kissed Man'naise and Mustard, then let Phil take my hand again. I heard my aunt crying as I unlocked the door. "We had such high hopes for that girl!"

I let that noise bounce right off me. I had a few high hopes of my own, and one of them was walking right beside me, holding my hand.

CHAPTER 29

FANCY

Raunchy? Right On!

*I*t was fifteen minutes before showtime and my stomach was in knots. Sparkle and I were in the ladies' room at the gallery and I sat trembling before a vanity mirror as she put some last-minute fussing on my hair.

"I swear, if I had a cigarette right now, I'd smoke it."

"You don't smoke, Fancy. Besides, it ain't tobacco you need. Only thing that'll calm your nerves at this point is some good weed or some good bone."

"Grow up, Sparkle," I said sharply. "I'm over here sweating down to my panty hose and you're making stupid comments."

She paused with the comb in midair. "What's the big problem, Fancy? This is your third major show and that one you did for *National Geographic* was a breeze. You know you're a gifted photographer. Your entire portfolio sold out in less than an hour at your second show. Relax, girl. Everything will go great tonight."

I'd been clasping my hands together to stop them from

shaking, but now I waved them around in the air. "It's not the sales that I'm worried about, Sparkle. It's the industry critiques that will be in next week's papers. Remember that nasty write-up I got after my first little trade show? The one that was held at the outdoor bazaar? They called my nude shots raunchy."

"They who?"

"They the critics. They don't always publish their names."

Sparkle shrugged, dismissing my concerns. "I don't remember the write-up, but I do remember the cash. You brought in beaucoup dollars, Fancy. When you're turning over that kind of bank you don't have to worry about what the critics say."

"No," I said, shaking my head. "That's not entirely true, even though I've been told that high sales usually accompany poor write-ups, and good critiques sometimes equal mediocre sales."

Sparkle rolled her eyes at me in the mirror. "So which do you care about more? What the rejects say, or what the real people buy? Seems to me that maybe the critics are out of touch with what the people actually like. I'd much rather have a critic talk shit about my work than have my customer base dry up. Plus, most critics are wannabe artists anyway. They critique the shit they can't create. They're probably so jealous they can't tell the difference between raunchy and realistic. Haters, girl. Just haters to the max. When they say raunchy, you say right on! Base your success on your bottom line, Fancy. As long as the cash registers keep cha-chinging, tell all those anonymous closet photographers who couldn't get their photos in a show next to yours to save their grandmama's life to kiss your jiggly ass."

———

THE show was turning out to be more than a success. I was so grateful to Sparkle, and to Emile's girlfriend Becky Ann too, who had come out earlier in the evening and purchased a few prints just to support me. The networking I'd done and the connections I'd made as a result of her hooking me up with Godfrey had really panned out.

Godfrey and his wife had taken me fully under their photographic wings, nurturing me and building my confidence. It was only through the lens of a camera, Godfrey determined as he pointed out minute details in my shots, that people like me could see the world for what it truly was. Working with him and Paula and watching the patient, loving way they responded to each other and how effortlessly Paula shared her man's time with another woman just amazed me. She had no reservations about the hours Godfrey spent helping me to "see" my subjects, and thus myself, for what we really were. Paula had no reservations because none were needed. She had a good black man and she knew it. Both of them honored their committed relationship and held their boundaries sacred, and not only was I grateful for their professional expertise, I was also grateful for the concept of balanced love that they had brought to my life. A view of the world and of relationships that, with Godfrey's encouragement, I could almost understand.

And Sparkle was right, I determined, shrugging away my fears. Forget the critics and their write-ups. It felt great to hear the wonderful praise my work generated and to see the prints disappear from the walls. A fair number of prints were selling to magazines and to online stock companies that later resold the images for a nominal fee. Unlike most artists, I didn't photograph a particular genre. I didn't specialize in wildlife, or architecture, or the like. My tastes and interests were broad and eclectic, which is probably why the critics didn't know what to do with me. Instead of giving an honest assessment of my individual shots, they constantly compared one set of shots to the next, even when it was obvious that there was no comparison to be made. It seemed they preferred that I go along with the status quo and make my round self fit into a square hole, but I refused to limit myself that way.

Tonight, as usual, I'd put out a mixture of shots that provoked a hodgepodge of emotions. There were photos ranging from the agony and desolation experienced by young AIDS orphans, to scarred and disfigured women who'd undergone radical mastectomies and had learned to love and accept their bodies. There were also a fair number of black-and-whites I'd shot of nude couples making love in various poses, the rapture on their faces clearly depicting the pleasure their bodies were experiencing.

We were about an hour away from closing when Sparkle tugged on my arm and whispered in my ear. "Who the fugg is *that*?"

I glanced over my shoulder and my stomach dropped all the way to the floor.

"Girl," she continued, "that is one phine-ass kneegrow with a capital pee aitch!"

Derek looked really good, I had to admit it. And as I knew from experience, he had a knack for knockin' boots. But it wasn't the sight of him that had my heart galloping in my chest. It was seeing Mica standing next to him that made me feel like I'd gotten caught with my hand in a cookie jar.

She'd called me several times since that morning we'd gotten busted, and each time I'd told her with no uncertainty that I simply couldn't see her again. Even behind my husband's back. My dismissal seemed to make her want me even more, and the last time we'd spoken I had to get nasty and threaten to have her charged with stalking me by telephone.

Before I could compose myself, Derek saw me and he and Mica rushed over.

"Well, hello, Fancy!" He reached for me and kissed me lightly on the cheek. "You're looking lovely tonight and your work is really great! I had no idea you were this talented."

Sparkle was still in my ear. "Fancy girl, you know him?"

Mica smiled and we exchanged a brief hug. She looked beautiful as usual, and every single thing about her was absolutely perfect. "He's right. You look marvelous and your shots are amazing. I read in the paper that you'd be here tonight and we wanted to come out and support you and show our love."

Sparkle elbowed me so hard she almost knocked out my kidney.

"Uhm." I staggered slightly, then regained my footing. "Derek, Mica, this is my best friend, Sparkle. Sparkle, this is Derek and Mica Bates."

I stood quietly as they exchanged greetings, my stomach fluttering like crazy.

Then Mica took my arm and said, "Derek, why don't you look around and see which prints you'd like to buy? Fancy and I need to have a little girl talk, okay?"

Mica hooked her arm through mine and swung me around away from Sparkle as she pulled me toward the back of the room.

"Let go of me," I told her, jerking my arm away. "What are you doing here?"

"Trying to talk to you, Fancy. Trying to understand why you keep refusing to see me."

I took a deep breath and faced her. "Look, Mica. I'm sorry, but you saw how Kevin reacted to us being together. This isn't something my husband is comfortable with anymore. How many times do I have to explain that?"

She shook her head. "I'm not talking about the four of us together. We don't have to do that anymore. But that doesn't mean that you and I can't still get together and have fun. I told you, we don't have to meet at your house anymore." She started ticking off on her fingers. "We can meet at my house, at a hotel, at a spa, you name it, Fancy, and I can make it happen."

"Wasn't it you," I said coldly, "who told me that women like us only get together for one thing? That we saved all that bullshit bonding for our straight girlfriends?"

She didn't answer.

"Look," I said, moving in close to her. "For the last time, Mica. Leave me alone. Be gone. I was weak when I met you, but my marriage means more to me than anything in this world. Now leave."

Her lips curled in a sardonic smile as she looked me up and down. "You didn't say any of that when I was eating your pussy, did you? Or how about when you were busy licking mine?"

"Fancy?" Sparkle was in my ear again. "Are you having any problems?"

"No," I said coldly, staring at Mica.

"Oh, 'cause you know me. Heh-heh. I'll kick a bitch's ass in a minute." Sparkle laughed again. "So you know, a bitch might just wanna step off before my foot gets to jerkin'!"

"Keep your foot on the floor, girlfriend," I said calmly. "Because a bitch was just leaving. Good night, Mica."

———

YOU know Sparkle was all over me.

"Fancy Gizelle Lawson. What in the hell was that mess all about?"

We had cleaned up the showroom and were packing the unsold prints into the back of my car. I'd transported them in a large suitcase that had wheels and a handle, and it was a whole lot lighter now than it had been when I arrived. There weren't many color shots left at all, and every single one of my nude pieces had sold, so to hell with what the critics might say.

"What mess, Sparkle?"

She cocked her head to the side, as serious as cancer. "Don't play with me, Fancy. I am not in the mood. I've heard a lot of crazy things about you that I know aren't true, but that chick just said something about you licking her snatch, and I'm trying to figure out how well I really know you."

I sighed, and slammed the trunk, then unlocked our doors with the click key. "It's a long story, Sparkle. A really long story."

Sparkle climbed in on the passenger side and I waited until

she put on her seat belt before starting the car. "Well, get to talking then, because I have all night."

As we drove toward New Jersey I began telling her my sordid tale. I expected her to recoil in disgust as I revealed all the crazy things I'd done for Kevin and confessed the enjoyment that I'd also derived from most of it. But she didn't. For once Sparkle had nothing sarcastic to say and she was totally out of jokes as well. I did my best to take my share of the blame as I told her about a few of Kevin's fantasies that we'd acted out, and as the words poured from my mouth I felt so relieved that I could finally unburden myself of the shame of it all. Finally, I was sharing the hidden and perverted details about my sexual relationship with my husband, and as I listened to myself recounting some of the twisted things we'd done, I was amazed that I still had my sanity.

Sparkle's bronzed skin had turned two shades of gray. "So that's why people say all those crazy things about you. Why so many guys claim they've had you. Damn girl. Have you thought about seeing somebody? You know, getting some professional help?"

I sighed. "Yeah, I had sessions with a counselor who works downstairs from me at Monmouth for a few months, but I started feeling like she was too judgmental, you know? She seemed to be more interested in getting me to leave Kevin than in helping me learn to cope with him."

"So now you like women?" Sparkle asked. Her voice was filled with fear and disbelief and, yes, a bit of disgust as well. "That chick said you licked her coochie! Fancy girl, please tell me you're not gay."

"I'm not," I said firmly, shaking my head. "I'm not gay,

Sparkle. I'm not even bi, although I have experimented sexually with women and enjoyed it. But that's not something I'm really comfortable with continuing, even though it might be a small aspect of my sexuality."

She was quiet for a while, and then narrowed her eyes and said, "Sneaky heffah. You never told me you were a stripper, Fancy."

I nodded. "Well, I was. A damn good one at that."

She leaned toward me and I was happy to see her grin. "You did lap dances and shook your ass on a pole and all that?"

"Yep," I said. "I did it all, Sparkle. I was the best."

"So what was your club name?"

I blushed. "Freak Nasty. It sounds so ridiculous saying it now."

Sparkled howled. "Freak Nasty! Go girl. I bet you had niggahs sprung."

"That's how I got Kevin." I giggled, but my laughter quickly died when I noticed the reaction Sparkle had to the sound of my husband's name.

"You're a good person, Fancy," she said, losing her good humor. "But Kevin did you wrong. Men make us do all kinds of crazy shit we would never do on our own. Kevin led you astray, that's all. He played on your love for him, and as far as I'm concerned, that shit is foul."

I reached out and patted her hand. "I know, Sparkle. But I'm also my own person with my own mind. Kevin might have had a lot of influence on the things I did, but ultimately I'm responsible for my own actions. He's my husband and I wanted to keep him happy."

"Girl, stop. There are plenty more trolls where that niggah came from."

"Then I *needed* to keep him happy. Okay?"

She cut her eyes at me, then smirked and looked out the window. "Whatever, Fancy girl. He's your man. If you like him, I love him."

CHAPTER 30

EMILE

Lickin' That Stamp

Something had gone way wrong. At first I thought she was planning on surprising me, you know? Springing it on me at the last minute, trying to play it off. I could imagine her saying it all sweet-like too. "Emile, honey, my car won't start. Could you give me a ride?"

Of course I'd go along with the program. I'd pick her up and follow her directions with a straight face. Turn left here? Get on the highway going south? And hours later, oh, is this the exit? Before I knew it I'd be sitting down on her family sofa, shooting the shit with her daddy and charming the cranberry sauce out of her mother.

Thursday morning came and I made a quick run to the super Wal-Mart a few blocks away from my house. "Good morning," I beamed at the checkout girl as she rang up my purchases. Three fifths of yak, some knotty-head gin, a bunch of Smirnoffs, five cases of beer, I was gonna make a damn good impression. My shopping cart was loaded as I headed back to my car, clutching my cell phone in my hand just in case she called.

I grinned. With what I'd just spent on bug juice for her family, she'd better call! Seriously, though, my wallet might have been a lot lighter but it was all for a good cause. Becky Ann was worth it. I would have come out a lot cheaper shopping at the base's Class Six store, but it had closed before I got off work the night before.

I made it back home in less than thirty minutes and, leaving the liquor in the trunk of my car, jogged up the steps and unlocked my door. The first thing I did was dash over and check my machine. No messages. Had a dial tone, though. I glanced at my cell phone, then called the message center even though I'd been holding it in my hand the whole time. No new messages. It was still early.

I'd put together my clothing the night before, and I glanced at the white Versace knit shirt and Italian black slacks hanging neatly over my valet. My plan was to take a shower right after she called, so I stripped down to yesterday's drawers and fixed myself a bowl of oatmeal and watched the Cartoon Network while I waited.

And waited. And then waited some more.

I must have checked my watch a million times. It was a two- to three-hour ride to the eastern shore of Maryland on the best of days, so you know holiday traffic was gonna be murderous. It was already after twelve, and we'd have to get on the road by two if we were gonna get there in time to chew the fat with her cousins and their friends before supper. I couldn't wait to meet her people. Yeah, some of them might be a little surprised when they first saw me, but I'd built my life around making great first impressions and I had a knack for getting white people to like me despite their biases. I'd dip their tobacco, admire their taxidermied game, and generally schmooze them up so good they'd forget I was black. All they'd be able to say about me was that I was a real nice guy. A great guy for their Becky Ann.

I started calling her at one.

Hi! You've reached the voice mail of Becky Ann Grantley. I'm not available to take your call at this time, but if you leave your name and number I'd be happy to get back to you at my earliest convenience. Have a great day!

"Uhm, Becky Ann? It's me. Emile. Happy Thanksgiving! I was just calling to see how you are, and wondering what you might be getting into for turkey day. You know it snowed again last night and it's looking pretty bad out there right now so be careful if you plan on driving very far. Uhm, give me a call when you get this message. Okay?"

By two thirty my stomach was all down in my balls, throbbing with disappointment. Did she leave without me? I wanted to get mad at Becky Ann, but instead I started feeling sorry for myself. Maybe she thought I wasn't good enough to meet her family. Did they even know she was seeing a black guy?

I called her apartment every fifteen minutes and now, nine hours later, I'd left so many messages that her machine was full. And that's when I finally got it. Becky and some other man were sitting around her parents' table drinking eggnog and carving the meat off a turkey while I was sitting around in yesterday's drawers drinking yak straight out of the bottle.

I couldn't believe it. My girl—okay, okay! She'd made it clear she wasn't just my girl. Still, my instincts told me she'd taken some duck-ass home with her instead of me. But why?

All of a sudden I wasn't good enough no more? Gimme a break! I'd done everything right in this relationship. I'd been tender and attentive. I'd paraded her around like she was my queen, staring sisters down when they walked past us frowning like I'd broken some unwritten rule. I'd spent so much money on Becky Ann that I should be claiming her as a dependent on my income tax return . . . but there was one thing that I hadn't done.

Come on, man! my inner voice was bitching. You know you ain't been righteous with that girl. How you gonna act when you ain't been keeping her satisfied? You gotta bring your A-game when you're dealing with a classy woman like Becky Ann. You can't be half-stepping and think your woman won't notice. Yeah, she might have said it was cool and all, and that she didn't really mind, but what woman do you know who deep down inside doesn't want her coochie kissed? If I wouldn't do it, nine times out of ten somebody else would!

I panicked. Jumping up from the couch, I ran into the bedroom and pulled on my clothes, then swept a shitload of running shoes from underneath my bed and pushed my feet into a pair. I knew what I had to do, and for the love of Becky Ann I was gonna do it too.

I rushed out the front door without bothering to turn off the television or hit the lights. The frigid air bit into me as I ran down the steps and I realized I'd forgotten to grab my coat. *Fuck it,* I thought, jabbing my car key into the lock. My baby would warm me up. We'd warm each other up. I blasted the radio as I drove toward Farmington Gardens, thinking about how happy Becky Ann was going to be after I ate her out like a starving man at a free buffet.

Her parking spot was empty. She hadn't made it back yet. I pulled up across from her house, right beside a fire hydrant, and shut off the ignition. Tomorrow was an early day for my princess. It was her day to open up the club for the breakfast buffet, so I knew it was only a matter of time before she came home. No problem. I'd wait. I'd do anything and everything for my sweet Becky Ann.

It was cold outside and getting just as cold inside my ride. I cranked her back up again and turned the heat up high. A moment later I glanced at my gas gauge and frowned. Damn. It was below empty. I'd been riding on fumes. I shut the engine off again and rubbed my arms as the tiny bit of warmth in the car dissipated into the air.

During the next couple of hours I turned the car off and on several more times, trying to stay warm. There was a good chance that I could find a gas station that was still open late at night on a major holiday, but what if I missed her? What if Becky Ann returned while I was gone and went inside and went to bed without knowing that I'd been there? Need heat? That's what good yak was for. Bracing myself against the cold, I flipped the lever near my feet, then jumped out of the car and ran around to the trunk.

Back in the car, I turned the bottle of Hennessy up to my mouth, then hissed as it burned all the way down to my nuts. *"B-r-r-r-r-r."* I shook my head like a dog. "Get ready, Becky Ann," I shouted, grinning into the rearview mirror as I stuck out my tongue and practiced my lick technique. Just because brothers don't dig eating pussy doesn't mean we don't know how.

"Yeah, boy-o!" I laughed and took another swig. My tongue danced between my lips like a snake, slithering and probing and lapping at the air. If keeping my baby meant I had to take a bite of the hairy taco, then watch out now! I was gonna eat that stuff until both of us were good and full.

———

I made the second trip to the trunk at midnight. By 3:00 A.M. I'd gone back in twice, and since it had started snowing again I went ahead and brought back a bottle in each hand. My thoughts were all over the place. Where could she be? Did she have an accident? I knew I should have changed those bald tires on her car! For all I knew my baby was stranded on the side of a road somewhere, hurt and needing me.

An hour later the ground was totally white and tears were welling in my eyes. Big fat don't-make-no-sense drunk tears. I should have known something like this would happen. As usual, things never went right for the poor foster kid. Every time I was due to cash in on something good, I got rocks instead.

I sat there a drinking and a weeping and a screaming, my pain running back and forth along the emotional spectrum. *Don't nobody lub me* . . . I moaned, icing the cake for my very own pity party. *Why sh-sh-she gotta do me this a' way?* I'ma *good* man, gawdammit! I gib my *all* for dat womannn . . . I do. You know I do. Awright, awright! Sheii . . . gimme a goddamn break, wudja? I'ma eat your frickin' kitty cat, Beck' *Ann*! Eat it righ' on up. Just lemme get my stomash righ' girl . . . Soon I get my stomash togedder I'ma tear tha' pushy up . . .

I must have dozed off because the next thing I knew I was freezing cold and I had to take a leak. My head was foggy even though my nose felt numb. I pulled the handle, leaned against the door, and almost fell out into the snow.

"Whoa," I said, my feet crunching in the icy whiteness as I blew in my hands and turned toward my car. With my back to Becky Ann's house, I whipped out my partner and took a piss right there in the street, splashing urine all over my back tire.

I had enough piss in me to fill up my gas tank, and it felt wonderful to release the pressure from my bladder and leave a big yellow stain in the clean white snow. But then I saw the headlights. A car was coming, slowing down as it approached me. I pushed harder as I tried to expel the last of my urine so I could stuff my partner back inside my pants before the car reached me, but it was too late.

I stood there dribbling piss and holding my partner as Becky Ann's car pulled alongside me and stopped. At first I tried to turn away so she wouldn't see me making a drunken fool of myself, but when I realized who was in the driver's seat, I knew for sure that fool was probably my middle name.

Ottenbach! That lousy square-headed West Point fucker! What was he doing driving my baby home at five o'clock in the goddamn morning?

"Emile?" Becky rolled down her window and stared at me. Stuffing my still-dripping ding-dong back inside my pants, I grinned and tried to lean into her window.

"Hi, princess," I said, my voice coming out a lot louder than I had intended it to. Her coat was off and she was wearing a red sweater. The strand of freshwater pearls I'd gotten her for Secretary's Day rested above her breasts. "I've been waiting all night for you," I told her. "I got a surprise for you, baby. Guess what I'ma do to you, Becky Ann? I'ma lick that stamp! I'ma—"

"You're going to kill her with your breath, buddy," Ottenbach chimed in. "Put the window up, dear," he instructed Becky. "Wouldn't want you to catch anything."

"You dirty son of a bitch!" I growled and stumbled around the back of the car, trying to reach the driver's door. Ottenbach just shook his head and drove off, pulling into Becky's parking spot as I ran alongside the car, yanking at the door handle like I was trying to get to him. Why, I do not know because Ottenbach was at least six foot four and had a body like The Rock. He'd kill me.

He turned off the car and climbed out, looking down on me from his muscled frame. "What?" he asked, then walked calmly around to Becky Ann's side, opened her door, and hustled her up the walkway and over to her front door.

I was right behind them.

"Becky Ann," I pleaded, elbowing Ottenbach and sandwiching myself between them. There was no way this fucker was getting up in her house. No way he was gonna tuck my baby into bed and slobber on my hundred-dollar pillows while I was standing right there.

"Are you okay, Emile?' she asked with real concern in her voice. "Why are you out here this time of night? Have you been drinking?"

I laughed. "Drinkin' and thinkin', baby. Thinkin' about what I'ma do to you, girl, the next time we doin' that thing you like to do. You know how you make that growling noise in your chest right before your eyes get all wide? Well, I'ma do somethin' that's gonna make your eyes pop right out your head, girl! I'ma do—"

"Look, Emile. It's late and you're drunk. Your shoes don't even match."

I looked down at my feet. Damn if one sneak wasn't white on black and the other one blue on white.

"It was a long drive down to Maryland," she continued, "and I've had an exhausting day. If you'll excuse me, John and I are going inside. You can call me tomorrow."

My bottom lip shook. You mean she'd taken this blond boy toy home with her for Thanksgiving dinner and left *me* hanging?

"Becky *Ann*!" I wailed. "Does this mean you like *white guys*?"

My whole world went dark. *"Baby!"* I shrieked, swaying on my feet with my shoes mismated. *"I* wanted to go home with you and meet your family! You should have taken *me*!"

There's nothing worse than a desperate drunk. I lunged at her, my words pouring out earnestly. "I'm ready to shop downtown now, baby. I'll stick my finger up your ass and lick you like a lollipop! I'll—"

Ottenbach's big hand was in my chest. He pushed once and I fell over. "Asshole!"

Becky Ann stood over me. "You're making a fool out of yourself, Emile. Get up and go home. It's freezing out here and you really should have on a coat."

"Not to mention a pair of rubber pants!" Ottenbach quipped. "Looks like Pinchback's pissed in his pants. Say that three times fast!"

I sat up partway and stared down at myself. Sure enough, the old water hose was still leaking and a wet stain ran down my pant leg.

"Fuck you, Becky Ann!" I yelled as loudly as I could as I

sat there crying in the snow. I didn't even have enough energy to climb to my feet as she unlocked her door and Ottenbach escorted her inside. "Just fuck you!"

Ottenbach's grin was a mile wide. He shook his head. "Damn niggers," he said, as he closed the door and locked it behind them.

———

FOR the next two hours I laid in the cut. Slouched down in the front seat of my car, I killed another bottle and waited for Ottenbach to come out of my woman's house. My mind took me all over the world and back, and rage boiled inside me as I imagined him putting those big hands of his all over my girl. He was probably laying on my side of the bed, flipping the remote, and propped up on both of my hundred-dollar pillows. It was all I could do not to rush over there and kick the door in. I wanted to so badly, but then what? What was my next move? I didn't want a fight. I just wanted my woman back. That's all. "Is that too much to ask?" I demanded out loud, crying again and slobbering down the front of my sweater. "Is wanting to be by Becky Ann's side asking too much?"

Before I could answer, her door opened. I slunk down even farther in my seat, peering up just enough to see Ottenbach step outside, then lean back in for a goodbye kiss. "You three-block-having, can't-shoot-worth-a-damn bolo'ing asshole," I whispered, ducking back down until I heard his ignition start and saw his car pull away.

I didn't waste any time. I jumped out of my car and ran across the street. I wasn't even cold as I stood there ringing Becky Ann's doorbell and getting wind-whipped. A curtain fluttered in an upstairs window, so I know she saw me, but the door remained closed in my face.

Ringggggggggg. Ringgggggggggggg. "Becky," I yelled. "Becky Ann. Come on, baby. Lemme in. I been out here all night. Don't be that way, baby. I got something to tell you. Open up, princess. It's me. Doggy Daddy."

Oh, so she was igging me? I let loose.

"BECKY ANN! OPEN UP THIS GODDAMN DOOR! OPEN IT UP RIGHT NOW SO I CAN EAT YOUR MOTHERFUCKIN' PUSSY!" Two seconds later, the door swung open and she snatched me inside.

"Oh, sugar," I pulled her close to me and stuck my nose in her hair. She pulled away from me, red in the face.

"You're disturbing my neighbors, Emile! And you're drunk!"

I laughed. "As a skunk!"

Becky Ann frowned. She was wearing a baby-blue silk robe that'd I bought her for Valentine's Day. "Emile, I want you to get in your car and go home! Leave. Now. Before I call the police."

"Call the police? For what, honey? I didn't come here for no trouble." I grabbed her again, holding her small waist and bending her backward as I tried to slobber kiss her. "Let's have a tongue fight," I teased. "First I'll stick it in your mouth, and then I'll stick it in your—"

"Emile!" She pushed me away. "Stop it right now! I do not want you here. I want you to leave my house and go home!"

I wasn't even trying to hear that. The only place I was going was shopping. Downtown. Where I'd get the most for my money.

I scooped her up into my arms and started up the steps with her protesting and flailing her arms all the way. She was naked under the short robe and one of her breasts peeked through, her nipple winking at me. She tried to grab hold to the door frame to stop me from entering her bedroom, but I barreled on in anyway and plopped her down in the middle of the unmade bed, then hurriedly jumped on top of her.

"Oh, Becky Ann," I murmured, my mouth covering hers, my hands on her breasts and stomach. I slid two fingers between her legs and saw that despite the fight she was putting up, her stuff was wet and slick, ready for Doggy Daddy. Damn. All this time and I was just learning that she was one of those babes who liked it rough. Got off on her man grabbing her by the hair and taking it like a Neanderthal. Well, not a problem.

I moved down her body, my fingers splashing inside her as she beat at my head and face and screamed for me to stop. I didn't want to think about what I was about to do. I just closed my eyes, pushed her thighs apart, and dove in. Head first, tongue on the ready.

I licked her out from one end to the other, stopping along the way to savor that pink clit that seemed to be swollen to twice its normal size. Becky Ann gripped my head in a vise clamp between her thighs as she fought and tried to push me away. Yeah, she wanted to play it rough. Well, I'd play her little game. I grabbed her ass cheeks and dug in deeper, swirling my tongue around and then stabbing it into her, drinking the nectar that flowed from her and dripped from my face and chin.

And it wasn't even nasty, either. All this time I'd been holding back on giving up the oral loving when I could've gotten through this without throwing up a long time ago. I did it right too. I bathed my woman with my tongue. There wasn't a centimeter of her stuff that I did not lick and kiss and savor like it was the sweetest thing that had ever touched my lips.

Both of us had broken out in a sweat, and with all that bucking around and fighting she was doing Becky Ann was getting pretty hard to hold on to. I didn't know if she'd come—she was still fighting me. But my dick was harder than Japanese statistics and I was ready to shove it in her deep and hard.

I took my face out of her crotch and rose up on my elbows, grinning.

"You loved it, right?"

Goddamn. I'd done that thing so good tears were coming from her eyes.

"Emile," she gasped, her face red and streaked with runny makeup. "You just fuckin' raped me, you know. You raped me, Emile! Get the fuck out of my house!"

I shook my head. Raped her? As hot and wet as that kitty cat was? Yeah, right. She was gaming all right. All that juice, she had to have come at least five times. "But was it good, baby?" I asked eagerly. "Did I do it the way you like it?"

She just screamed at me again. "Get the fuck out of my house, Emile!"

Get out of her house? She couldn't be serious. I dried my face on the sheets, then reached into my mouth and felt around on my tongue. I looked down as I pulled a long strand of black hair past my lips and held it in the air. For a moment we both just stared at it.

"W-w-what's this?" I asked, wiping my hand on my sweater.

She scrambled toward the top of the bed. "Just get out, Emile."

"But hold up," I said, my erection dwindling, my drunk completely blown. I peered at the eight-hundred-count white satin sheets I'd gotten her for her twenty-eighth birthday and cringed. Several prominent strands of silky black hair seemed to wave at me like little tentacles. I looked down. Three, no four more strands had grabbed ahold to the front of my white sweater.

"Becky Ann." My voice quivered even though my words were now a mere whisper. "What the hell is this?"

An image of Ottenbach flashed through my mind. Superman-looking asshole. Blue eyes, dark hair . . . I tasted her juices on my tongue and my body failed me. I opened my mouth and the bottom of my stomach pushed up through my throat, splashing the bed and Becky Ann's legs, and burning the surface of my tongue.

"Becky Ann . . ." I heaved again, spewing vodka and hot yak and pulling her down the sheets by her thighs. I just knew she had an explanation that would somehow make this all better. "Baby, please," I slobbered and wiped at my mouth, pointing at the strands of black hair that seemed almost alive. "What is all this?"

Her evil voice straight blew my high.

"It's exactly what it looks like, Emile."

I lost it. Suddenly, I was stone-cold sober with juices drying on my face as the love of my life calmly confirmed my fears.

I'd just sucked Ottenbach's dick.

"Nasty bitch!" I shrieked and reached for her neck.

Sweet little Becky Ann brought her knee up and broke my damn nose.

Blood squirted everywhere. I grabbed my face while she kicked and punched and screamed at the top of her lungs. Somewhere in the depth of my mind I saw the drama playing out on a big screen. It was the middle of the night. Big old black me, wrestling in the bed of a naked, just-fucked strawberry blonde. Her screaming and fighting. Me drunk and bleeding. It didn't take an idiot to figure out where this was heading.

I jumped out of the bed, holding my nose and swallowing blood.

"Now wake up, Emile," Becky Ann screeched, reaching for the telephone. "The black women of the world are just fine. *You're* the asshole who has the problem!"

"You dirty little whore," I breathed, backing toward the door. "You're no better than those ghetto bitches out in the streets."

"Who ever said I was?" she yelled as I turned around and stumbled down the stairs. All I wanted was out of there. I wanted to be far away from Becky Ann, and as close as I could get to a toothbrush and some mouthwash. Maybe even some bleach.

I flung open her door and ran out into the snow. Blood bubbled from my nose and pooled into my mouth and I cursed as I dropped my car key twice before getting it in the lock, my bloody fingers leaving bright red splotches in the snow.

Cranking up my ride, I looked in the rearview mirror and nearly screamed at my reflection. That bitch had some bobcat in her. She'd scratched my head and face raw. I was going to get Becky Ann back if it was the last thing I did. I swore on the graves of my future children, I was gonna pay that low-class trailer tramp back!

With blood dripping from my face and thoughts of revenge racing through my mind, I stomped down on my brake and put the car in drive, and that's when the lights lit up the inside of my car and I realized that several black-and-whites were surrounding me, blocking my path. I counted twelve high-beams. Six cars. Enough Jersey troopers to Rodney King my ass without leaving a trace.

I put the car back in park and played it cool as a half-dozen officers rushed over and surrounded me, praying that this was all some kind of crazy nightmare that I'd wake up from in just a moment, but deep inside something told me that life, as I had known it, was over.

CHAPTER 31

EMILE

First Sergeant Kevin Lawson

The phone call came sooner than I'd expected.

By Friday morning the police had taken me to get my nose set and then released me on my own recognizance, but things weren't over by a long shot. It didn't take a Breathalyzer to determine that I was drunk, but it did take a police detective to explain that simply getting behind the wheel of a car in my condition and putting it in drive constituted a DUI.

I had called Kevin to come pick me up, even though we still weren't talking. I was thankful that he arrived right away and didn't ask me a single stupid question either. I was virtually stranded because my car had been impounded and my license revoked, so I asked him if he planned to be around for the weekend, just in case I needed a ride. He reminded me that it was Fancy's birthday today, and said he was taking her up to New York on a shopping spree and they wouldn't be back until late Sunday night.

I didn't have anywhere pressing to go anyway. The court

date they gave me was two weeks away, but it would take a miracle to keep me out of jail for that long because the moment I saw that filthy Becky Ann I planned to snap her scrawny neck in three places.

And why not? Whichever way I sliced it, I was ruined. It was just a matter of time before Colonel Turner called me on the carpet, and after the way I'd treated her there was no way she'd have mercy on me. I could see it now. My job, my rank, my driving privileges, all gone. Pissed away behind some white girl whose magnificent qualities had only existed in my mind.

I couldn't sleep and I couldn't eat. Hungover and scared, I spent all day Friday rinsing my mouth out and pacing the floor, battling Ralph as I tasted Becky Ann's nasty kitty cat on my tongue.

I could never face Ottenbach again in life, and, yeah, the embarrassment of losing a command would be awful, but things could get much worse. There was a range of punishments for officers who had a drinking problem. And, yeah, as far as the army would be concerned I'd developed a drinking problem the moment I got arrested whether it was my first drink or my last. A career-ending official reprimand was almost guaranteed, but a dishonorable discharge was pretty unlikely.

The phone rang and I answered on the second ring. "Hello?"

"Good day. This is Colonel Turner calling for Captain Pinchback."

Like I said, I'd known the call was coming. I was just surprised they'd gotten the police report down to my battalion so soon. "Good afternoon, ma'am. This is Captain Pinchback."

"I apologize for calling you during a holiday weekend, but we have a critical problem here."

I apologize for calling you? That caught me off guard.

"Er, uh, no problem, ma'am. I was just uh . . . uh . . . spit-shining my boots."

"Well, put your Kiwi down and keep your spit in your mouth, soldier, because you're gonna need it. I want you in my office in fifteen minutes flat, and don't be late."

———

I looked pitiful on that ten-speed. I hadn't ridden it more than twice since meeting Becky Ann. The chain was rusted and the seat gouged at my ass, but even in all that cold and snow I made it up the hill toward battalion headquarters the best I could, huffing and wheezing like the fat little asthmatic kid I used to be.

Thoughts of my younger self brought me great pain, but thoughts of my last night with Becky Ann made me want to chew a mouthful of concrete, so I pushed them both out of my mind as I chained my bike to a rack, then ran up the two flights of stairs leading to the battalion commander's office and stood before her door in a cold sweat.

I saluted. "Captain Pinchback reporting as ordered, ma'am."

"You're two minutes late, soldier. At ease," she said, returning my salute and motioning me into her office.

"Have a seat right over there. This"—she gestured toward a middle-aged white man who was already seated in a row of chairs that were bordered by two small rubber tree plants—"is Dr. Bledsoe. Dr. Bledsoe is the chief of infectious disease medicine at Fort Monmouth Hospital. Regulations state that the battalion chaplain has to be present in a case like this as well. He's next door making coffee, so while we're waiting for him to return, I'll fill you in."

I nodded but remained silent, totally confused.

Colonel Turner flipped through a few papers on her desk, and then spoke quietly but directly. "I understand that you recently received a new cycle of Advanced Noncommissioned Officer Course trainees."

I nodded. "Yes, ma'am."

"Well, as you know, part of the preactivation medical testing for National Guard and reserve forces involves HIV antibody screenings." She glanced at me for a brief moment, and then went on.

"One of your soldiers has tested positive for the antibodies that cause HIV, and according to Department of Defense regulations, he must be notified of his preliminary HIV status and counseled by a medical officer and his company commander.

"You, Captain Pinchback, must give this soldier a safe-sex order, and you must also obtain a list of his sexual partners dating back over the past ten years."

I nodded again. Here I'd been worried about saving my career, and I had a soldier out there who'd soon be worried about saving his life. We sat in silence for several moments, and then two men were standing in the doorway.

"Colonel Turner?" I recognized the battalion chaplain even though I'd had very little professional interaction with him. "Sergeant First Class Duncan has arrived, ma'am. Can we come in?"

I sat there grimly as they stepped into the office. Colonel

Turner motioned to the soldier to take a seat beside me, and as we gave each other the black man *What's up* chin lift, I could tell that he was clueless as to what this was about.

"Sergeant First Class Duncan," Colonel Turner said, "this is Kirk Bledsoe, a chief medical officer from Fort Monmouth Hospital, and this is Major Morris, the battalion chaplain. You already know the academy's company commander, Captain Pinchback, so let's get down to business."

Actually, I didn't know him. The cycle had just begun a few weeks earlier, and I hadn't gotten to know many of the new soldiers. My blood ran cold for this guy, though. He couldn't possibly know the size of the hammer that was about to hit him in the head.

Dr. Bledsoe spoke next. "Sergeant First Class Duncan, as Colonel Turner stated, I am a medical officer assigned to Fort Monmouth. During the initial medical screening you took before being activated for duty, an abnormality was discovered in your laboratory results."

For the first time the guy spoke. "What kind of abnormality?"

"Your HIV screening," Bledsoe said quietly. "Your lab results indicate that you have been exposed to the virus that causes HIV and AIDS, and your body has begun producing an antibody to this virus."

The room was so quiet I could hear waves from the Atlantic as they lapped against the shore.

He shook his head. "So what does that mean? What am I supposed to do?"

"Right now," Colonel Turner explained, "Captain Pinchback will give you a safe-sex order and he'll collect a list of your sexual partners. Since this is a holiday weekend the laboratory at Monmouth is closed for routine testing, but you'll be required to submit another blood sample on Monday. They'll use different screening techniques on this sample and send it to a totally different independent lab. The results take a few weeks to be returned, but in the meantime the chaplain will be available to you and so will each of us sitting here in this office."

He was taking it better than me. He looked shocked, but composed. I wanted to bust out crying. Colonel Turner looked at me and nodded.

"Er, yes," I said, taking my cue and reading from a laminated card she'd given me. "Sergeant First Class Duncan, as your commanding officer I am issuing you a lawful and enforceable command. As of this moment you are to cease having unprotected sex of any kind. If you do engage in sex acts or sexual intercourse, it is mandatory that you disclose your current HIV status to your sexual partner, and mandatory that you use a latex condom during all sex acts whether or not your partner requests such protection. Do you understand?"

He nodded, his eyes on the floor.

"In addition," I went on, "you must at this time provide me with a comprehensive list of your past sexual partners. This list must go back at least ten years. I realize that you may not be able to give a complete accounting of those partners at this time, but we would like you to give us the best approximation that you can. As per Department of Health guidelines, we will notify these partners that they may have been exposed to the virus that causes HIV. Your confidentiality will not be disclosed in any form, nor will there be any of your identifying data contained in their notification. Do you understand?"

He nodded again. Yes.

"Well," Colonel Turner breathed heavily. There was real sadness in her eyes. Three of the five people in the room were black, and that probably meant something to a woman like her. She passed me a notepad and a pen, which I passed on to Sergeant First Class Duncan. "Take a few minutes to process all this, young man," she said, rising from her desk. "We'll step outside and leave you and the chaplain to discuss things and to write your list."

I followed her and Dr. Bledsoe out into the hallway, where the smell of hot coffee met my empty stomach. I loved the taste, but never drank the stuff. "Get me a cup of coffee, Pinchback," she ordered curtly.

It'll make you black, I almost warned her, but then I shut my mouth, realizing how stupid that sounded. Obediently, I went into the office next door to pour her a cup, and while I was in there, I poured myself one too.

WE waited around killing time by drinking coffee and trying to make small talk for about twenty minutes. I stayed on the edges of the conversation as Colonel Turner and Dr. Bledsoe discussed everything from hammertoes to gardening.

As badly as I felt for Sergeant First Class Duncan, I was a little bit scared for myself too. I mean, I'd fooled myself into thinking that Becky Ann was only having sex with me. Thursday night had killed that illusion in a major way. Not only was she knockin' boots with playas like Ottenbach, she'd let him slide up in her bareback too.

My stomach lurched at the thought of it and I sloshed coffee in my mouth to mask the foul taste that had risen in my throat, but the truth was the truth. I'd had unprotected sex with Becky Ann on several occasions. I'd known she went out on occasional dates with other men, but she was supposed to be my special princess! I was the one who brought her designer sheets! She laid up on my hundred-dollar pillows at night, and even claimed to like the way they smelled after I slept on them.

By the time the chaplain called us back into Colonel Turner's office and handed me the list Sergeant First Class Duncan had compiled, my fears of a DUI and a ruined career were on the bottom rung of the ladder. I couldn't wait until the lab opened up on Monday morning. I was getting myself tested too, and never again would I play Russian roulette in the bedroom. Pretty white girl or not.

I accepted the sheet of paper and sat back down to look it over. Names were listed in a single column from the top of the paper all the way down to the bottom. The front page was completely full, and there were tons written on the back. Ol' boy had been busy, and I guess he noted the surprise on my face.

"Those were all that I can remember right now. I have more in my address book at home."

Well goddamn! I nodded calmly, my eyes still scanning the list. It took me a moment to understand exactly what I was seeing. To realize that Sergeant First Class Duncan had listed both male and females as his recent sexual partners. I tried to keep my face neutral as I flipped the paper over and skimmed the names back there, but when my eyes touched the bottom of the page, when I read the very last name listed, my ears started to buzz and the room went dark. I felt myself slipping from my chair, and just before I hit the floor my mind registered the name that had frozen my blood.

First Sergeant Kevin Lawson.

CHAPTER 32

SPARKLE

A Thief in the Night

*A*re you sure you don't want me to come with you?" Phil asked, talking through his nose. He'd caught a nasty cold and I could hear him sniffling in the background. He probably looked like Rudolph by now. Red nose and all.

"Nah, baby," I answered, cradling the phone between my shoulder and my ear. "You just stay in bed and chow down on that turkey soup. Miss Sparkle made it from leftovers so you know it's slamming." We'd spent Thanksgiving Day at his place and I'd returned to my apartment a few hours ago to get dressed for Fancy's birthday party. Our dinner for two had been simple, but Phil didn't seem to mind.

Deebo had called on my cell to wish us a happy Thanksgiving and boy was I surprised. At first I thought maybe Aunt Viv had put him up to it as a way of saying she was sorry, but I should have known better because apologizing wasn't her style. But Deebo gave me props for sticking with Phil.

"I like your friend, Sparkle," he said. "And I'm sorry that

drama went down. He seems like a solid guy, and there's no reason you should be alone just because the brothers haven't been able to see you for the prize that you are."

"Tell that to Aunt Viv," I told Deebo drily. "Your woman hates Phil and she doesn't even know him. She never even gave herself a chance to know him."

Deebo agreed. "It ain't easy loving somebody your people don't approve of. Look at me. Your aunt is old enough to be my mother, and then some, but I still love her. Now, my family is another matter. My sisters think I'm a gigolo and my mother thinks Viv is a nasty old freak. Yeah, I could go out there and get myself a young hottie, but I wouldn't be nearly as happy. Bottom line, Sparkle, we gotta take love where we find it. And that's a fact."

Deebo was right, and coming from a black man his approval set me all the way at ease and made me dig Phil even more. I'd found something real in white boy Phil, and like Deebo suggested I planned to take as much of that good feeling as I could get.

Still cradling the phone, I pulled on a pair of black calf-high Prada boots and then wrapped a colorful scarf around my hairline, allowing my emerging forest of three-inch dark-brown twists to explode from the top. I'd gotten rid of all that weave. The blond dye, the tons of makeup, and the green contact lenses too. All that extra shit had been holding me back.

Phil sneezed into the phone and damn if my chest didn't start to hurt. A tickle jumped on my throat and I wondered if I was catching the same bug he had. Or maybe it was just that I had caught a bug for him. "Be careful driving in the snow, love. Which hotel are they holding it at?"

I grinned. My man was all concerned! "You must be for-getting that I'm a New York City girl," I told him. "You know we drive in snow like it ain't no thang. Kevin's having the party at the Ritz-Carlton. It's pretty inside and out, but why he picked that stuffy-ass joint all the way out in Philly, I do not know. We could have stayed right here in Jersey and rocked the Zodiac all night long and had just as much fun. But it was his call, and I couldn't really protest because it's a surprise party, so Fancy doesn't know about it."

"Great," Phil said and then yawned in my ear. "I'm freez-ing, baby."

"Let me let you go," I told him. "Take your butt to sleep. You're probably running a fever. I'll swing by as soon as the party's over and check on you. Maybe I'll climb in bed with you so we can stoke up a little body heat."

He sneezed again. "That sounds like a plan. You have your key, right?"

I blushed so hard my feet started to sweat. We had recently exchanged keys to our apartments and I still couldn't believe we had taken our relationship to this level. "I got my key, baby," I reassured him. "I'll let myself in like a thief in the night, and I promise I won't steal anything."

"You already did," Phil said sleepily. "You've stolen my heart."

———

THE hotel Kevin had chosen was one of those upscale joints with bellboys in red jackets, curbside check-in, valet parking, the whole nine. I fit right in pulling up in my hot little Z and stepping out in my Tracy Reese faux fur coat. The circular driveway had been shoveled until there wasn't a drop of snow or ice to be seen, and I was cool with that because my Prada boots were meant to look good, not keep my feet dry.

Handing the valet my keys, I slipped the car-check stub into my handbag and braced myself. If Fancy wanted to forgive Kevin for all the dirty shit he'd made her do over the years, then that was cool in the gang. Sister had to live with that nasty rodent and I didn't fault her for that. But me? It was hard to believe that I used to love and respect that clown. As a first sergeant and as a friend. Now just the thought of his foul ass made me wanna start throwing punches, and I had no idea how I was supposed to grin all up in his face when I really wanted to stick my foot in his perverted ass. But he was still my boss, though, and Fancy's husband too. I had to try and keep the peace for both of our sakes, but it was gonna be rough.

Well, guess who was waiting on me as soon as I pushed through the glass carousel of doors? Mister Me-So-Horny himself.

"Hey, Sparkle," he called out, waving me over. He put his arm around my shoulder and went to kiss my cheek, and I jerked away.

"Damn, soldier! What's wrong witcha?"

I made myself smile and elbow him in the side. "Catching a cold," I said, faking the funk. This creep didn't even realize that I was up on his shit. He thought he was still safer than a snake in the grass. "My friend Phil got sick and now he's spreading flu germs everywhere. I took some echinacea, but ain't no telling what's already on me."

Kevin laughed. "If you hadn'ta ducked out of work the day we were taking flu shots you wouldn't have to worry about it." He looked around the lobby real quick, then put his eyes back on me and grinned some more. For those who didn't know what he was about, Kevin looked finer than fine on the outside. But on the inside, I knew he was as twisted as they came.

"C'mon," he said. "Fancy just left me a message and said she's running late. I told her that we were having dinner here with you and your date, but in reality I have a hooked-up suite up on the eighth floor with a crew of friends waiting to scream happy birthday. I got you and me a table in the bar 'cause that's where she's expecting us to meet her."

I followed him through the hotel lobby, noting the expensive sculptures and the real marble floors. There was a sculpture of some Greek guy with a tiny dick sitting in the middle of a fountain, and it was all I could do not to laugh out loud as I thought about what Phil was packing. My baby didn't have an ounce of Greek in him.

The bar was huge and Kevin led me over to a dim booth in the back of the room.

"Damn," I said, taking off my coat and sliding in on one side. There was a bottle of berry-flavored wine cooler on the table and two empty shot glasses. "How's Fancy supposed to find us way back here in the cut?"

Kevin shrugged. "She'll call when she's pulling up outside and we can stand up and wave her over." He signaled to a waiter to bring him a shot of gin, then reached for the wine cooler and twisted off the cap. "I got you a little something to get you started."

"I drove here, First Sergeant," I said wryly. "Don't you remember that briefing you just gave on drinking and driving?"

He laughed. "Hell yeah, I remember. That's why all I got

you was a wine cooler. Not enough alcohol in it to mess you up. Besides, you'll dance most of it off in an hour or so. Go ahead and drink up my money, girl."

He slid the cooler across the table and I lifted it to my lips. It was ice cold and ultrasweet, just the way I liked it.

"So," Kevin asked. The waiter had returned with his drink and I watched as he deep-throated the gin in one gulp. "How's everything going in the supply shop? We've got a pretty large cycle going through this time and everybody's gonna have to jump through hoops to get those folks out of here in the six weeks we've been allotted."

I shrugged and took a long swig from my bottle. "That's your brother's fault," I said. "Nobody told him to say we could make that shit happen. All he had to say was no can do and these troops would have gone through on a regular ten-week schedule just like everybody else. And now, just because he opened his mouth and got involved in NCO business, *I'm* supposed to put in more hours and jack up my social life?" I shook my head. "It ain't happening, Top."

Kevin nodded in agreement. "I know. I told him it wasn't gonna work, but you know how he is. Hardheaded. I didn't even feel right telling you and the rest of my staff that y'all gotta support this mess, but you do."

I waved my hand and leaned back into the booth. I was getting a buzz on and the last thing I wanted to do was talk about some work-related drama.

"It's hot in here," I said, slipping out of my bolero jacket. Normally I would have had something two sizes too small beneath it that showed my cleavage all the way down to my nipples. But tonight I'd worn a deep chocolate shirt that had tightly spaced buttons up the front and long sleeves. It was fly, I'll say that, but it didn't shout *hoochie,* which was just fine with me.

Kevin went on talking, but I wasn't hardly listening. Even with my jacket off I was still burning up, and suddenly my vision got blurry and I felt sick to my stomach.

"Damn," I muttered. I felt like putting my head down on the table, but Miss Sparkle was nobody's slouch and that would be just too tacky. Instead I closed my eyes and took a deep breath, hoping it was just a little rush from the wine cooler that had me. Kevin was still talking when I reached for my purse. My fingers felt like rubber as I fumbled inside for my cell phone, dropping the valet stub in the process.

"Callin' Phil," I said out loud even though Kevin's voice was droning on. My tongue felt heavy and thick, and for the first time I noticed how big Kevin's head was and how much he looked like my dead father.

I pressed Phil's number on speed dial and put the phone to my ear. The bar music was suddenly killing me, louder than any I'd ever heard before, and I had to stick one finger in my other ear just to be sure Phil's phone was ringing. And ringing. And ringing. He must have been knocked out sleeping.

The phone was still next to my ear when I felt my forehead hit the table. And then I felt Kevin next to me, sitting beside me in the booth instead of across from me.

"Sick . . . ," I managed to whisper as he took the phone from my limp fingers. "I'm sick," I told him as I sprawled there with my cheek on the table and my hand across my face. My tongue felt swollen as slobber leaked from the corner of my mouth, and I was grateful when Kevin put his arm around me and pulled me upright.

"You're cool, girl," he said as he leaned me against his shoulder, holding me close. "Everything is cool."

And that was the last thing I heard as the whole room went silent. The last thing I felt was a pair of hungry hands. Reaching between my legs. Moving under my shirt. Pulling on my breasts, stroking my nipples. And then complete blackness.

CHAPTER 33

FANCY

The People You Love Most

hanks anyway," I muttered, standing beside my car and fuming as my neighbor detached his cables from my battery. It was so badly corroded that it was probably beyond revival. Or maybe my car had some other mechanical problem. Either way, this bad boy wouldn't start. Add that to the fact that it was cold as heck outside and the catsuit I was wearing under my coat wasn't doing a damn thing against the biting wind. Me being buck-ass naked underneath it didn't help either.

Kevin was expecting me in Philadelphia in less than an hour and arriving late wasn't really an option. I'd called his cell phone as soon as I figured out that my car was dead, and when he didn't answer I left him about four voice messages telling him I was having car trouble and would probably have to take a cab.

I slammed the hood closed and rushed back into the house to find a phone book, and fifteen minutes later I was riding in the back of a warm sedan, courtesy of Security Car Service.

I closed my eyes as we sped down the rural streets and toward the Ben Franklin Bridge. Somehow a year had passed and another birthday was staring me in the face. I'd begun my special day with a long soak in the bathtub, surrounded by lit candles and enveloped in aromatherapy, which I really needed. With everything that was going on at my job and Kevin's Thanksgiving obligations to his soldiers, it had been a hectic week.

As the company first sergeant, Kevin was obliged to share a holiday meal with those soldiers who lived too far away to travel. Most of them were grateful because they couldn't stand the idea of chewing on a rubber turkey from the base's mess hall, and there were even a few soldiers who were stationed here or who lived close by, but who came over to our house anyway because they had no families to share the day with.

I'd put on the hog up in my little kitchen. Baked the biggest damn turkey I'd ever seen in my life. Tom was so fat, I was scared the sides of him would stick to the inside of the oven and burn. I'd also made a huge pan filled with tender short ribs of beef, some baked macaroni and cheese, candied sweet potatoes, you know the deal. A Thanksgiving meal with all the fixings.

Our house had been full too. A bunch of soldiers had shown up with their hearty appetites, and we were more than happy to pile their plates high and to even fix them doggie bags to take back with them to the barracks.

And Kevin had helped in every way imaginable. From

chopping and washing the collard greens to peeling potatoes and basting the turkey. He'd been so sweet and helpful. Just like a little boy. Eager to please. And before long, I knew why.

We'd just finished cleaning the kitchen, me putting the left-over food away in plastic containers and him washing and drying the dishes, when I decided to check my e-mail account. I had finally reached the HIV-positive soldier I'd been trying to contact, and Dr. Bledsoe had added two more soldiers to my case file. My co-worker Millie was assisting me on these cases, and although she planned to visit her sister in D.C. over the long weekend, she'd promised to e-mail me any updated information that she received.

Kevin had gone outside to take out the trash when I logged on. What I found waiting in my e-mailbox came as no surprise:

Happy Birthday, Baby!

Fancy Lawson, you mean the world to me, and just to prove it to you I plan to throw you the best birthday party you've ever had. Meet me in Room 748 at the Ritz-Carlton in Philadelphia on Friday evening, and make sure you're there on time. See your instructions below and get ready to enjoy a special night with the people you love most.

The instructions he listed were pretty similar to many I'd seen before. Get the key. Come up to the room. Enter quietly and slide in from the foot of the bed. Enjoy the birthday treat you find waiting for you.

As had become my habit of late, I refused to allow myself to think too deeply when Kevin thrust me into these situations. I just performed on demand, like a good little call girl, which, minus the pay, was pretty much what I was. But not for much longer. Tonight would be the last time I'd go along with any of Kevin's sexual dramas. It was my birthday, yes, but I knew this intimate party was more about acting out my husband's fantasies than celebrating another year of my life. So whatever scenario Kevin had cooked up, I hoped it was a good one, because it would be the last one I'd participate in. This *was* the last time.

Traffic was heavy, even for a snowy holiday weekend, and it seemed to take forever for us to get into Philadelphia. Once there, I could tell the snowplows and salt spreaders had been doing their job as the streets were much clearer on this side of the river even though the volume of cars was still thick.

Over an hour after climbing into the hired car, I paid the fare and got out at the top of the Ritz-Carlton driveway. Hurriedly, I looped my purse strap around my wrist, and then scurried into the warm lobby, smiling at the doorman who greeted me.

"Room 748, please," I said to the male receptionist at the desk. He was a nice-looking Hispanic brother. Neat facial hair, low-trimmed nails. He looked at me with the usual in his eyes. *Damn, baby, you so fine. I'd like to fuck you right where you stand.* You know the look. I slid him my driver's license, and without even glancing at it he gave me a plastic room key.

"Is there anything else I can do for you?" he asked with a crooked smile. I stared at him for a second. He was just a baby, I realized. Barely into his twenties. I'd eat his little ass up in the sheets and then spit him right back out.

"No, honey," I answered, slipping the credit card–sized key into my pocket. I'd had both bigger and better than him. At the same time. "Not a thing."

————

THE moment I stepped onto the elevator my heart began to pound. *Yeah, Freak Nasty,* something inside of me mocked. *Get in there and get your nasty freak on.* My hands were shaking as I pressed the floor button, and I took several deep breaths in an attempt to calm myself down.

Nevertheless, my nipples were aching by the time I reached the seventh floor and turned left into a long corridor. I'm ashamed to say it, but as I approached Room 748 my mouth was watering. And that wasn't the only thing wet.

I swiped the lock with the card key and pushed open the door, entering the suite. I was standing in the foyer of a sitting room, and there was a dim light coming from across the way. I could hear them. The bed moving, my husband urging, talking his talk.

This is the last time.

Dropping my coat and purse on the sofa, I crossed the sitting room silently and peered into the bedroom. Things were exactly as Kevin had said they would be. The love game had already begun. Two forms were entwined in the bed, and just as he'd instructed, I stripped out of my catsuit and slipped naked beneath the loose covers, crawling in from the bottom and inhaling their aromas.

This is the last time.

Kevin was on his back, and the woman was lying on her back too, on top of him spoon fashion. He had her knees up and her legs spread, and my husband was banging her from behind, holding her tightly by the knees.

"Oooh, yeah," he groaned as he felt me crawling in toward them. He was very close to coming, I could tell by his frantic pace and the throaty sounds he made. "Come on, baby. Get you some of this good pussy, Fancy. Get you some of this shit. Get you some."

This is the last time.

I straddled my husband's legs and kissed upward from his knees to his thighs. My lips found the base of his penis as it pounded inside of her, and I tasted their mingled juices on my tongue. Grasping her thighs, I pulled her legs down as Kevin pressed on behind her. I licked the inside of one of her thighs, and then the other. She moaned something, then murmured a protest and tried to close her legs, and that's when I froze.

"Get the fugg offa me . . ."

"What?" I whispered, and in that split second horror engulfed me down to my very core. Ripping off the blankets I screamed in disbelief. She had a belly ring. Surrounded by a tattoo of the sun. It was identical to mine.

"Sparkle!" I cried out as Kevin gripped her breasts and climaxed, his orgasm rushing from him in a mighty roar. The moment it ended he pushed her aside and lay there panting on his back, gripping his still-hard penis and pumping it in both hands.

Sparkle flopped over on the bed like she was boneless.

"Kevin!" I screamed. His eyes were closed as I jumped from the bed and grabbed the wrought-iron art deco lamp from the nightstand. Yanking the cord, I held it high over my head with both hands, then slammed it down on his face with all the strength I could muster, feeling immense satisfaction as his blood spurted warmly, splattering me, the headboard, Sparkle, everywhere.

The scene was surreal and the room swam in circles as I came close to fainting. Their nude bodies lay side by side in the mess of the bed. One moaning and trying to vomit, the other with his face bashed in. Bloodied and lying completely still. Commanding myself to move, I paused just long enough to dial 911 from the hotel phone, then fled naked out into the hallway, yelling and beating on doors as I desperately tried to summon help for my friend.

CHAPTER 34

EMILE

From Bad to Worse

I'd been trying to make contact with Kevin all afternoon, calling his cell phone and even his crib. Nothing. I remembered him saying that him and Fancy were going to New York for her birthday, but I still should have been able to reach him on his cell phone.

Colonel Turner had been highly sympathetic when I passed out in her office, hitting my head on a coffee table and knocking over a rubber tree plant. "My brother . . . ," I'd whispered, still clutching the list as she held a cold cloth against the lump that was rising on my head. "My brother's name is written on here." It was all true, I realized miserably. Becky Ann had been right. Kevin was bisexual, and his name being on that list proved it.

Colonel Turner had hustled everyone out of her office and shut the door. Then she pulled over a chair and sat down beside me and gently took the list from my shaking hand.

"I don't see any Pinchbacks listed here," she said after a few moments. "What's your brother's name?"

I motioned for her to turn the paper over, and then pointed toward the bottom of the page. My head was pounding and I was scared to look again and see Kevin's name there in writing. It was just too painful to think about what this might mean in terms of the rest of his life.

Colonel Turner was surprised. "First Sergeant Lawson? Isn't he assigned to your company?"

I nodded through my tears.

"I'm sorry," she said. "Obviously this raises a lot of issues, his health being one of the most primary, and his sexual behavior being yet another. I'm not surprised that you two have such a close relationship but I thought you meant your biological brother had been exposed to this virus."

"We were raised together," I said miserably. "He's my foster brother and he's all the family I've got."

Again she looked surprised. "In that case, we have a serious conflict of interest here. I know this is difficult for you, but as a commander you should have disclosed your familial relationship to First Sergeant Lawson before allowing him to be assigned to your unit, but at this point that's neither here nor there."

She stood and rubbed my shoulder gently, and if my grief for Kevin hadn't filled up every inch of my heart, I would have surely been ashamed of how I'd behaved toward her in the past.

"Take some time to pull yourself together. Obviously, we need to identify and contact any other military personnel who may be on this list, and then turn it over to the Department of Health for their disposition. I'll give a copy to Dr. Bledsoe, who can pass it on to his staff members. In the meantime, I suggest you locate First Sergeant Lawson and talk to him. As a commander, and as a brother. You're obligated to give him a safe-sex order and to direct him to Fort Monmouth for immediate HIV testing."

I'd sat through the rest of her instructions in a fog. All I could hear was *immediate HIV testing*. Immediate HIV testing. Immediate HIV testing. I didn't even think about my own sad predicament until I was standing outside the battalion looking for my car. And then it all came crashing down on me and I remembered that I'd pedaled myself here on a purple Huffy ten-speed.

It was all too much. Just too damn much. I looked at my bike chained to a rack, and then sat down on the curb and cried. Forget that I looked crazy, a commissioned officer and company commander crying like a baby in the deserted battalion square. Forget that the woman I'd loved had cheated on me and turned out to be someone I didn't even know. Forget that it was cold as hell and my ass on that concrete was getting a serious case of freezer burn. Who cared that I would probably lose my command and would most definitely be humiliated before the entire battalion.

Because the only thing worth caring about right now was the thing that mattered most. And the only thing that mattered to me was the fact that my brother might be in trouble. And if my brother was in trouble, then so was I.

————

THINGS went from bad to worse in a matter of hours.

The second call from Colonel Turner came at 8:32 P.M., and woke me out of an exhausted and tear-filled sleep.

"Captain Pinchback?" Her voice was formal and full of authority.

"Yes?"

"Colonel Turner here. I've got two things for you."

I noticed there was no apology for calling on a holiday weekend this time.

"Yes, ma'am?"

"One, I've been informed by the staff duty officer that a blotter report has been sent to the battalion. It has your name on it and I'm sure you know what charges it involves, but we'll deal with that later. Two, I just got off the telephone with a detective from the Philadelphia Police Department. He was calling from Temple University Hospital. Do you know anything about this?"

I shook my head and rubbed my swollen eyes. "No. No. Ma'am. I've been right here in New Jersey all weekend."

"Well, the good news is, I know where your brother is. The bad news is, he's been arrested and is currently in custody at the hospital. He'll be transported to the city jail for arraignment as soon as he's discharged from the emergency room."

I only heard one word. *Arrested.* I snatched my rumpled designer pants from the floor and pulled them on. I had to get to Philly and see about my brother.

"Arrested? Arrested for what?"

"Assault, sexual battery, and administering a date rape drug."

"That's insane! Who did he assault? Sexual battery on who?"

Colonel Turner's voice was dry.

"On your supply sergeant, Pinchback. Staff Sergeant Sparkle Henderson."

———

THE next week was one of the most painful in my life. I went over everything at least a million times in my head, trying my best to understand where Kevin and I had gone wrong and which elements of our early lives had led us to our personal crossroads.

For the longest time I'd blamed Dirty Sue for everything that was wrong in my life. I'd assigned her value to every black woman whose path I'd crossed, and it was easy for me to treat them all with the same deep-seated contempt that I felt for her.

But if Dirty Sue was responsible for all of my baggage, then that meant she was responsible for Kevin's too, right? I mean, we'd slept in the same bed and eaten out of the same pot. But somehow this excuse didn't fly with me. In fact, after spending five straight hours talking to Fancy and listening with my jaw dropped as she revealed a dark side of my brother that I had never known, there was no excuse that could justify the things that he'd done to women.

And if there was no excuse for him, then there was none for me either. Looking at your own shit is never very easy, and for someone who had spent his whole life dumping blame on one woman, eating my own crow was quite a difficult load for me to swallow.

I'd visited Sparkle in the hospital and apologized to her. For Kevin's actions as well as for my own.

"I'm sorry, Sparkle," I told her. She was sitting in a chair looking out the window when I arrived. Her hair was full of little twists and she didn't have a drop of makeup on her face. She looked younger and prettier without it. "For everything."

She nodded. "I owe you one too. An apology, I mean."

I shook my head, no.

"Yeah I do. I ragged you out. And I was wrong. I apologize."

I shrugged. "Well, maybe we were both wrong. About a lot of things. But I really hope your situation works out for you."

"Thanks, Emile. I do too. I just don't understand why Kevin would do something crazy like this to me. To Fancy." She frowned and adjusted the blanket that was covering her legs. "It just doesn't make a bit of sense."

I just shook my head. I agreed. I couldn't understand it either.

"I think it's a sickness," I said quietly. "Something mental. From what I've been able to learn, Kevin has a sexual addiction that got twisted into an obsession over you."

She shuddered and closed her eyes. "Fancy called," she said with her eyes still shut. "I know what you told her about Kevin and that guy. I know he might have been exposed to the HIV virus."

I sighed. "Yes, that's true. We don't know anything yet for sure because Kevin won't be released into military custody until later on today. But we'll get him tested. We'll get all of you tested."

I saw a tear slide down her cheek and my heart went out to her. I stood there helplessly as she cried inside, then I touched her shoulder and left.

IT was one of the hardest things I've ever had to do.

They were waiting in Colonel Turner's office when I arrived, and while the scene was eerily familiar, the cast was much closer to my heart.

"You okay?" I asked, as Fancy clutched my arm. Her eyes showed deep grief and she looked drained, but she nodded and stepped firmly into the office and stood beside me.

Colonel Turner was at her desk and Dr. Bledsoe sat in an armchair. Kevin and Major Morris, the battalion chaplain, were sitting in two of the four folding chairs along the wall, and I led Fancy over and made sure that I sat between her and her husband.

Fancy had insisted on witnessing this, but as far as I could tell she didn't look at Kevin once. But I did, and as soon as our eyes met I almost fell out of my chair again.

He looked bad. Fancy had done a job on him with that lamp, but of course the damage was mild in comparison to what he'd done to her. Like mine, the bridge of Kevin's nose had been broken, but his fractures were multiple, and one of his eyes was horribly black and swollen almost shut. There was a huge bulge on the ridge between his eyes, and the doctors said he might need to have surgery on his damaged sinus cavity.

Colonel Turner closed her door and spoke. "Good morning, Mrs. Lawson. I'm Colonel Bonita Turner and I understand that you already know Dr. Bledsoe. The other gentleman is Major Morris, our battalion chaplain. Each of us offers our condolences for what you must be experiencing, and if there is anything that I, or any member of my staff, can do to make this time any easier for you, just ask."

"Thank you," Fancy managed to whisper.

"The purpose of these proceedings today," Colonel Turner

continued, "is to comply with Department of Defense regulations as they apply to cases where military members have potentially been exposed to the virus that causes HIV. While First Sergeant Lawson has not tested positive for HIV antibodies, he was identified as a sexual partner by a member of this battalion who did, in fact, test positive in preliminary HIV screenings. Captain Pinchback?"

I stood up and approached her desk, then took the laminated card she was offering me and once again read from it. "First Sergeant Kevin Lawson, as your commanding officer I am issuing you a lawful and enforceable command. As of this moment you are to cease having unprotected sex of any kind. If you do engage in sex acts or sexual intercourse, it is mandatory that you disclose your potential HIV exposure to your sexual partner, and mandatory that you use a latex condom during all sex acts whether or not your partner requests such protection. Do you understand?"

Kevin looked so pitiful it hurt me to my heart.

"Yes," he said quietly, speaking for the first time. "Yes, sir."

"In addition," I went on, "you must at this time provide me a comprehensive list of your past sexual partners. This list must go back at least ten years. I realize that you may not be able to give a complete accounting of your partners at this time, but we would like you to give us the best approximation that you can. As per Department of Health guidelines, only if your initial laboratory testing returns positive will we notify these individuals that they may have been exposed to the virus that causes HIV. Even then, your confidentiality will not be disclosed in any form, nor will there be any identifying data contained in this notification. Do you understand?"

"I understand."

Colonel Turner came over to comfort Fancy, who was now crying softly. Kevin got up from his chair and rushed over to embrace her, but Fancy shrank away, burying her face in the battalion commander's neck.

Colonel Turner threw up her arm, blocking Kevin with an open palm.

"No," she said coldly. "Leave her be. Go next door and write your list, then report back to medical hold and wait there for further instructions."

Kevin's broken face crumpled into a lumpy mask. His knees sagged as he stood rooted in place. "I'm sorry, Fancy," he sobbed. "Baby, please believe me. I'm sorry."

"Pinchback," Colonel Tuner said, nodding at me as Fancy began to cry harder. "Go with him. I'll stay here and take care of her."

I stood up and put my arm around my brother's shoulder, gently guiding him toward the door. His whole body shook as he sobbed out loud, turning around for one last look at Fancy. "I'm so sorry, Emile," he whispered through his tears.

"I know, Chief," I answered, shedding quite a few tears of my own. "I know."

CHAPTER 35

FANCY

Coping Strategies

Two weeks had passed since that bomb had gone off in the middle of my life. I'd spent the better part of that time trying to understand how things had gotten so far out of control, and asking myself what role I'd played in causing the explosion.

I'd only spoken to Sparkle a handful of times since that horrible night, although I would have liked to have been with her every day. It was hard losing a husband and a sister at the same time, but I understood how she felt. After all, Kevin had violated the sanctity of our friendship, and while I knew she still loved me, it was possible that our relationship might not ever fully recover.

Phil had called, both to give me messages of comfort and to keep me abreast on Sparkle's condition. We were all waiting for the results of our HIV tests so I could only imagine that she felt as fearful and as uncertain as I did.

I had never been one to ignore God during times of ease

and run begging him for favors during times of need, but I sure did a lot of praying during those hours after I summoned help for Sparkle. Kevin had given her quite a large dose of a date rape drug, and they'd had to pump her stomach at the hospital to bring her around.

It was all so very scary, and between the police and the doctors and the visions of what Kevin had done playing out in my head, I got so hysterical they ended up admitting all three of us.

As it turns out, Kevin had gotten the worst of it, physically that was. I'd broken six bones in his face with that big heavy lamp, and if I could do it all over again I would have bashed him twice. My anger at him hadn't nearly been realized, but I was too busy hurting for Sparkle and grieving the possible death of our friendship and the definite death of my marriage to allow anger to take hold. That would come later.

Today, though, the movers had come. An army-sponsored team who had packed up all of my things and most of the furniture, and who would move it all over to the small apartment I'd found in Browns Mills. It was close to the base and not very expensive, and my drive to work would actually be a few minutes shorter.

Kevin was responsible for getting his own things out of the house. He was living in the barracks over at a medical hold unit, and had been restricted from entering our quarters, and the housing area at large, until forty-eight hours after I'd turned in my keys. We'd only spoken once since that tragic night, and I'd hung up right in his face as he babbled some nonsense about how he got raped in a downlow club.

Too ridiculous.

I'd gone to see my counselor again, and to my relief she

was gracious and accepting, even though I'd basically given her my ass to kiss the last time we'd talked. Without sharing every detail, I gave her a summary of what was going on in my life. Aside from the pain I felt for Sparkle and the fear that each of us might have been infected with HIV, my next biggest stressor came from doubting Kevin's sexuality. I'd never once suspected him of having sexual feelings for men, and to find that he might have been infected by one of his own male soldiers was devastating.

The first thing my counselor suggested I do was get some information on sexual addiction and the difficulties experienced by those who love and live with people who are addicted to sex.

Since this would be my last night in the home I had shared with my husband, I decided to put it to good use. My coffeemaker had been packed and shipped, so I fixed a cup of instant tea and sat down at Kevin's computer.

In less than ten minutes I had discovered a cache of pornographic files of women in every imaginable pose. Of course I searched his computer for photos of naked men as well, and to my relief there were none.

I surfed the Net for quite some time that night, and during my travels I lit upon a website that explained my husband's attributes to a tee. I learned that sexual addiction was something that affected millions of people each year, and that more families had been hurt, marriages destroyed, and friendships permanently damaged than you would believe.

To my surprise, I found that there were degrees of sexual addiction, and the symptoms that people experienced were not always manifested in the same way. I also learned that it wasn't strictly a male thing. There were countless women in the world who battled sexual addiction each day, and while it might sound like a fun thing to be married to a woman like this, for the men in their lives it could be anything but.

One site in particular really brought things home. It was called S-Anon, and it offered support for people who had been negatively affected by someone else's sexual behavior. It talked about coercion, manipulation, and co-dependency, and to my surprise I discovered that many sex addicts chose spouses who were also addicted to sex to some degree as well. How insightful. What an interesting truth.

I printed out several key pages from those websites, then found other sites that provided additional information and treatment options and I printed out pages from those as well.

I slept in the guest room that night. Partly because both my bed and the sofa were en route to my new apartment, and partly because I was beginning to gain a greater understanding of my husband and also of myself. With tears in my eyes I climbed into the guest bed and inhaled the scent of wood shavings and cherry stain, as memories of my husband plagued me throughout the night.

In the morning I left early, anxious to be on my way. I planned to drop my keys off at the housing office before driving to my new apartment, and I felt good about the finality this gesture would bring. On Kevin's desk I left one of the two copies of information I'd printed out about sexual addiction and coping strategies.

And in my hand I held the other.

CHAPTER 36

SPARKLE

Get Ready to Rumble!

*W*e were laying across Phil's bed eating popcorn and watching a movie when he whipped it out. "You up for it?"

I looked at the backgammon board and smiled. We hadn't played in weeks and it was something that I'd missed.

"If you don't know, you better ask somebody!" I teased, looking totally unsexy in a red-and-white-striped nightie with a red bandanna tied over my hair. "Hell yeah, I'm up for it. Miss Sparkle is like bubbly, don'tcha know? She *always* rises to the occasion. Humph. You better ask yourself if *you're* up for it."

I jumped on him and sat on his chest, and he flipped me over easily until he was on top, pinning my arms above my head with a grin.

"Is Miss Sparkle up for anything else?" he wanted to know. I felt that rocket trying to bust out of his pocket, but I shook my head. Phil had been my everything. He'd been by my side every step of the way, and had even taken leave from work to stay home with me while I recovered.

"Not yet, mister. Not yet."

He kissed me. "I'm not rushing you, baby. Just want you to know that I'm not running from you either. I'm right here if you want me. We've always used condoms so nothing's changed."

With his body pressed tightly to mine, I put my arms around him and ran my fingers through his dark hair. I had fallen in love with this man, and I'd finally reached the point where I wasn't ashamed to feel it or to say it. While ya bull-shitting, Miss Sparkle was actually ready to declare that love in open court or even on national TV if it came down to it. But I wasn't ready to put his life on the line. Not for anything.

In twenty-four short hours the results of our HIV tests would be in, and while I was a little bit nervous I was no longer afraid. I'd been deep in the process of shedding those excess layers and shaking off some of my stifling old habits. I'd been choking myself with negative energy just to keep up a crazy front for society, and the peace that I'd found in truly loving myself was greater than the fear of any disease.

I won't lie and say that I wasn't still pissed with Kevin, because I was. I had no idea that he was such a monster or that he was even looking at me that way. And poor Fancy. She surely didn't deserve any of this. Fancy was still my girl and all, and you know heffahs like me are loyal to the core, but I gotta 'fess it. I was having a hard time getting us back to where we were. As much as I loved her, all that pain and guilt I saw in her eyes kinda messed me up. She couldn't even look at me without breaking down, and while I truly didn't fault her for a single thing that Kevin had done, he was still her husband and she felt responsible for his actions.

But she wasn't, I reminded myself, squirming out from under Phil. The only person who was at fault here was Kevin, and even though Fancy had messed around and let that fool forget who the queen was, she was still my best friend.

"Set it up," I told Phil, throwing a kernel of popcorn at him that he tried to catch with his mouth. "Get ready to rumble, baby, 'cause Sparkle ain't taking no mercy and she damn sure ain't taking no prisoners!"

Phil laughed and dug into the bowl, flinging a handful of popcorn back at me. "You think you're so bad, huh? Well, hurry on back so Big Phil can spank that booty for you!"

I lifted my gown, then turned around and flashed him a quick hit of my naked ass, stretch marks and all. Then I snatched up the cordless phone and ran into the living room.

I dialed Fancy's cell phone and smiled when I heard her voice.

"Hello?"

"Hello?" I shrieked. "*Hello?* What happened to *Hey, ho!?*"

She chuckled. "I'm sorry. I didn't recognize the number on my caller ID. Hey, ho. How's it going? Where are you?"

I sat down on the sofa and folded my legs beneath me. "At Phil's," I said. "I've been staying over here a lot, especially at night. Dude is sprung, Fancy." I giggled. "Straight bent. But then again, so am I."

"Wow, Sparkle," she said, sounding happy. "That's awesome, girl. Phil is a wonderful person. I think he's good for you too."

I agreed. "We're good for each other. What's been happening with you? Did you get all your stuff unpacked or is your lazy butt still living out of boxes?"

"You know it. Boxes, girl. Boxes. I'm planning to start unpacking next weekend."

Rare was the moment when Miss Sparkle couldn't find the right words to say, but there was an awkward little pause as I took a few deep breaths and reached for what was in my heart.

"Fancy," I said softly. "I want you to know something, okay?"

Her voice was even softer. "Okay."

"I want you to know that no matter what happens tomorrow, no matter what the outcome turns out to be, you're my friend, Fancy. My sister and my friend, and I love you."

"Me too, Sparkle," she said, and I could tell she was starting to cry. "Me too."

"Well!" I said, trying to lighten things up. "If you want some help digging shit out of those boxes, I'm available this weekend. Matter of fact, you need me, gurlfren', 'cause that setup you had going in the old crib just wasn't saying a damn thing."

"Sparkle, you are crazy."

"Nah, for real, though. You had your spot looking like an old folks home. Let's go to IKEA and get you some new stuff for your new space. You know I can pick out nicer shit than you, Fancy, so don't even front."

"Sparkle, hush. All your taste is in your mouth, girl."

"Whatever." I laughed. "Just be ready to get your shop on."

"I'll be ready, Sparkle. I'll be ready."

"And Fancy?"

"Yes?"

"I'll see you tomorrow, okay?"

I hung up and sat in the darkness, but only for a second.

"*Let's get ready to rumbbbbbbbbbbbbbbbbbbbble!*" I screamed at the top of my lungs, then wiped a tear from my eye and charged back into the bedroom to wear Phil's butt out.

CHAPTER 37

EMILE

Like What You See

Just like the fat wheezing foster kid of Brunson Hill Road, I was at the mercy of a black woman again. But this time it wasn't Dirty Sue who held a belt in her hand, it was Colonel Turner who was wielding a pen.

I saluted. "Captain Pinchback, reporting as ordered, ma'am."

She returned my salute and left me standing at the position of attention.

"Captain Pinchback, we are here this morning to take action on the DUI you received during the early-morning hours of November 25, 2004. According to state regulations your blood alcohol level tested above the state legal limit of .080, which constitutes driving while intoxicated as per New Jersey state law and the Uniform Code of Military Justice. Do you have anything to add that is not contained in this report that might influence my decision regarding your punishment?"

I nodded. "Yes. Colonel Turner, I admit that I was drinking

heavily that night, and that I behaved irresponsibly by getting in my car after consuming a large amount of alcohol. However, I'd like to make it clear that I was not driving when I was arrested. True, I was behind the wheel, but I had not moved that car. Not one single inch."

Colonel Turner looked up from the report and gave me such a look of disgust that I wished I had kept my mouth shut. She pushed her glasses up on her head and nodded toward the door.

"Close it."

I shut her door and returned to the position of attention, just knowing she was gonna eat me up one side and down the other. And she did.

"Listen, Pinchback," she said with a sigh. "I'm going to talk to you like you're my son, because I'm old enough to be your mother. I've seen plenty of men like you. Young, intelligent black men who get so enamored with themselves and their so-called status until they crash and burn before they really get started in life.

"The problem with you is, you're oblivious. You think just because you chew tobacco and yuk-yuk with these clowns that it makes you one of them. Well, you're wrong. You are not one of them, and you will never be one of them. But that's okay, soldier. Because you're you, and that should be good enough for the world. But first"—she held her finger in the air and stared me down—"*you* has got to be good enough for *you*."

I nodded. I had been coming to that same conclusion myself.

She flipped back through the report. "Now let me put a little bug in your ear. You know those young captains you shoot the shit with? Those guys you've been working so hard to impress? Well, it was one of your buddies, Ottenbach, who gave you the shaft. He bent you over and rammed you with it good too, you know. Didn't much matter that you hadn't moved an inch when they caught you. The police received a telephone call from a concerned citizen who thought you just *might* get your drunken tail behind the wheel of that car and drive.

"How do you think they knew where to find you? Why do you think they were sitting outside just waiting for you to get in that car and turn on the ignition? Bottom line, Pinchback, you were stupid and gullible and now you have to pay for it."

I felt sick. Not only had Ottenbach rammed me good, the good colonel was getting ready to run up in me dry. I braced myself for the fatal blow that was about to come.

"Captain Pinchback, for the offense of driving under the influence, I am hereby relieving you of your command of the Twelfth Army NCO Academy effective immediately. You will be reassigned to a brigade of my choosing, which I will designate as soon as a slot for you becomes available.

"I am *not* placing a letter of reprimand in your official record, nor am I recommending that any further disciplinary action be taken against you at this time, but I am mandating that you attend drug and alcohol counseling through the Army Community Services office here on base. Do you have any questions, soldier?"

I shook my head, surprised that more than half of my ass was still left for me to sit on. "No, ma'am. Thank you, ma'am."

She looked up at me and sighed. "Do yourself a favor, Pinchback."

"What's that?"

"Develop a sense of self-worth."

"Ma'am?"

"I know you have your preferences, but it could be that those preferences aren't based upon what you actually like in a person, but rather on what you don't like about yourself. So do yourself a big favor. In fact, do me and the rest of your sisters and brothers out there a big favor."

"What's that?"

"Practice looking in the mirror and actually liking what you see."

CHAPTER 38

KEVIN

Our Lives Have Become Unmanageable

The meeting wasn't supposed to start until seven, but the room was filling up quickly. I looked around for a seat toward the back and headed that way.

There were all kinds of people here. Black, white, young, old. There were executives and laborers, beautiful sisters and ordinary-looking women too. I had to keep myself from staring because a lot of them amazed me. They looked so normal that I couldn't even see them having the same kind of problem that I had.

Squeezing in between a thin Asian man and a middle-aged white woman, I sat down on the folding chair and held my hat in my hands. There was a table with coffee urns and plastic cups to my left, and while I could have used something hot, I didn't feel like getting back up. And not because it bothered me when people stared either, because let's face it, I deserved to look the way I did. My doctors were willing to do surgery to correct some of my nasal disfigurement, but I had refused. What I saw in the mirror every morning was exactly what I needed to see. It was a small reminder of those I'd hurt.

And hurt them I did. It was almost like another Kevin, another me had done all that crazy shit and had all those whacked-out fantasies. The military had come down hard on me too, hitting me with charges of rape, dereliction of duty, administering a date rape drug, and even kidnapping. Honestly, the thought that I'd be raping Sparkle had never crossed my mind. I wasn't conscious of the aggressive nature of my fantasies toward her. Instead, I'd deluded myself into believing that she was just another hot chick who loved dick, and therefore setting her up to be had was no big thing.

I cringed inside at the thought of what I'd done. My hearing was in a week, and I planned to plead guilty to everything, no matter what my lawyer said. I didn't have a chance in hell of getting Sparkle to forgive me or of winning Fancy back, but if I was gonna have any hope of getting right with myself, I had to own up to my wrongs and admit that this thing in me was just too big and ugly for me to battle on my own.

I won't lie and say I wasn't scared about what tomorrow would bring, because I was. I didn't know what the odds were that any of us would turn up positive, but I prayed that at least Sparkle and Fancy would be okay.

I reached into my jacket pocket and pulled out one of the sheets of information that Fancy had left on my desk. I read it for what must have been the millionth time. Each time it reassured me that I was not alone, that help was available if I wanted to seek it.

Which was exactly what I was doing.

The room had been buzzing with side conversations, but now everyone fell quiet as a young man walked up onstage.

He was about thirty, dressed in an expensive suit, and looked like somebody you'd find on Wall Street reading the stock market reports.

"Good evening, friends!"

"Good evening," the crowd said.

He smiled out at us. "My name is Arthur, and I'm a sexaholic."

"Welcome, Arthur!"

"Yes," he said, straightening his tie. "It's so good to see each and every one of you here tonight. As most of you know, we are a fellowship of men and women who share our experiences, and the only requirement for membership is a desire to stop lusting and become sexually sober!"

Applause went up.

"But not only do we share experiences, my friends, we share a common problem. Early in our lives we learned to feel inadequate, undeserving, lonely, and afraid. What we felt on the inside never matched what we saw on the outside of others."

I saw a few heads nodding, and realized that mine was one of them.

"We disconnected from ourselves, from the people who loved us, from our husbands and wives and significant others. We tuned them out by using sexual fantasies and compulsive masturbation, we plugged into strip clubs, prostitutes, and cybersex as we fed the pictures in our minds and gave life to the images of our lust by pursuing the objects of our sexual fantasies."

Arthur was talking to me. I knew it, and he knew it too.

"We became true addicts, through fantasy, promiscuity, infidelity, compulsive masturbation and manipulation, and then even more fantasy. We got it through the eyes and through the flesh. We bought it, we sold it, we gave it away for free. We were addicted to the mystique, to the tease, to that which was forbidden. The only way to be free of it was to do it! And we did!

"Our lust caused us guilt, shame, self-hatred, and pain, and we were propelled away from reality, escaping inside our secret selves. We took sex and dignity from others to fill up what we thought was missing inside of us. Lust was the driving force behind our sexual acting-out, and true sobriety can only be gained when we face up to that lust and conquer it completely. So stand up and join me, my friends, my sisters and brothers, in reciting the twelve steps that we've adapted to help us overcome our pain."

I rose with the others and read from a projection screen on the stage.

1. We admit that we are powerless over lust. Our lives have become unmanageable.
2. We have come to believe that a Power greater than ourselves can restore us to sanity.
3. We have made a decision to turn our will and our lives over to the care of God, as we understand him.
4. We have made a searching and fearless moral inventory of ourselves. . . .

As I read along with the hundred or so other people in the room, I felt my first real sense of relief since I was a little kid. Maybe I wasn't just some oversexed stereotypical black man who banged anything in a skirt just for the hell of it. There was a proper name for the beast that had been riding me since my childhood. The beast that had stolen all of the good out of my relationships and killed my marriage. The beast that had led me to manipulate and betray my wife and rape her best friend.

They were reading the eighth step, and I quickly joined in.

8. We have made a list of all persons we have harmed, and become willing to make amends to them all.
9. We have made direct amends to such people wherever possible, except when to do so would injure them or others.

And that's when it hit me. I stood there in the midst of my own personal madness and broke down like a baby. I'd do anything to be able to make direct amends to those I'd hurt. To tell Fancy and Sparkle, and even Teesha and Lil Mama, how sorry I was, and to have them believe me.

Five minutes later, Arthur had opened the floor for sharing, and I found myself standing on the stage with a microphone in my hand.

"Good evening, friends," I said quietly, gazing out at the crowd as my entire soul yearned for sexual sobriety. "My name is Kevin, and I'm a sexaholic."

"Welcome, Kevin!"

If you or someone you love has a problem with sexual addiction and its consequences, help is available. Learn more about sexual addiction at:

The Sexual Recovery Institute
www.sexualrecovery.com
(310) 360-0130

Sexaholics Anonymous
www.sa.org
(866) 424-8777

S-Anon International Family Groups
www.sanon.org
(615) 833-3152

Hello, wonderful readers!

Thank you for selecting my fourth novel, *Knockin' Boots*. I take great pride in bringing you highly crafted stories on a range of topics, and each of my works delve into unique and multi-faceted scenarios that spring from the blessed wells of my creativity. From illicit love affairs between soldiers in *Black Coffee*, to the heartache of intra-racial prejudice in *Chocolate Sangria*, to the inherent strength in good black men in *A Woman's Worth*, I have served my readership with the utmost respect and above all, obeyed my literary muse with pride and dedication.

Knockin' Boots is a spicy novel filled with hidden agendas and secret desires. Between the pages of this novel you will embark upon a risky journey. A journey into the world of sexual addiction and self-deprecation that is an unfortunate reality for many members of our society. You will meet husbands and wives, sisters and friends, addicts and enablers, and witness firsthand the destruction and devastation that boundary violations and sexual obsessions can wreak on those we love.

As such, I hope you feel my characters' pain and experience their conflicts as events unfold that challenge their relationships and impact their very lives. And as usual, I ask that you hang on tight and enjoy the ride.

ACKNOWLEDGMENTS

As always I thank God, the merciful Owner of the world and Master of the Day of Judgment for blessing me with clarity of vision and the wisdom of discernment in my life and in my friendships. To my husband, Gregory for his everlasting love, friendship, and companionship, and for being the best husband and father a family could pray for. (GWIWGDFY!)

To our children, Kharim, Erica, Greg Jr., Kharel, Kharyse, and Khaliyah. We are so proud of each of you and of your accomplishments and we love you more than words can say. The joy of our lives dwells in each of you, and we thank you for knowing yourselves and for being the wondrous beings that you are.

To my sister Michelle Carr, and to my wonderful nieces and nephews. Thanks for being supportive and nurturing. I love you all!

To my cousin Annetta Jones. Twin, that Johnson blood runs strong in our veins. Thanks for your support and encouragement. I love ya!

Thanks to Mel Taylor, acclaimed author of *The Mitt Man,* for your counsel and wisdom and the gift of your friendship. I'm lucky to have you in my life and I value you more than you know.

To my friends, Kim and Jimmy Kendrick, Yvette Williams,

Tawana Harrington, Carmelia Scott-Skillern, Linda King, Phyllis Primus, Rhonda Tatum, Dee Gilbert Woodley, Stephie Howard Easton, Edie Hall, Susan Goekner, Michelle Vollmer, Vicktoria Eichelberger, Sherrie L. Respass, Jackie McGuire, Dawn Williams, Pat Houser, Robin Oliver, Lenell Lopez, and Alfreada Kelley. I thank each of you for not only being true friends, but for actively supporting my writing and championing my career and encouraging others to read and enjoy my works as well.

To those fellow authors who truly have love and generosity in their hearts, you know who you are. It's always great when we sincerely wish the best for each other and our words and deeds also reflect those wishes. To Pat G-Orge Walker, whose heart is pure and whose pen drips with wit, thank you for your constant support. To Jamise L. Dames and Christine Young-Robinson, thanks for being steadfast in your friendship and with your love and encouragement.

To my agent Ken Atchity and to Margaret O'Conner, thanks for providing me with an attentive and nurturing home. I'm proud to be a member of your team and look forward to many years of success. To my wonderful editor, Melody Guy, thanks for your kindness and understanding, your expertise and your ability to see my vision. Thanks for *everything*!

Biggest thanks go out to my readers who take time from their busy lives to blow up my mailbox with love and praise. It is for you that I write, it is for you that I create. You can visit my website at www.tracypricethompson.com and I can be reached at tracythomp@aol.com. I look forward to hearing from you.

Peace and balance,
Tracy

Knockin' Boots

TRACY PRICE-THOMPSON

A Reader's Guide

A Conversation with Tracy Price-Thompson

Q: Tracy, you know how to tell a terrific story! And your ear for dialogue and the different speech cadences . . . It reads so naturally and so strongly. You know that's your gift. Were you born with this natural storytelling ability and ear for dialogue? How did it manifest itself when you were growing up?

A: I was the youngest child in my family—my mother's baby—so, of course, I spent a lot of time listening as she interacted with family and friends. A vivacious, outgoing woman, my mother had a knack for comedy and was always engaged socially, so just hanging on to her skirts and being exposed to her conversations, which were filled with wit and humor, gave me a good foundation and ear for dialogue.

Q: The military world was the setting of your first novel, *Black Coffee*. Why did you return to that backdrop for *Knockin' Boots*?

A: I live in a military community, an environment that I think is largely unfamiliar to most people. Military communities differ greatly from those on "the outside," yet shocking, scandalous things happen among people regardless of their locales. In *Knockin' Boots* I wanted to depict a successful soldier who, because of his profession and position, had to keep his desires hidden and his addictions secret. A mean feat when you are restricted by rigid rules and regulations.

Q: **What other novels did you have in mind when you conceived and wrote** *Knockin' Boots?*

A: None, really. Not many works of contemporary African American fiction deal with military themes, and fewer with themes of sexual addiction and interracial relationships among soldiers.

Q: *Knockin' Boots* **takes a fun, trendy theme in contemporary fiction—erotica—and puts a self-help, cautionary twist on things. Why was it important enough to write about this?**

A: Because such debilitating consequences can arise from risky sexual behaviors, and the repercussions of this type of addiction need to be acknowledged, even in fiction.

Q: **Out of all the addictions, why focus on sex? It's an addiction only recently labeled.**

A: Yes, I agree that it is only recently labeled, but I believe that this addiction has very long roots. I chose to examine the consequences of sexual addiction in *Knockin' Boots* because we all have sexual desires, but not all of us can control them. Kevin committed boundary violations that were due in part to his early sexualization, and that is something we must guard against as it pertains to our children today. In examining this type of sexual addiction, I wasn't interested in duplicating a plot that was already out there in some shape or form, but rather in analyzing the effects on the enabler of the addicted person, and how, quite often, that person is also battling the same addiction but to a much lesser degree.

Q: What sort of research did you do to depict varying levels of sexual addiction fully and accurately?

A: I did a fair share of research for this novel because, above all else, I want my work to be credible and plausible, even if it is fiction. I believe there are thousands, if not millions, of Kevins and Fancys out there, who suffer from uncontrollable sexual urges. And if only one such person walks away with a small bit of insight after reading *Knockin' Boots,* I'll be satisfied.

Q: Do you have any advice for people struggling with sexual addiction?

A: Only as I state in the novel: Help is available but you must seek it. Enablers must do the same thing—recognize that they are enablers and seek assistance for themselves.

Q: Tracy, you delve into some dark territory here. Sexual freedom and expression turned into sexual depravity and violence. Did you dread or fear writing a particular character or story line? Which one and why?

A: No. None of the characters or aspects of the plot were fearsome for me. I enjoyed writing Sparkle's character and getting to know a good guy like Phil. I thought Becky Ann had a lot of insight that Emile could have benefited from, and I believe black women are giving birth to and raising far more self-hating Emiles than we would like to admit. It really does take a village, you know.

Q: You explore some very provocative and powerful relationship, friendship, and family themes: interracial dating, the lengths people will go for "love," sexual abuse, rape, self-

hatred, child trauma, the sexual continuum, sexual shame, sexual freedom and acceptance, loyalty to friends, and how well we can ever *really* know someone. What was the most difficult, the most painless, and the most exciting theme to explore?

A: The most difficult theme to explore was the threat of contracting HIV. Many people get tested and wait with bated breath for the results, unsure if the lives they've been living have caught up with them. I think a lot of us have been in a similar position at one time or another, afraid that there will be consequences for our carelessness, and that was difficult for me as HIV and AIDS have touched my life very intimately by striking several of my family members. The most painless part to explore was that of Emile as he battled his severe case of self-hatred. As a great lover of self, it was fun to examine and uncover the motivations behind some of the ills of Black on black relationships, and to peel back the complicated layers of many black men who harbor dislike, disgust, and ill will toward their own women. The most exciting theme to explore was Sparkle's self-actualization as the very thing she abhorred ended up firmly rooted in her heart. Amazing!

Q: Will we be reunited with Kevin, Emile, Sparkle, and Fancy in a future novel?

A: Whew! At this point, no. I am already thinking thoughts of other characters, places, and plots!

Q: What or who are you addicted to?

A: Peace! I'm addicted to peace. I gotta have it and I raise hell whenever mine is disturbed!

1. Emile is shocked when he learns about his brother Kevin's sexual predilections. Similarly, Sparkle is dumbstruck when she learns about her best friend Fancy's affair with another woman, as well as the lengths she went to to please Kevin. In your life, how well can you ever really know someone? Have you ever been that surprised by a loved one's confession or revelation?

2. Fancy goes to great lengths to sexually satisfy her husband, Kevin. In her world and in real life, at what point does one go too far?

3. By the end of the novel, Kevin starts to deal with his sexual addiction. What do you think of this recently identified addiction? Do you conceive of it as an addiction similar to alcohol or drugs or food? Why or why not?

4. There are some erotic scenes in *Knockin' Boots*. What are some other memorable love, sex, and intimacy scenes in books you've recently read?

5. Have you or a loved one ever excluded a particular racial or cultural group from our dating/love lives? Why or why not?

6. Do you think Emile is justified in trying to oppose everything his tormentors Dirty Sue, Lil Mama, and Teesha stood for by acting in such a reactionary manner?

7. How did Emile's self-hatred manifest itself? In what other ways are many African Americans' self-hatred revealed?

8. Sparkle was taught by her mother to "use what you've got and not be shy about it." In sexual matters, when does this theory become dangerous and take away from a woman's mental and emotional worth? Does it ever?

9. In an ironic twist, Sparkle falls in love with a white man, the very race she condemned Emile for loving. It ends up being her richest, healthiest relationship ever. What are your beliefs about interracial dating? Do you find black man/white women coupling easier or more difficult to accept than black woman/white man love?

10. Fancy has a physical and emotional affair with a woman, but does not consider herself bisexual, rather that that is a facet of her sexual identity that she chooses not to explore further. Do you think this makes her bisexual or heterosexual, or that it places her somewhere along the continuum?

11. Emile gives Kevin a wake-up call about his sexual behavior and possible HIV status. Similarly, in a strong dose of girl power, Fancy sets Sparkle straight about how she uses her body and gets involved with married men, and, at one point, Fancy even saves Sparkle's life. What do you think would have happened if these two friends hadn't so strongly intervened? When in your life have you had to take a similar course of action for a loved one in trouble?

12. Emile and Kevin were exposed to sex in an unloving and traumatic way at a very early age. With Emile, Kevin, Sparkle, and Fancy, what—if anything—about each of their pasts led to their current relationships with sex?

13. What is the level of health or dysfunction in each of the four characters' relationships with sex?

14. How has addiction touched your and your family's lives?

15. How has this novel changed or reinforced your thinking about sexual relationships and HIV prevention?

16. What do you think will happen to Fancy, Emile, Sparkle and Phil, and to Kevin after he is treated for his addiction?

17. What do you *hope* the future has in store for them?

TRACY PRICE-THOMPSON is the nationally best-selling author of *Black Coffee, Chocolate Sangria* (a Main Selection of the Black Expressions Book Club), and *A Woman's Worth*. She is a highly decorated Desert Storm veteran who graduated from Army Officer Candidate School after ten years as an enlisted soldier.

A Brooklyn, New York, native and retired army engineer officer, Price-Thompson is a Ralph Bunche Graduate Fellow of Rutgers University who holds an undergraduate degree in business and a master's degree in social work. She lives with her husband and their children in Hawaii, where she is currently at work on her next novel. She can be reached at tracy thomp@aol.com.

Tracy is happily and healthily addicted to her husband, Gregory Thompson.